A Trilogy of
Love Triangles

To Arthur & Janet
beloved brother & sister
in law

Jack

A TRILOGY OF
LOVE TRIANGLES

The Misconception
The Borrowed Plumes
The Disconnected

Decker designed the cover!

Jack K. Campbell

Library of Congress Control Number: 2017919210
ISBN: Hardcover   978-1-5434-7254-7
               Softcover   978-1-5434-7255-4
               eBook   978-1-5434-7256-1

Print information available on the last page.

Rev. date: 03/01/2018

To order additional copies of this book, contact:
Xlibris
1-888-795-4274
www.Xlibris.com
Orders@Xlibris.com
771670

Contents

DEDICATION

Dedicated to the co-authors of my life, Helen and Don Campbell

THE MISCONCEPTION

Bear with this —

It begins in a terrible
slaughterhouse world —

but ends in a world as the
womb for spiritual conception,

I

The Life to Come

At the word, "Daddy-O," Eugene Baran panicked! Not much more than a kid, he lost his cool at the sudden prospect of a bastard kid to be, a shotgun wedding to be, the wrong wife to be! He had the conception of pieces of meat getting put together on an assembly line, coming to life, pushing his own life off track! No more running around. No more doing his own thing!

Geno, v'at ya gonna do?

At the cry of a high-pitched voice, his eyes snapped open with a flash, pictured no one, only the dark shadows of an unknown bedroom! Not knowing where he was, he knew he wasn't a kid anymore, hadn't been called "Geno" since he was a stud on the South Side of Chicago, Back of the Yards, Polish Chicagoski. He'd been slugging his way up in the fight racket, punching the clock in a slaughterhouse, killing time in that dead-end job.

Unraveling out of strands of sleep, he dropped the pregnancy rap as a bad dream, no sweat, but a thread of memory drew him back to a tangle of recollections knotted around the bloody meat packing strike of his youth! He went out with his union, broke with it and turned scab, had to take off in the Air Force to get away from union goons and neighborhood scorn. At the same time he'd been playing around a lot, could have put his meat out one too many times! The Air Force took him out of union hands, maybe out of marriage banns as well! He tried to wind-up his memory, get it flying back in time.

The Air Force sucked him up in the Berlin Airlift, put him to the loading of planes in West Germany, unloading them in West Berlin. Germany had been divided by the victors in the war against Hitler, but one of the allies, the Soviet Union, suddenly blocked the rails and roads to the American zone in West Berlin. World War III was on the line, but the AirLift supplied West Berlin with food and fuel, kept it from falling behind the Iron Curtain. The Soviets finally reopened roads and rails. World War III was averted, but his recollection of a bastard kid to be was still blocked off. His memory was in ruins, like the gutted German cities he'd been flying over.

Now, in the shadows of night, he didn't know where he was! In some woman's bed? He was past it! On a business trip, waking up in a motel? He was retired. On his deathbed, viewing the instant replay of life? Was he running out of time?

A clock began beginning to tick him back in time! Past time? He pictured himself as a kid again, cigarette sticking to a lip, baseball cap pitched to one side, loose curl dangling down front. Illuminated under a street lamp on Forty-Ninth Street, he was shedding his shadow over a girl, eyeing a silver crucifix throbbing at the crack of her breasts. The word, "Daddy-O," came out of her upturned mouth, a big mouth smeared with lipstick, slashed from ear to ear like a bloody wound. There was a space between the two front teeth, thin as the space between the breasts. He knew she had him by the balls! Her people would make steer-meat out of him if he didn't marry-up. He had to listen to the tap-tap of her saddle shoes, the snap-snap of her bubble gum, the blah-blah of her words. Geno, v'at ya gonna do?

He didn't remember what he did do, now knew he was reliving his youth, not dreaming it up! The girl of big mouth was Kozy Koczur, Liv to her people, Livia to the nuns, Livie to the neighborhood, "Kozy" to him, "cozy" in the snug of a hug! She was a highschool bobbysoxer with the G.I. Jive in the bop, be-bop of her saddle shoes. She was related to him by marriage, carrying his kid without marriage!

The sound of a clock kept ticking him back and forth between worrying about his whereabouts, and wondering about the bastard kid to be. How did he beat the rap? Did he knock the bun out of the oven? He had the killer punch, but not the killer instinct! He could run with the gang, roll drunks in back alleys, sweat-out the cops. He could hammer the brains out of a pug in the ring, couldn't put him away when he had him on the ropes. No killer instinct! Trainers couldn't put it in him! He knew he was only tough on the outside.

What happened? Did he fly off, leave Kozy holding the bag? Did the bastard kid to be come to be when he was overseas? There were holes in his memory. It got through to him that forgotten times are dead, might as well have never lived! He was leaving little deaths behind, outliving himself!

Could he have murdered a memory? Why else would the shadows in his mind be haunted by the ghost of Kozy?

Did he slip the bobbysoxer into a back-alley operation? The A-word didn't come easily, even after all these years. Abortion was a deadly sin, a murderous crime, would cost an arm and a leg, if not a soul, but the world had turned all the way around on it. Abortion was now a choice, not a crime. It wasn't even a scandal for a broad to bitch-it-up and raise a bastard on her own, but it struck him, in the tick of a clock, that the Church had not gone round with the world. He hadn't taken Mass in years but knew the priests were still against abortion! He'd always wondered why it was preached that bodies were born in sin, but it was a sin to keep a sinful body out of the world?

No religious freak in the old days, when he was full of life, he was now confronting his mortality, thinking about the afterlife! If life after death was in the cards, and he played the mortal sin card, he was out of the game!

Maybe he didn't ring-up a kid in the Kozy slut-machine! Maybe another stud hit the jackpot, and Kozy put the finger on him? A second thought put it out of mind. Kozy only went for him, for sure.

Maybe she wasn't knocked-up at all, just putting the hit on him! On second thought he didn't think she was that cunning! On third thought, she might have been mistaken, got her periods mixed up, but he couldn't count on that. On fourth thought, she might have gone into seclusion when he was overseas, put the kid up for adoption! He didn't play the mortal sin card! He had a middle-aged son or daughter running around somewhere, and a bunch of grand kids!

He liked the idea of his genes running around, but it would freak-out his little woman. The wife wouldn't even let him have a feel before marriage. After marriage, she let him have his way, but didn't have the right kind of tubes for kids.

Where was the little woman? It struck him, in the tick of a clock, that she was on a pilgrimage to Rome, for an Easter audience with the Pope. The next tick of the clock sent him on a pilgrimage of his own, back to the Back of the Yards, but he only ran down empty alleys and dead ends. He found himself back in the dark of night, still carrying the dark of the past with him. He knew he'd find his way out of the dark bedroom by light of day, but might never find his way back to the dark of his Kozy past! Whatever happened didn't seem to have made a mark on him, but when he closed his eyes, the girl with the big-mouth reappeared under the street lamp on Forty-Ninth Street. He heard the clang of a streetcar, and its sound faded into the words, "Daddy-o! Old Man gonna kill me!" His eyes snapped open. Kozy's Old Man appeared in the mirror of memory. Big Zur, a beer-barrel of a man, carried a lot of weight in the Yards, and Back of the Yards. A foreman in Hog Kill, he could salt Geno down like a pork belly, serve him up to Kozy like a slab of bacon.

Tick- Tock. The ticking clock ticked him back and forth, from present to past. In the dark of the past he feared he'd screwed himself out of the American Dream, would never get out of the Yards, never get rich, never fart through silk! In the dark of the present he knew he was living the American Dream, living it up in a suburban dream house. In another look back, he pictured another girl, Marya Nowak. He had the hots for her, thought he'd shot his wad on the wrong girl. Marya was choice meat, prime cut, but never let him have a piece. She led him around by the sugar string, never gave him any sugar. He knew she liked him, called him her Genie, told him about the "genie" in Aladdin's Lamp, but never rubbed him for a thrill, only wanted marriage out of him!

In the dreamy dark of night his dream girl came to light. She'd grown up around the corner, spinning cartwheels in a whirl of wavy blonde and flashy underpants, round and round. She was the "fancy-pants kid" of "Doc Nowak," a big time meat inspector! Marya was the only girl, last of the litter, thought she was a boy, wanted to run with boys. She only got herded round with boys by the hooded Mercy Sisters, but he always wanted to get out of line with her, lost track of her for awhile when the Old Man couldn't ante-up tuition. He had to play the public school game. By the time she joined him in public high school, she no longer wanted to run with boys. She was way ahead of them, had Quiz Kid brains! She made the varsity debate team, waved arms when making points, touched her breast at every reference to patriotism. She had plenty of room up top for patriotism, and the war against Hitler swung plenty of patriotism her way!

Marya took the affirmative in the national debate question, whether the League of Nations should be reconstituted after the war, but took the negative on any entangling alliance with him! It was hands off, even when he got her in the dark of picture shows. A flash of the neighborhood movie house popped up on his screen of memory. It was his royal refuge, arching up amid rows of shops, shabby tenement flats, rickety stoops, rotting clapboards and shingles. It had a golden lobby, crystal chandeliers hanging high, marble stairs that led to a world where Robin Hood drew bow and arrow, Tarzan swung from tree to tree, and The March of Time took him around the world at war. He was always afraid the war would be over before he was old enough to make the scene.

The scene was flickering out of mind. He was in the dark, but not the dark of the neighborhood movie house. There was no lighted blue dome overhead, no footlights along the aisles. He still didn't know where he was, wasn't sure who he was? Was he the kid on the make, or the old man who had it made? He could hardly move, felt connected to a cord. Umbilical cord? Was he stuck in a womb, a bastard kid to be?

....

"You're stuck in the hospital!"

A black nurse in white cap and uniform answered Eugene Baran's question. Black and white, she was bending over him in a white-walled room divided by a white curtain.

"I'm your Nurse, Rose," she said with a white smile framed in black.

He knew he was in a hospital room, not a womb, attached to a feeding tube, not an umbilical cord. He hoped the nurse wouldn't treat him as a piece of meat. As a kid, the only black women he knew in white frocks were workers in the canning rooms of the packing house.

Adjusting himself to a world of black and white, he saw a crucifix hanging over the doorway. As a kid, he tried to hide from the eyes of Jesus on Church and family walls. Now, he hoped Jesus kept an eye out for him.

"What happened to me?"

"Had yourself a bang-up smash-up," the white-frocked nurse was saying as she whipped a thermometer up and down.

"Is this St. Joseph's," he asked. The crucifix over the opened doorway suggested the Catholic hospital near his suburban home.

"It's the Good Samaritan," the nurse corrected him. She stuck the thermometer in his mouth, used her own mouth to tell him the Good Samaritan was taking a beating for doing good. She complained about getting hassled on the way to work, told her patient that pickets were protesting the hospital's "abortion clinic!"

"Abortion was illegal in my day," Eugene Baran managed to say as soon as the thermometer was out of mouth and recollection of Kozy back in mind. The A-Word was still hard for him to get off the tongue.

"Maybe you not be here," the nurse smiled with a spark of a gold tooth, "if abortion be legal in your Mama's day."

"Why am I here?"

"Here on earth?"

"Here in the Good Samaritan."

The nurse took up a clipboard, told him he'd been in a car accident, admitted for a "broken femur, lacerations, cracked ribs, internal injuries."

"Don't remember any smash-up," he mumbled.

"Good Lord put pain outa mind."

"Got me a pain!"

"Got pills for it!"

"Got a pill to take me outa here?"

"Mr. Eugene, you be scheduled for emergency hip surgery, soon as a surgeon gets through picket lines."

Surgery was not the word Eugene Baran wanted to hear. He'd gotten laid up in hospitals when falling off scaffolds, after he got out of the Yards and worked his way up in the roofing business, but never had to be cut open like a side of beef.

"Routine hip surgery," the nurse assured him, reading his mind.

"Little woman's gonna skin me alive if I wrecked our spanking new Caddy."

"Woman gonna be glad you still in your skin." In another breath the nurse asked where his wife could be reached, told him she needed to be contacted.

"She's in Rome, for Easter. Don't want my smash-up to wreck her audience with Holy Father."

"Woman not married to Pope Man," Nurse Rose said, waving a hand to hold his attention before his eyelids dropped all the way down. "How we get hold of your woman? She gonna need to approve procedures."

"Contact my company, Baran Roofing."

"You got your own company! Must make a body dizzy, so high up!"

"Had to work my way up from the pits, Union Stockyards."

"My old countrified folk came up from Miss-A-Sip for nip of free air in stockyards. Got lots of stinky air."

"Body get used to smell."

"My countrified folks got penned-up way off on other side of State Street, got plenty whiffs."

"You folks got free pass, nowadays, can live anywhere."

"World sure was sick, back then," the nurse replied, "not cured yet."

"Stockyards got sick and died," Eugene Baran brought up, trying to change the subject. As he mumbled, he shut eyes, and eyelids screened scenes of the Yards getting torn down. He let the memories roll.

"Got me a child-eye view of stockyards in its hay day," Nurse Rose told him, cutting off his rushes of mental pictures, "before bulldozers run bulls off."

"Had me a hand in running bulls out," Eugene Baran smiled back. With closed eyes, he pictured himself in a wrecking crew, saw the cattle pens shattered, and buildings knocked down, slaughter houses, fertilizer plants, Glue House, Hair Works. The neighborhood around the Yards got put down. When the saloons on Whiskey Row got bulldozed, the remains were hauled away, except for the smell of beer.

He opened his eyes to shut out the flicker of the past, heard the nurse say she was leaving him to his rest. She snapped off the light, flooded the room in darkness, left him adrift in his stream of thought. He hoped it would carry him to the scene of the accident. Poker chips and poker hands came to mind, poker faces, potato chips, beer and bourbon. He'd gone off the wagon, remembered falling behind the wheel of his new Cadillac. Headlights began spooling up a ribbon of highway. He couldn't wind it up fast enough. The ribbon snapped. His looking glass of memory broke in pieces. Sifting through the debris, he got hauled out of the driver's seat, manhandled into a siren-screaming ambulance. He remembered the hurt of bouncing on a hard surface, and the sudden relief when the ambulance jerked to a stop. He got a window view of a lighted hospital entrance, and snarling faces and waving picket signs.

"Right to Life!"

"Right to Living Wage!"

The living present and the union strike of long ago seemed to have gotten mixed up. Had the broken hip gotten him out of joint with time? Had it taken him out of mind? Was he hallucinating? Beside his bed stood a brawny youth, baseball cap swung to one side, cigarette stuck to a lower lip. It was his own youth, Geno, bare arms folded, forearms big as hams. His ice blue "Slavic eyes" were staring out of a face frozen in a perpetual frown. His jaw was so big and square it dragged down his mouth, made it look small, pinched-up, frowning. He remembered getting told the frowning mouth came from Mama Stara, "the old one." She told him he also got his crop of straw-blond hair from her side of the family, but nobody could remember her without gray hair. He could hardly recall when he had any hair, but saw his youth standing beside the bed with a harvest of straw-blond hair raked back with Vaseline to a "Duck's Ass," except for a wayward curl hanging down in front.

Eugene Baran thought he was dreaming, but the youth touched him, gave him a physical spark! Science-fiction comic books filled his mind as a kid, now he pictured himself in a time- traveling frame of mind. He could talk to his youth, find out what happened to the bastard kid to be.

His youth talked first, asked why he got left behind, stuck in 1948? Eugene Baran said that was the unforgettable year he enlisted, reminded his youth of labor union and female union problems. "Why didn't you come with me," he asked.

"Fly boy don't vant me no more." The voice was in an accent that Eugene Baran had left behind, with his youth. "Tired of low life," he said, "tried to make something of myself."

"Couldn't get no better life, always made out."

"Balls played Geno around."

"Geno be our name, passin' genes our game!"

"What happened to the knocked-up Koczur kid?"

"Ain't your memory same as mine?"

....

Out of memory, and dreams, Eugene Baran opened eyes, didn't know where he was? It finally came to him that he was in the dark of a hospital room, and his youth came back to him in a drugged sleep. He'd outgrown Geno a long time ago, packed him up with old Sunday clothes and Air Force uniforms. Why did his youth come out of the mothballs of memory?

In the dark of the hospital room he let himself time-travel to the so-called "Dark Days" of his youth. Teresa, the sister assigned to his upbringing, blamed him for the "Dark Days!" When he came in the world, the Stock Market crashed, banks failed, and the world went "dark!"

Back then, he didn't know why the "Depression" days were called "Dark?" Days seemed bright enough, except for a stockyard fire that blackened the skies for awhile. It was mostly dark in the Sunday Room after the old man got his final pink-slip. He kept the shades drawn, filled the room with pipe smoke, let his whiskers grow. The Sunday Room was always dark after his coffin lay next to the wind-up Victrola, and there was no more smoke or music in the room.

It must have been dark for the neighborhood men who walked around with hats pulled down over eyes! It must have been dark for those street people who shaded their eyes in shame as they plodded through the back alley with all their possessions in push carts or beds on rollers. Panhandlers kept their eyes down when they begged for food at the back door. Sometimes Mama Stara let a shabby man come in for a cup of tea, and crust of bread to soak up the last drop. Geno never had to beg for food. Mama Stara always put something on the table, if only bread and lard. The coal stove was always fired-up, water always on the boil. Mama Stara used the same tea bag, over and over. She kept adding scraps of food to a pot of soup. Whenever one of his brothers got work on a government work-project, Mama Stara bought a chicken. Back then, when he was at the second table, he thought a chicken only had a neck and a back, and made soup. He heard about pork chops, never tasted one. Mama Stara said pork was still full of the demons Jesus used to cast into swine. She did allow ham-meat. The Old

Man claimed ham was cured, the devil salted and smoked out of it. Ham was for Easter, one year.

Church filled every Sunday. Most other days of his youth seemed filled with opposition to the Company Union, fights to get a worker's union. He remembered street fights, and reports of tear gas, brass knuckles, police night sticks. After riots, and Roosevelt's intervention, they got the United Packinghouse Workers of America. It drew no color lines. Race People had been resented when their cotton-picking hands came up North as strike breakers, but they were turning into good union people. The UPWA got all workers a voice and an arm, but couldn't make jobs! The "Dark Days" hung over the neighborhood, but were bright days for him when he got a streetcar excursions to White City, the remains of Chicago's last century Columbian Exposition. Its rickety roller coaster was still riding high, creaking up and roaring down. There were "magic carpet rides" down the polished mahogany slides in the Fun House, and a boat ride in the Tunnel of Love!

A new World's Fair, the Chicago's Century of Progress, hit the South Side when he was too young to remember much. The big brothers got jobs working in it, and time off to get a Sky Ride, and an eyeful of Sally Rand's Fan Dance. The Fair brought light to everyone's eyes.

The Tree Army got all the old brothers, took them out West to shoot tree seedlings in the ground. They sent money and letters home, bragged about the grub they got to eat, complained about the book-learning after chores, and the dead silence of the nights.

As he lay in the dark of Dark Day memories, he got a thrill at remembrance of "work papers!" He was eligible for after-school jobs. Many underage kids tried to quit school and get full time work, but mostly got truant officers!

All the while he was in school, and working part time, he was running with the gang, the Forty-Niners, rumbling with the Marshfield High Balls, banging with all outsiders. The Forty-Niners held the turf along 49th from Loomis to Paulina, tried to hold all the streets between the railroad tracks and the City Dump. They saw plenty of action, back fence to back fence, and ran the rackets, shot craps in alleyways, rolled drunks on Whiskey Row, skipped out of many "paste and paper" school days, went skinny-dipping in the Drainage Canal or Bubbly Creek.

They didn't know why the days were called "Dark," but liked the dark nights. The dark was good cover for "junking." The gang swiped scrap iron off freight-cars parked in railroad sidings. The "Junk Man" paid a penny a pound for the stolen scrap, and most of it got sold to Japan. After Pearl Harbor, it was said the "the iron came back to us!"

The war put the slaughterhouses back in full production, but took away most of the slaughterhouse men. Old men, boys and women, kept the plants in killing trim. There was money for meat, but most meat was going to the military, got rationed for civilians, gave Black Market jobs for the gang.

Geno was more interested in his own meat, thought he was turning into a good piece! He was discovering his own body, and the bodies of women. His sisters kept their bodies covered up when running round the house. His first sight of raw female meat was from his bedroom window that looked across the way at a neighbor's bedroom window. Marie Wojciechowski, the neighborhood songbird with a great pair of lungs, got herself shown off in her bedroom window on nights the blinds weren't pulled all the way down. The show went on the road when she married the neighborhood hunk, Antanas. He got drafted and she followed him to some city down South where he was put into radio school. He made the rate as a radioman, shipped out on a "tin can," and Marie came back home, began making the scene in the back window again. He could still see her in his window of memory, remembered when she got the "government telegram," and a gold star appeared in the front window, but her backside kept showing in the back window.

When the war ended with the blast that shook the world into the Atomic Age, the boys came back as men, swaggered around in new civilian clothes and parts of old uniforms. One of the boys, now a man, was Casimir Koczur, the boy Teresa had been waiting for all through the war. A big redheaded hunk of a meat packer, he wanted to marry Teresa, but didn't want to be hung-up in the stockyards for the rest of his life. He told Teresa the war put him through the "meat-grinder" and he wanted out of the meat business, into the mind business. He needed a college education, but the G.I. Bill wouldn't pay enough for him to keep a wife. Teresa got him to marry her, promised to stay on the job in Armour's General Office. She put him through the University of Chicago, one degree at a time. The big redhead did all right for himself, got to be a college professor, and Geno did all right, too, went from "trucker" on the killing floor to "boner" in the packing plant, and up to "checker" in the canning rooms. All the while he kept up with his fists, could whip the punching bag into a blur, and warm the canvas with most pugs who got into the ring with him. Trainers at the Settlement Project figured he might make it to the Golden Gloves, and Olympics. All he needed was the killer instinct.

Those were the days Geno was sporting girls on his arm and wing-tip shoes on his feet, and the time he got from under the wing of the uneducated ones, got his own "roost" behind the barroom in the neighborhood family saloon, World's End. He had to share toilets and washbasins with patrons, but had his own shower rigged-up in the liquor storeroom.

He was living it up, until the Koczur Kid pulled him down with the bastard kid to be, and he went to the Forty-Niners for a hand-up! He pictured all their unshaved faces looking up at him in their abandoned tool shed headquarters. He thought they'd be impressed by his fertility, but got called a "dumb ass." He should have stuck his "Polish kielbasa in a rubber."

"Rubbers fer feet, not meat," Geno laughed it off. He knew about contraceptives, didn't want to buy them. Contraceptives were illegal, but available behind the counter in almost any drugstore.

"Rubbers cramp a man's style," Slick spoke-up for Geno. Slick was respected as a make- out artist.

"A man gotta take chances," Geno bragged, "like shootin' craps."

"Only roll bones of sportin' gals," Splinters advised. He was skinny as a rail, but tall enough to look down on everybody. He asked for the name of the "bitch" carrying his "cargo."

Geno didn't want word to get out to the Koczur's, said it was nobody's business but his own.

"Guess it be no business of Forty-Niners," Splinters shot back, looking down on everyone.

Up came the voice of a fringer, proclaiming the Forty-Niners should be one for all and all for one, but no one paid attention to a fringer, a kid catching on as a gang member.

"Geno make bed," a voice of authority proclaimed, "gotta sleep in it!"

Members looked up to Basil Walski, gang council member. Known as "Rabbits," he had a big swollen nose, broken in fights, and pinkish eyes that never learned to read. He was called "Bits" for short, but was a big man. "Pole get smart, too late smart," he said with a twitch of his big nose.

Geno said, "Bits only know street smarts."

Bits said it didn't take book smarts to know Geno had no choice but priest, or crooked sawbones!"

"Choose me a crooked sawbones."

"Too rich fer your blood!"

"Abortion be cheap an' legal in Cuba," Moucher the Mouth spoke up. His words came out of a mouthful of rotten teeth, and he didn't speak much, except to borrow money and smokes.

Someone thought Cuba was a foreign country. Someone thought it was across water. Someone thought it would cost a lot to get there, "midwife cheaper." Another voice suggested quinine injections, a chew of Argo Starch, mustard powder and kerosine. Another voice thought a douche full of Draino would wash a body out. Someone mentioned a coat hanger. The fringer cautioned against killing, and getting "jug time."

"Ain't no killin' if nature do it," Bits proclaimed with a gleam in his pinkish eyes. He said nature could make a "miscarriage" on its own with a little help from the outside.

Geno wanted to know how to get a date with a "Miss Carriage?"

"Miscarriage come in anti-life pills," Bits said, wiping his big nose on a sleeve as he talked and sniffed.

"Give my left ball fer a Misscarriage pill!"

Bits said he got wind of a Voodoo Man in the Beef House, a dude who could brew-up the killer pills.

....

"Time for your pill."

Nurse Rose startled Eugene Baran out of his drowsy thoughts. He asked if it was a killer pill, and she said the pill would only shut him up. She laughed as she shook a thermometer at him, plugged it in his mouth.

"My temp's got the hots for you," her patient spoke up as soon as the thermometer was out.

"Mr. Eugene feelin' better," Nurse Rose said with another white and gold smile, "but actin' worse!" She handed him a pill and paper cup of water, told him she'd be back to trim him up for surgery.

As the pill went down, the name of the killer-pill man came up in Eugene Baran's memory. His first name was a biblical character. His last name was the same as the man on a ten dollar bill. Moses Hamilton! Bits gave him the name and his Beef House work station, but the memory was slipping into darkness.

....

Looking for the "Moses Man" in the light of the Killing Floor of the Beef House, Geno knew his way around. He'd been a trucker, still knew some of the boys trucking scraps to the Dump Chutes. Not one of them heard of "Moses Hamilton," or the "the Moses Man," not even the head lineman, and he got no better responses from the Skinners and Trimmers. As he inquired along the Skinning Bed where cattle were losing identity, their hides coming down like aprons, no one knew the "Moses Man." No one knew him on the Viscera Tables where piles of intestines were slithering along a stainless steel conveyor belt. One pile of entrails bulged with a calf embryo, a miniature hoof sticking out of the slunk bag. Geno knew the skin of a calf embryo was valued for women's gloves and purses. He wondered how much a human embryo might worth! He put it out of mind when he saw a familiar face, black as the ace of spades, the face of a player in the floating poker game between shifts. Everybody called him Boast. A Beef Lugger, he bragged about his back, broad enough to hold half a side of beef.

"Vat's a Beef Lugger up to at Viscera Tables?"

"Pickin' up policy slip from pick-up man," Boast replied. "Gonna strike it rich! Why Kitty hangin' out round pile-a-guts?"

Geno knew Boast called every white boy, Kitty, and let it pass, asked him if he heard of the Moses Man, Moses Hamilton.

Boast said he knew every union brother, and the Moses Man was a Ribber by trade, a Jumpin' Jack Preacher by grace. "Geno be sniffin' roung wrong fireplug, Moses Man be in Number Two Freezer House."

"Two-bits," Geno promised, pulling a quarter out of his pocket, giving it a flip, "if ya get me to Ribber Man."

"Be on way back to Loadin' Dock," Boast said, grabbing the coin out of the air with a swish of his big hand. "Got yourself a deal. Why Kitty want Moses Man?"

"Anti-life pills."

"Been messin' with black meat?"

"Polska meat!"

"Dark meat sweetest meat of all," Boast bragged, turning his broad back on Geno, waving him to follow.

Geno could hardly keep up with the long, loping strides of the Beef Lugger as they headed for the elevator shaft. The elevator lowered them down five floors, creaking all the way, and they made it outside the Beef House, on the walkway with the smog rising out of the Lard Rendering Plant. Geno followed Boast to the covered bridge hanging over the railroad tracks. The bridge connected the East and West Loading Docks, brought them to the high-rise Freezer Houses.

Ducking into Number Two House, they parted their way between hanging sides of gauze- shrouded carcasses. There was a pleasant whiff of pine sawdust in the cold air as they waved past Beef Lifters amd Baggers.

"Meats hangin' pretty," Boast said as he squirmed between hanging sides of beef, "all dressed-up, no place to go."

"Boast gonna date 'em on Loadin' Dock!"

"Boast gonna hang 'em up, not lay 'em."

They laughed their way toward a gang of Pole-Men. Pushing sides of beef with long poles, they reminded Geno of African warriors swinging spears in Tarzan movies. They let them pass.

Boast pointed ahead. "Moses Man be hangin' out yonder."

Geno caught sight of a black man looking up at a side of beef much bigger than himself. Wrapped in a white cooler frock, he was standing in oversized rubber boots and slipping a hand- saw between beef ribs.

Boast piped up, asked if Mr. Moses Man could take timeout to "chew rag, make a buck?"

"Oh, Precious Lord," the Ribber was humming, paying no attention to the newcomers.

He was looking over a side of beef, picking up a roller-brand, running it down the white-marbled flesh, printing "choice" in purple ink. He pushed the branded side of beef on its way, the steel trolley groaning under its weight. He turned to his visitors, asked why they "be hangin' out in cold beef country?"

"Kitty wanna get hands on anti-life pills," Boast spoke for Geno.

The old Ribber didn't answer, only stuck a knife blade up to the hilt in a side of beef, opened it up for his hand-saw. While he sawed, and hummed, Geno sized him up. The Moses Man looked like Fu Man Chu in the movies, a man with arching cheek bones and a drooping mustache. His face was a yellowish black. Strands of wooly black and white hair stuck out of his black skull-guard.

"Land-a-Goshen," the Ribber finally said as he pushed a side of beef off on its way. "Why Whitey want to keep whitey chile outa whitey world?"

"Chile be accident," Boast spoke for Geno again.

"Reckon all Lawd Boss Man's human critters be accidents," the Moses Man said as he brought his whirling hand-saw to another set of ribs, "all men accidents 'cept Mr. Adam. Lawd Boss Man only want Mr. Adam, but Mr. Adam want Miss Eve for company keeper, so Boss Man ribbed Miss Eve out Mr. Adam. After Miss Eve sin, Lawd Boss Man allow more sinners. We all be accidents of sportin' life!"

"Mister Moses Man be flamin' sword Baptist," Boast explained to Geno. "Preacher for Uplifting Humanity Church," the ribber announced to Geno as he brandished a knife. "Man not to kill, 'cept to feed mouth."

Boast asked why "Mr. Preacher Man" made killer pills?"

"Chile got right to be wanted," the Ribber proclaimed with a slash of his knife. "Whitey kid not wanted," Boast spoke up for Geno again.

"Whitey might not know what Whitey want!"

Geno talked for himself, said he didn't want to bring any more sinners in the world.

The Ribber lay down his hand-saw, picked up his roller-brand and printed "choice" on a side of beef. "Reckon we all be fixin' to get graded by Lawd Boss Man," he said. "Some of us critters be prime meats, some choice, some cutter scraps, some be condemned meats." He waved his roller-brand at Geno. "Brand ink be made outa sweet berries so don't spoil meat none. It taste like elderberry wine. Whitey boy, try a nip."

Geno took a lick off the roller-brand to oblige the old man. "Tastes choice," he said, lips turning purple.

"Choice," Moses Hamilton pronounced slowly. "Whitey got choice. Boss Man don't put hedge round us to keep off Devil Man. Boss Man give freedom to make choice. Can't be no sin without free choice!"

"Choose killer pills," Geno spoke right up. "Free choice got a price?"

"How long little woman got thorn in flesh?"

"Got rag off, time, or two."

"Unblessed chile be caught in time! Sawbuck see Whitey outa accident."

Geno figured he was getting ripped-off, but jabbed a hand under his white frock, came up with a roll of dollar bills, stripped one off at a time.

"Don't know why Mister Adam want company keeper," Moses Hamilton kept talking as he counted and piled up the dollar bills. "Boss Man live by self, all by self, in heavenly bliss, but it be written, man not to live alone."

"Don't live alone," Geno said, wishing the Ribber would cut the bullshit. He held out his hand, turned it up.

"Pills gotta get brewed-up," the Moses Man said with a snort. "It take time to get born, time to get unborn. Boy get magic beans day after today, after five o'clock bell, Freezer House Number Two, Locker Room. Locker number four an' twenty-two."

....

Geno found the locker room, next day. It was walled-up with insulation board to hold out the cold and wrapped-round with wire netting to hold out the rats. The Moses Man wasn't at locker 422! Men in all stages of undress were crowded round the lockers. They were slipping in or out of pants, coming in or off shift. Hairy cockroaches and men's hairy feet were running between the rows of lockers and benches.

"Four-twenty-two be spare locker for Moses Man," Geno heard from a man raising arms into a sport shirt. The speaker's mouth disappeared for a moment, popped out of a collar to say that if the Moses Man said he'd be there, he'd be there. The man tucked-in his shirttail and waved off.

Geno slumped down on a bench to wait, tuned into conversations. Talks in different dialects were airing round the room. Talk of the upcoming strike held sway, arguments for and against, mostly for.

"Packers gonna chicken out, can't make a buck vithout us."

"Vartime price controls off. Packers makin' a killin'!"

"Price-a cow-meat jumpin' over moon!"

"Packers offer nine cent more an hour. Get it vithout no strike."

"Strike get us twenty-nine-cents more."

Geno tuned out of strike talk, like changing radio stations, got into sport talk. Cubs and Sox were hitting it off in Spring Training. Recent scores were coming up.

"I'm into scoring, not baseball scoring," someone spoke up. "Any man vit a good bat can get to first base vit a woman."

Geno wished he hadn't hit a home run! He switched off the locker room talk and tuned into his own thoughts. Had the Moses Man pulled a fast one?

Looking down, between his square steel-toed work shoes, he caught sight of a cockroach looking up, antennas twitching. It vanished before his shoe could stamp it out. Another pair of shoes appeared, brown shoes with white spats. Geno looked up at the old Ribber who'd been transformed into a man of the cloth, dapper in collar and coat. The Moses Man opened the locker, handed Geno a brown envelope, told him he got his choice.

....

"Choice beans," Geno opened up when he made contact with Kozy in the shed behind the Koczur flat. Kozy was at her rosary, and he assured her that he had the answer to her prayers. He shook a brown envelope at her.

"Been livin' bead to bead, day to day," she said, fondling her rosary. She told him she feared the "Blessed Lady" might not bless her anymore!

Geno assured her there was no blessed child in her, only pieces of meat trying to get put together.

"Be good to get my body back!" Kozy sighed, and squeezed the beads in one hand, made the sign of the cross with the other, said it would be good for them to be a twosome again, no more threesome.

Geno nodded, told her the pills would wipe her slate clean. Kozy pouted, asked if she had to take the pills all at once? Geno said one or two would ring her bell. She said she rather hear a wedding bell. He said wedding bells would ring after she rang-up the school graduation bell. She didn't think a school certificate would do a girl any good. He didn't think a bastard kid would do a girl any good. She said the kid would not be a bastard if wedding bells rang before she "bigged-up." He said her "old man" wouldn't let her quit school to marry "a loser like me," and if she played the "shame card," she'd lose a big Church "Do!" He knew she was a wedding freak. First time he met her, at Teresa's Choosing Party, she only talked about her own wedding, had no husband in mind, only the union hall for a wedding reception. It would make for a good union!

He was surprised to hear her say she'd rather have him than a Church "do." A day with him, she said, was worth a lot more than "five days of a Church do." She said she only wanted the "puttin' to bed" part of the wedding do, didn't care about the virgin wreath, and all the trimmings.

He asked if she wanted to sleep in a single bed, back of a bar, for the rest of her life? She said a married pair would fit "good" in a single bed. He said that even if the union got its wage demands, he couldn't afford meat for two on the table. She said she loved every inch of him, could eat him up. She snapped her bubble gum as she talked, fished it out of mouth, stuck it behind an ear for future use. He said if he could keep punching his way up in the fight racket he'd hit it big, buy her a diamond ring and a golden wedding! She grabbed the gum from behind her ear, put it to work chewing words of resignation. "Guess I gotta take my medicine."

....

"Take your medicine," Nurse Rose was saying, waking Eugene Baran, lifting his head to coax pill and water down the throat.

"The pills didn't work," Eugene Baran spoke up as he broke into consciousness, still in the grip of memories, recalling the killer pills only made Kozy sick.

Nurse Rose said, "pills guaranteed to make you feel cozy."

....

Thinking of Kozy, Eugene Baran opened eyes to the white of his hospital room. The nurse was gone, the white curtain alongside his bed was parted for the first time. A hulking big man with thinning hair was shaped-up in the opposite hospital bed. He was eying him like a judge, asking, "you awake, old man?"

"Awake, as charged," Eugene Baran answered-up, not sure he was telling the truth. He might still be dreaming. He tried to get a better look at the man on the other side, but took a shot of pain as he turned his body.

"Been lying in wait to get a word with you," sounded the voice from the opposite bed. "Orderlies called you Eugene Baran last night. Long time ago I hung out with Eugene Baranowski, Back of the Yards. You remind me of him."

"You see what's left of him! Who are you?"

"Ski! Dropped the rest of my Polska name as a kid, never knew the man who gave it to me. Ski rhymed with me!"

"Dropped the ski from my name, when dropping the Polska life," Eugene Baran talked back, trying to imagine the old man in the next bed as a youth.

"What dropped you in here?"

"Car wreck," Eugene Baran replied.

"Guess we're a couple of old wrecks," the man called Ski said with a laugh in the sound of his voice. "Hit and run driver put me in the hospital, hit and run father put me in the world."

Eugene Baran didn't think a man from his old neighborhood would let on he was a bastard. He asked where they "hit it off?"

"Name of Ski ought to ring a bell. We went round in the square ring together, way back at the neighborhood Settlement!"

"Spared with a stable of pugs, punched 'em all out."

"I hit it off pretty well with you," Ski said. "Always looked up to you, remembered your name, and left punch."

"You pack a good memory."

"Packed a good punch, too! Remember our trainer, Toothpick Nick?'

"Nick the Prick!" The name jumped out of Eugene Baran's mouth. "Old Nick ran Settlement Gym."

"Chewed us out like his toothpick," Ski joined in, "taught us fighting had rules."

"Called me Corky, said I could uncork a good left."

"Called you Corky because you had that corkscrew hanging down."

"That too," Eugene Baran agreed, "but said I had a shot at the Olympics."

"Didn't he old boy say you didn't have the killer instinct?"

"That too."

"Told me I was a natural," Ski said. "Fighting was my way of life. I lived on the streets!"

"Said I was a natural, too," Eugene Baran spoke up. "I fancied the streets more than home. Did we hangout, outside the ring?"

"Armour Beef House, time we scabbed."

"Screwed myself up, back then," Eugene Baran remembered.

"I was screwed up, too," echoed back. "Would still be a Joe Palooka comic strip boxer if it hadn't been for Doc Godfrey. Remember Doc, Settlement Project Director?"

"Doc Not Free of God," Eugene Baran remembered. "Wasn't he a professor at University of Chicago?"

"Sociology professor. Our Settlement was his project, modeled after Hull House, couple miles up Halsted from us. He taught me life had rules, and English had rules."

"Tried to socialize all us punks."

"Labored for the birth of a better society."

"What happened to the old boy?"

"Went to a better world. I kept up with him, to the end. Did you know his wife made him give up the Settlement to make more money in full time teaching at the university?"

"Didn't he put us in books, make money off us?"

"Studied us, first generation Americans in transition between cultures, but didn't make money off us. No money in professional journals or research papers."

"He stepped on our mother tongue," Eugene Baran kept talking and looking back, "made us drop the old accent, tried to make us melt into the American Cultural Pot."

"He always said immigration, now integration, but when all kinds of computer technology came along, he figured we were all immigrants in a new kind of world."

"I got up in the world, got my own roofing company. What you been up to?"

"Doctoring. Old Doc got me into cultural study, but I took to the test tube kind."

"Thought of going into doctoring myself, but my wife had brothers in the roofing business, and I went up that ladder."

"You doctored roofs."

"How does a medical doctor feel as a hospital patient?"

"Impatient to get back to my free clinic."

"You give doctoring away?"

"Retired from my practice, set up a volunteer project in the low rent district."

"You're a goodski, like old Doc Godfrey!"

"I am Doc Godfrey, Doctor Ski Godfrey. Ski rhymed with Godfrey, and the Doc didn't have kids. I took his name when he didn't need it anymore."

"What are the odds of two punks from the stink of the Yards coming up smelling like roses, and getting together in the same hospital room after all these years?"

"Wouldn't bet on it! It must be in the cards!"

"You figure deck's stacked in game of life?"

"I don't figure life's a game, believe predestination's in nature, or science wouldn't be possible."

"I figure there's no way to predict human behavior," Eugene Baran contradicted. "This old boy thinks life's a game of chance. Some players figure the angles, some cheat, some are winners, some losers."

"Thought I was a loser, got dealt a bad hand," Ski admitted from the other side, "wanted Jesus to come off the wall, fight me." After a long pause, he said he got hung up at the Cook County School for Boys, had a good priest who got Christ to come off the wall "take me in hand."

"Did the good priest tell you why Jesus put you in the can?"

"When I was a Coffee Grinder, that good priest told me everybody's in the can, serving a life sentence in this world. Good behavior gets us out, into the world beyond."

"Never drew the faith card," Eugene Baran talked back. "Didn't play along with any creator who makes us kill to live, and then die."

"Life for life," Ski proclaimed from his side of the room.

Life for life!

Eugene Baran remembered hearing that!

"Got wind of that in Beef Kill," he told the man in the opposite bed.

"You're memory's getting its sights on me! Think I made that up."

"Thought it didn't mean a thing, like the wind."

"It meant the lower life sacrifices itself for the higher."

"We sure have a higher life than beef cattle!"

"And we die for a higher life."

"Higher life's over my head."

"It must be as hard for us to understand the higher life," Ski thought out loud, "as for those cows to understand our way of life."

....

Thinking of the higher life, Eugene Baran was carted off to surgery, but discovered himself looking down, down on himself! He'd left his body! Had he turned into a spirit? He remembered being drugged, remembered how much, as a roofer, he liked to look down. When he was on the job, he carried binoculars to get a better look at windows with shades up.

He got plenty of peepshows during lunch breaks, some soap operas every day, same time, same station.

Long time ago, he thought there might be a Big Roofer in the sky looking down on him. It made him uneasy. Now he was looking down on himself, looking into windows of his past.

His life had been built-up, one story at a time, like a high-rise apartment building. Through a lower window he saw himself running with the Forty-Niners. In a higher window he got a glimpse of Kozy, but the shades came down. Higher up, he saw himself in the Air Force, then in college classes, then up to marriage, up and up. His world of life kept changing. Chicago was no longer "Porkopolis," no longer "Polackville!" The old neighborhood wasn't even down there anymore. He couldn't go back, like the Old People who couldn't go back to the Old Country. Nothing but the Stockyard Gate was left standing in the old neighborhood, reminding him of the Brandenburg Gate amid the ruins of Berlin. Weeds were struggling for life between rusty railroad tracks and uneven bricks. The great churches left standing around the Yards were abandoned, standing like cemetery monuments. The lofty church where he used to kneel and take communion was boarded-up. The Dan Ryan Expressway, the "Dangerous Dan" shot traffic over the remnants of the old neighborhood. People were driving over his old country!

He stopped looking down, looked up at a masked face. A stickup on the Dangerous Dan? It was his doctor looking down on him, and he fell into thought of a referee counting him out in the ring.

....

In the ring, Geno was looking through the bars of his boxing helmet, seeing the street kid, called Ski. He was bobbing between his bulging boxing gloves. Toothpick Nick was yelling at the two of them to keep guards up. Geno always liked to drop arms, tempt sparing partners to make a move.

"Keep eye contact," Toothpick Nick yelled at him.

Geno was in the habit of looking at the direction of opponent's feet, not the aim of his eyes. He saw the street kid's feet aimed to the right, felt the wind of Ski's glove glancing off the left side of his chin. Ski was sputtering at him that it was more blessed to give than receive!

Geno was gasping for him to turn the other cheek! They maneuvered around each other at close range, jabbing and hooking, mixing it up.

Ski was a tough street kid, built like a Sherman tank, armed with rapid firing fists. Good legs on him, too, rising on tiptoes. He had good footwork!

A voice shot through the ropes, the voice of Walski, the big-nosed punk called Bits!. He wanted Geno to get on with it, wanted his own turn in the ring.

Geno, uncorked a left, popped a right, set Ski on his tail, but the street kid pulled himself up on the ropes, started swinging again. Toothpick Nick yelled for the "pugs" to "break it up," and called for "Walski" to "muscle-in" on the Cork.

Basil Walski, the "Bits," was already sucking his mouthpiece into place, and ducking between the ropes. He sidestepped toward Geno, hit him with a flurry of words, "got fuggin' mind on knockouts or knock-ups?"

Bits couldn't read a newspaper, but could read Geno's mind. He knew Geno wasn't concentrating on boxing. Bits caught him off guard, jarred him with a left, hissed something about "poppin' it to the Pop to be."

"Put cork in it," Geno hissed through his mouth guard. His brother-in-law, Kozy's cousin, was one of the judges on other side of the ropes.

"Gonna take ya down," Geno warned. "Only babes fall fer Geno!"

Geno back pedaled, kept Bits in his sights. It seemed, all at once, his old buddy"s face looked obscene. It had taken on the look of a man's privates. His bulbous nose was pointed up, quivering like an erection, and his flabby cheeks were hanging down like the balls on a bull.

"Bits look better if he put trunks on face!"

Geno dodged a left and threw a right, caught Bits on the button, put him down on one knee. He was stunned, managed to stand, couldn't get his gloves up.

"Get bad ass outa ring," Toothpick Nick ordered with a splinter of toothpick, "give Delaney dude a pop at the Cork."

Jamie Delaney was at ringside, running in place, looking good in silk trunks and fancy footgear. He was a college kid volunteering at the Settlement.

Already parting through the ropes, Delaney ducked in the ring. Geno fell back to his corner, eyed the rich dude getting set, punching his gloves together. He really knew his way around the ring, got private lessons from a pro. Geno knew he could whip the rich kid's butt, but didn't want to knock himself out of free rides in the dude's four-door Nineteen-Forty-Seven Frazier sedan. Taking a drivers-ed course at the Settlement, Geno got to borrow the dude's wheels for practice, but practiced mostly on girls, in the back seat.

"Canvas fancy pants," came the yell from Bits on the other side of the ropes. He was shaking out of his headgear, brushing back his hair. Geno knew Bits fingered the Delaney dude as "a sneak-spy." Why else would a rich kid volunteer to help out at the Settlement? Geno knew the rich kid was a sociology major researching "gang culture," and wanted Geno's help.

As the Delaney dude made his moves, around and around, Geno kept him in his sights. The slick dude had a good build on him, Geno thought, but it went to waste, never went down for the long count with a woman, never got its bell rung. The dude even admitted it! Geno offered to fix him up, but the dude said he was "saving" himself for the right girl."

Geno kept his range, measured the space between them with the length of his arm, kept in mind the distance between their ways of life. The dude lived way up high in an apartment house in Hyde Park, next to the "country club," and the Lake Front. Geno had a couple of invites, got a ride on a private elevator to a door with a "Colored" for a housekeeper. The Delaney dude even had a room to himself, college pennants on his wall, and a window shot at Lake Michigan.

There was a lot of distance between them.

The pair finally swung into each other. Geno put Delaney on the ropes with a left, but let him get away.

"Meat packing boy pack punch," Toothpick Nick spit out with another splinter of toothpick, "but got no killer instinct!"

The bell clanged. The three minute round had gone round the clock too fast for Delaney, too slow for Geno. It was time to hit the showers. Geno and his sparing partner touched gloves, jumped through the ropes, headed for the locker room with all the others.

As Geno and Bits banged open their adjoining locker doors, Bits made a stink about Geno giving the "dude" a soft touch. Geno said Bits smelled like he slept in a wheel of cheese. Bits bent over and aimed his rear end at Geno. He had a talent for farting at will.

They skinned out of trunks, in silence, strutted into the showers where other bodies were already dissolving in streams of water and steam. Geno got a filmy view of Ski and Delaney unfolding armpits to the spray, like budding plants to the sun. It occurred to him that he could see more of others than himself. He wondered if others had as much to hide? As he caught another flash of Jamie Delaney's slippery skin flickering in and out of the spray, he thought of palming Kozy off on the dude's dumb ass. If he could get Delaney in the sack with Kozy, he'd fall for the pregnancy rap, but he let the scheme go down the drain. She wasn't his kind of girl, and Kozy wouldn't go for anyone else.

He came up with a blurry view of the street kid known as Ski. He was standing on sturdy legs, body rotating, soapy blond hair thinning under the pounding splash of water. He might go for Kozy, but he was too street smart to take the pregnancy rap. Geno looked down. His toes were spreading out, squashed, flattened, depressed like his spirits. He looked up, wanted to get inside one of those other bodies, any body not hung with pregnancy troubles. He wanted to get out of his own body.

....

"Got your old bones back in joint!"

The voice of the man called Ski sounded in Eugene Baran's ears, and he opened his eyes to the white of his hospital room, and the sight of Ski in the opposite bed. He was not the Ski with hair streaming thin in the shower of memory. He was the Ski with hardly any hair at all.

"Mind's out of joint." Eugene Baran heard his own voice groaning at Ski. "Legs don't do what I tell 'em."

"Restrained to keep you from rolling over on the hip. In my early practice, a body would be sandbagged."

"Can't sleep on my back, damn it!"

"Can think on your back. Lay back, take time to get in joint with your past."

"Will looking back get me back on my feet?"

"Keep you in balance. We embody the past, stand on it."

"Broke with my past."

"Past and present are joined at the hip."

"My past was a pain in the ass."

"Past kicked me around, too, you know," Ski said, and the conversation between beds lapsed. Ski sank down in bed, remembering growing up in one folding bed after another, one foster home after another. He preferred sleeping in empty fright cars on railroad sidings, or under back stairs in alleys.

"Lived in the streets," he spoke up, mostly to himself, "ran against the law, and my police record grew faster than grade school height and weight reports."

"My story, too," Eugene Baran talked back. "Past is past!"

"Past put us here. Got the book thrown at me, but turned a page in reform school, turned up a better life. One page leads to another."

"What makes you relive the past when it was so hard to live?"

"It wasn't all hard. Remember the Corner Candy shop?"

"I sure liked the penny candy-counter."

"A penny for your thoughts about the girl behind the counter, the Candy Girl, Christina Josowski?"

"Crippled-up kid with a stovepipe for a leg?"

"She was a lollipop on a stick, with one good leg."

"Saw better meat in barrels."

"You only saw her withered leg. She had the face and heart of an angel. Too bad girls couldn't wear pants in those days."

"Girls in pants seemed to go against nature, girls in pants," Eugene Baran remembered. "Nowadays, women have taken to pants, and taken the jobs of men."

"Men and women are finally getting in joint as equals."

"Men should be on top."

"You're out of joint with the times!"

Eugene Baran let it pass. He was trying to get the Candy Girl in the cross hairs of memory sights. He remembered neighborhood punks took potshots at her, mocked and tormented her. "Back in our time," he mentioned to Ski, "people blamed a deformity on the sin of the father!"

Eugene Baran mentioned that gossip put the blame on the Candy Girl's old man. It was said he tried to fuck-up the pregnancy with a coat hanger, only hooking a leg."

"God-awful thinking," Ski sighed from his side. "Some of my patients still blame sickness on sin."

"Josowski people should have done something about their kid's leg."

"Prosthetics not so good back then, and very costly. Every other part of Christina was made in Heaven."

"You got to know every other part?"

"God blessed us with a child to be. I scabbed during the strike to get cash to support a family."

Eugene Baran could hardly believe they'd scabbed for opposite reasons. He asked what happened to the kid the Candy Girl was carrying?

"Taken away, aborted!"

"How's that? It was against the law in those days!"

"Her people got medical approval, probably claimed a crippled girl couldn't carry a child. Maybe they claimed rape?"

"Didn't the Candy Girl throw a fit?"

"Girls had to go along with parents, in those days."

"Girls didn't have much voice," Eugene Baran granted, "but their old ladies did!" He remembered how Mama Stara ruled the Baranowski roost, especially after the Old Man passed on.

"Christina's mother sent her away," Ski explained, "somewhere I couldn't find her, but I came across a girl who needed help, and we married and took care of each other!"

"Now I'm the one with a bad stick of a leg," Eugene Baran heard himself saying.

"Now you know what a cross the Candy Girl had to bear!"

"Christina had Christ in her name," Eugene Baran tried to say something good about the girl with the withered leg.

"She had Christ in her heart."

They both fell into separate world's of thought about the Candy shop and the Candy Girl. Eugene Baran's world had a vision of the Candy shop with a glass candy case and wooden counters. Owner, Joe Josowski, was always chewing his cigar at the tobacco counter. Joe's Sow, as she was known, was always at the magazine counter, always on the lookout for shoplifters. The Candy Girl was always behind the candy counter, hiding her withered leg. Ski's world only had the Candy Girl in it.

Eugene Baran broke the silence, said a penny would buy a lot at the penny counter.

"Red and black jawbreakers, red and black licorice sticks," Ski mentioned, "a long time to make a decision, whenever we had a penny."

"I went for the bubble gum with the Indian or War cards," Eugene Baran remembered. "Collected and traded 'em."

"Only wars in Spain, and China, back then," Ski remembered.

"No war cards when big war came along," Eugene Baran said. "No gum."

"Josowski's didn't think I was worth a penny," Ski brought up in turn, "but Christina made me feel like a million."

During the space of silence between beds, Ski began collecting memories, sorting through them, picking out the time he first laid eyes on Christina. He'd been reformed in reform school, eligible to be tried out in another foster home. A County Officer, an uptight, stringy woman, had him in tow. He remembered the long, single hair hanging on her chin. He didn't have a hair on his own chin, back then. He carried a letter of recommendation from

Father Gregory, and a drag-around suitcase tied together with a rope. He remembered standing ramrod stiff in pants too small and shoes too big. Joe Josowski looked him over, revolving a cigar in his juicy mouth. Joe's wife, round as a fatted hog, gave him a lot of lip. Christina blended in with the bright-colored sofa she was standing behind. She seemed to be part of the furniture.

He dreamed on. He was accepted by the Josowski's. The County Officer commanded him to be "good" and rushed off, shaking the house as she stomped down the stairs. He had an after-school job in the Corner Store, and a room of his own, and room in his heart for the girl with the withered leg. He began calling her "Trinka." She liked to call him, "Ski-Boy." He escorted and protected her on the way to parochial school. He carried her books, protected her, went on down the street to the public school, came back in time to walk her home. He got to love books, and Trinka! In free time, Trinka read to him. They lived together in the volumes of My Book House, and were especially at home with "Hansel and Gretel." Trinka had to be told what it meant to be "abandoned." Ski had to be told what it meant to be "loved." The candy store was their Gingerbread House. The mother turned into the wicked witch, turned him out of the house. She found them playing "doctor." He wanted to become a doctor and fix Trinka's leg. She wanted to become a nurse, and take care of him. The same County Officer with the single hair on her chin came to collect him, and his suitcase with the rope around it. He was marched back to the Cook County School for Boys, and reformed some more, until he was of age to be turned loose. He found work in the Yards and a kitchenette apartment, Back of the Yards. Memory furnished that one-room with a sofa-bed, a table and chair, kitchen with sink and hotplate, bathroom down the hall. The room was at window level with the elevated tracks, and trains shook him up at night. Memory shook him up with walks to work, step after step over bricks caked with dried blood and manure. He thought his life was stagnating between days of meaningless work, but he was saving money for medical school, planning to learn how to fix Trinka's leg! All the while, he avoided the Corner Store where

Trinka still stood behind the candy-counter. He didn't think he was worthy of her, not yet. He lived on revelations of her at Mass, but never let her see him in his secondhand clothes. He loved the lofty jeweled spaces of the church. The Latin of the priests was beyond comprehension but sounded heavenly. He understood corpus and sanquis, thought God loved flesh and blood, must love the slaughterhouse. When not at work, he began attending the Settlement Project, took night classes to prepare for college, took up boxing to get rid of tension. He borrowed books, read into the nights. Some nights he was so tired the book print seemed to scurry across the page like cockroaches on the floor. Sometimes the printed words bubbled up in his mind like gruel from the tank-house. Sometimes the rattle of an elevated train almost shook the thought of Trinka out of mind.

....

The clatter of breakfast trays in the hallway shook the past out of Ski's mind. The curtain between hospital beds was now drawn, but the man behind it, and the life that went with him, was still in mind. A train of thought began carrying him back, Back of the Yards, to his lonely kitchenette apartment. Walking saved carfare, and memory walked him through the Switching Yards. He often got held up by the unloading of cattle cars. Bumping flank to flank, the big animals snorted and clattered out of railroad cars and up ramp to slaughter. He wondered if they knew where they were headed? He used to wonder where he was headed. He still did.

The voice of Nurse Rose scattered his thoughts, and he saw her as an apparition in white, standing amid the ghosts of the past.

"Abortion protestors still out in force," she was telling him as she set down his breakfast tray. "Pickets won't like what you got to eat." She pointed at the easy-over eggs. "You got aborted chickens for breakfast!"

"Not fertile," Ski said, crossing himself before taking a bite.

"Protestors against contraceptives, too," she spoke up with a gold-tooth smile. "You're a good egg, Doc. Bet you never took an egg outa nest."

"Abortion was against the law, most of my time in practice, and I always obeyed the law."

"Bet you had yourself an easy-over-egg kind of life."

"Not so easy. Got hatched out of the nest, had to bring myself up."

"Well, you got yourself a Mama hen! Be takin' you under my wing." She smiled, said she had to "fly off."

Ski poked a fork at what the nurse called "aborted" chickens. They were nested in corned-beef hash, got him stirring up memories of his job in the Potato Room where the potatoes were peeled for the corned-beef hash. Promoted to Industrial Engineering, he was put to work gathering production data for the Efficiency Experts. Assigned the Potato Room, he kept track of the number of pans of potatoes each worker peeled. They were on piece work, got fifteen cents for every pan beyond the required seven an hour.

Breakfast got him hashing-up a mess of memories.

....

The potato peelers started lining-up in Ski's memory, lining-up on both sides of two sets of conveyor belts. One belt streamed steamed raw potatoes at the peelers, and another belt carried the eyed-out potatoes away. The peelers were all women, fifteen to twenty of them, depending on how many showed up on the Monday after Payday. They stood in stalls, swishing their backsides, swatting occasional flies, inspecting and eyeing out potatoes, tossing them into overhanging pans. He walked back and forth, judged when pans were full, dumped them, credited the peeler. Faces and badge numbers and names began coming up in mind, bite after bite of corned-beef hash.

The name of Number Six-thirteen was "Rubamalinda," and her face appeared with crystal drops of sweat on pencil-drawn eyebrows. Silver hoops, big as a ring in a bull's nose, always hung from her ears. She stood in worn-out ballet slippers, bare heels sticking out the back. She often complained of "the misery" in her in "feets." He told her to get good work shoes, but she said "feets wedded to dance." She even danced in place as she peeled, often told him, as he dumped her pans, that she "pitched the boogie" at the Savoy and Regal theaters, did "gigs" all over her side of town, but couldn't make a living with her feet, had to keep a hand in potatoes.

Another pretty face along the line was round, round as her body. He didn't remember her number or name, but had been told she would strap a slabs of bacon under her dress and sneaked it by the guards at night. He only knew for sure that she had a big belly and smelled like bacon.

A name, without number or face, came to mind, Faustine. He'd read about Faust in night school, told her that a man called Faust sold his soul to the devil for wealth and fame. She didn't know about Faust, or how she came by the name of Faustine, but might have to sell her body if she couldn't make the "rate." She could hardly peel seven pans an hour.

And there was "Sara," who'd sell her soul for a different name. Her name was too "old fashioned." She wanted to be called "Shara." Once, she invited him to her place for "country- fried eats." He told he was "engaged," couldn't be unfaithful. He really felt betrothed to Trinka.

And there was Belinda, with plump ruby-lips and hair bejeweled with ringlets of black. She bragged about her "smokey color," promised a lot of fire under the smoke. She got her color off a "daddy from Smokey Mountains," and a "Mommy from Smoke House," kept telling him she was poor at peeling potatoes but good at a-peelin' to men.

Number Six-Twenty-One wanted to know what a "nice white boy" was doing in a "shit house," and why he wasn't married? He said a woman wouldn't want a man without a good job. She said, "a man ask me to marry-up, ah says, wait till ah gets mah hat."

And there was Ruby with a bush of hair that stood out, and up, in leaps and bounds. She said she'd be getting out of the "spud business" and into the "beautification business." She was learning to "process" hair. He wondered why dark women wanted to straighten hair, and white women wanted to curl it?

And there was Zetta, with the slant of oriental eyes, and the long eyelashes. Her face was bronzed like a South Sea Islander, reminding him of a woman in a painting he'd seen on a school trip to the Art Institute. The girl in the painting was grasping a round basket of breast-shaped fruit, and Zetta was always grasping a big, round potato. She was the slowest girl on the line, but assured him that she was "real fast after work." One day she came to work in a fur cape bulging under her white canning room frock. She opened and closed the white frock for everyone to see what she could earn, "after work."

The only white face came up in a row of recollections, face of an old woman from the "Old Country," known as "Stara," the Old One. Old and wrinkled, with a pinched-up mouth that never smiled, she was scrunched-up in white cap and frock. Her shapeless legs were bound-up in white cotton hose. Her shoes were cut open to let out bulging toes. She was the fastest peeler on the line, piled up the highest piece work record every day. Day after day she'd ask if "Sonny boy okay?" She let him know she had grown sons and daughters, and a strapping boy his age. Sometimes she'd address him with old country words, "ty," or "pani." She never questioned his tally at the end of the day, like some of the peelers, but her voice was always crabby, with a mix of Polish and English jammed-up in her pouting mouth. Between scowls she tried to push hard- candy on him. He had no idea what she wanted for her favors? She needed no cheating on his piece work record sheet. Maybe it was her habit from the old days, when a woman had to "pay off" the foreman in one way or another, to stay on the payroll. He wanted to think she was mothering him, thought mothers must be giving persons.

The only man in the potato room was "Nate," the "Steamer." He worked the boiler with black hands, white seams around knuckles. His hands kept the boiler belching and spitting out steamed potatoes. His hands knew their way around machinery, and around women. He had the "gospel truth" on the "canning room sisters." There were "sweet meats," and "leftovers," and he kept his mouth busy during breaks, often bragged about his gold tooth, and his ways with machinery and women. With a lingering thought of Nate, and what happened to him during the strike, Ski finished the breakfast of corned-beef hash, wiped his mouth, but couldn't clear his mind of his time and motion work in the Potato Room. He used to spend all his time counting, potato pan after potato pan, break times and changing clothes times. He even counted the bloated, pregnant drops of water dripping off overhead pipes in the Potato Room. Now it occurred to him that time and motion study wasn't so far removed from his work in medicine.

He had to keep patients in time and in motion.

It was Easter time and he knew he couldn't get in motion to the Stations of the Cross. Bedridden, he couldn't attend Mass! Another Easter time came to mind. The parishes of Sacred Heart and Saint John of God joined in celebration of "the farewell to flesh." It was Carnival time, and he showed up. Trinka appeared amid the girls waiting for dance partners. She had been turned into a princess by the magic wand of time!

She got sight of him, waved, limped his way. He bowed in his uncomfortable new suit, and his mind memorized every part of her. She was gowned in satin, down to the floor, no hint of a withered leg beneath the folds.

"Good to see my old Hansel!"

Her words came back to him as he lay in bed, herwords of complaint. Why did Hansel abandon her?

She gave her long skirt a little kick.

"Your Hansel got thrown out!"

"Hansel could have dropped breadcrumbs, little notes to let me know where he was."

Ski said he wanted to make something of himself first. She said she always liked the way he was made. He said he wanted to make himself a doctor, mend her leg. She said both legs were ready for a dance. He said neither of his legs knew how to dance.

"We're all cripples, in one way or another," she said, pointing the tip of a slipper and a flash of flesh-colored hose. "Let me give you a hand," and she led him into the music, the old hit song, A Sentimental Journey!

Before he could step into the memory of the dance, a hospital orderly cut off his journey back, took his breakfast tray and memories away, but the vibrations of the cart of breakfast trays shook him back to the apartment next to the elevated tracks. An elevated train was passing at the same time Trinka appeared in his doorway. Her voice shook with the tremble of the apartment as she told him she was out on her own, wanted to be on her own with "Ski-Boy." She said she'd walked all the way from the Corner Store, and all the way up his steps, one step after another. She said he lived "up close to heaven." He didn't know how she knew his address, but was quick to say she brought "heaven" with her. She settled on the couch that he used as a bed at night, asked him to join her.

When it came time for another elevated train to make its approach, the apartment began quivering again. The rolled-up window shade started to spin and sputter. The paper calendar on the wall was flapping. Trinka was vibrating in his arms, one part of her at a time.

Another time she made it up the back stairway, bearing tidings of great joy. "A child is to be born unto you."

....

"Daddy-O!" The word kept popping up in Eugene Baran's mind as he lay awake on his side of the hospital curtain. He still wondered how he beat the pregnancy rap? He remembered the anti-life pills didn't work any better than mustard baths and other home remedies. It came to him that Bits suggested a car bump. It would bump the bastard kid out.

Sinking into memory, he came up with Geno in the Delaney dude's wheels, with Kozy at his side. Looking back, through the rearview mirror of memory, he saw the Chicago skyline sliding over the horizon. Kozy was rolling down the window, letting the wind whip her ponytail into a gallop. His knotty hands were vibrating at the steering wheel, feeling all eight cylinders bucking like a team of horses. He imagined himself in the movie, Stagecoach, whipping horses, keeping ahead of a horde of Indians. He thought he was leaving his troubles behind. The car was obedient to his will, seemed to be part of his body. He didn't want to hurt it, but kept looking ahead for a place to bump out the bastard kid to be. The hood ornament, a ballet dancer, was poised in a never ending leap, pointing ahead, at a lonely country road.

"Man alive," Kozy screeched! "Scarin' life outa me."

He'd never thought of scaring the "life" out of her. It would save the car from busting a fender or springing a spring!

"Look, no hands," he yelled, speeding up, but letting up at thought of Teresa's ugly birthmark. It came from Mama Stara's scare. Pregnant, she was almost hit by a runaway milkwagon horse.

He let the car slow down, looked for a place to skip off the road, but a glance to the side caught Kozy at her beads. Had she ratted to a priest? Holy Shit! If word got out that she was knocked-up, a little crack-up in a car might not be seen to be an accident.

"You been to confession?"

Kozy nodded head and ponytail, said she went to Holy Cross where priests didn't know her.

"Priests got a bead on everybody."

"Gotta make confession to make Mass. Don't make Mass, make folks mad."

He told her pregnant women shouldn't show their faces in Holy Places! She said only the old people believe in wywod, and her people would skin her alive if they knew her condition.

"No more talkin' to priests, no way!"

Kozy laughed, said she used to have to make up sins, and priests told her to mend her ways. She thought she had to sew something.

Geno told her to sew-up her mouth. Kozy agreed to lie about confession, take Mass in sin, mend her ways later. She bent forward to flip on the radio, couldn't line up a music station, settled for the news. It was reported that the Russians might close the roads and rails to Berlin, and Geno let the car slip off the road. It rushed to an explosion.

In the silence of the hospital room, Eugene Baran thought he could hear the crash, remembered the Indiana clinic where Geno had been told his "little woman's baby's safe, safest passenger in the car." Everything went black again.

....

Coming out of blackness, Eugene Baran looked up at the black countenance of a man with a doctor's stethoscope hanging loose.

"I was your surgeon," the man said, "Dr. Hamilton, making my rounds. Your surgery went well."

The black face with dangling mustache and name of Hamilton gave Eugene Baran remembrance of the Moses Man, and the killer-pills that didn't work. As the doctor made his examination, Eugene Baran wondered if he'd been cut open by the son or grandson of the black Beef-Ribber.

"I knew a Moses Hamilton when I worked in the Yards."

"You might have known one of my kin. Long time ago, a good number of family put their time in the stockyards."

....

"Black an' White brothers gotta pull together!"

The words floated around in Eugene Baran's head as the doctor examined him, and by the time the doctor left, Eugene Baran thought he was Geno again, scrunched-up in the headquarters of the United Packinghouse Workers of America. The place was bursting with black and white people, smoke and swearing. Geno saw Moses Hamilton with union leaders on the platform, saw himself with a bandage round the top of his head, a reminder of the car bump that didn't bump away his troubles.

The command for brothers to work together bellowed out of a local officer, a black man in a turtleneck sweater. He was standing on the platform with other union leaders, shaking his fist at the "sins of Management," announcing that talks with Management had broken down. The Federal Mediation and Conciliation Services had dropped out of negotiations! The "Sixty- Day Cooling Off Period" was over. It was time to make it "hot for the Packers!"

As the cheers of union members settled down, the national president was introduced. He was a "college man," a lawyer. In coat and tie he looked like a company man, but was greeted with a respectful clap of hands.

"It's a hundred years after the Communist Manifesto," he spoke up, "and labor's still in chains!"

Geno didn't know he was in chains, only wanted to keep out of ball and chain!

"We got to take down the slave masters," the President lashed out as soon as there was a break in the uproar. He talked about the strength of their union. It was over a hundred thousand strong, "spread from sea to sea in one hundred and forty plants." He went on to report the Amalgamated Meat Cutters and Butchers were going to join them in a strike, and while the Teamsters settled with the Packers, they promised not to cross picket lines. "We strike at stroke of midnight!"

After a roar went up, the president took his seat again, and the local union director took his place at the podium, yelled out, "Let rulin' class tremble!"

Stamping feet gave the floor a shake, and the walls a tremble.

"Cops, National Guard, nobody stoppin' us!" The Director held up a pack of cigarettes. "Lucky Strikes, an we be lucky strikers, gonna kick butt!"

Moses Hamilton roared out, "Let Lord's trumpets blow! It be Judgment Day!"

II

Labor Pains

The day came, Tuesday, St. Patrick's Day, March 16, 1948! All across the nation newspapers headlined the strike!

National Butcher Block! Panic For Pork Chops!

Chicago newspapers heralded the Yards as the Busiest Square Mile in the World, and it was now Out of Business!

Elevated trains and streetcars had carried off the last of the night shift. The Yards were stripped to the bone. Only skeleton maintenance crews hung on. Clouds of fading white smoke and steam hung over the Yards, like swirling ghosts. When sunlight slanted through the morning overcast, it caught its reflection in overhanging particles of soot, sparkled like diamonds above the smoldering smokestacks.

Daylight brought the pickets out in force, Geno among them. They closed off all fourteen gates to the Union Stockyards, and built fires in steel garbage cans to warm their hands. Newspaper boys were flashing headlines along the streets between the pickets and the police. The Chicago Tribune and the Dziennik Chicagoski branded the leaders of the United Packinghouse Workers of America as "Communists," blamed the "Reds" for the coming shortage of "Red Meat." Other newspapers branded the Packers, "gluttons for meat profits!"

Hungry, without breakfast, Geno lined up in front of the Main Entrance to the Yards, at the arched limestone gate on Halsted, across the street from the Stockyard Inn, the "in-place," Back of the Yards. Geno knew a writer stayed there a long time ago and wrote a novel about bad meat packing. It led to government meat inspection. Marya's father told him that.

While Geno was brooding about government inspection, and stamping feet to keep warm, a WGN radio truck eased up to the curb. A radio crew got out, set up equipment. Word spread along the picket line that the truck was bringing WGN's morning radio broadcast to the strikebound Yards. A reporter, getting wired-up, announced to the crowd that he was going to conduct interviews. He raised his microphone, told radio listeners he was "on the meat beat at the Main Gate of the Union Stockyards," he said he was surrounded by "cops an' pickets an' bystanders," and would get their "slants" on the strike. He held out his microphone, asked a man in topcoat and derby to "tell my listeners your take on the strike?"

"Pickets are taking the law in their own hands, blocking traffic on public streets. I'm management, can't get to my office."

The management man took aim at the microphone, said the public should be protected from "bare-knuckle unionism!" The interviewer asked why management wasn't willing to meet union demands, and the management man said higher wages would lead to higher meat prices. "Inflation's a tax on everybody, hurts poor people most of all!"

"It costs more to live these days," the interviewer agreed. "Do union men make a living wage?"

"Average full time worker gets a buck-fifteen an hour! That'll buy a couple pounds of steak, every hour."

"We don't live by meat alone."

"Can't live without it."

"No meat at all if the industry can't afford to stay in business."

"How much is a man worth?"

The interviewer didn't wait for an answer, started moving on.

"I'd like to speak for the working man," someone in the crowd called out, elbowing his way to the roving reporter. "I'm Doctor Kip Godfrey, professor and social worker. Meat packing workers don't work all the time, wait on seasonal farm animal shipments. The Back of the Yards Council came out on the side of the workers! The City worker's Family Budget reported that a man with a family of three can't live up to the American standard on what the Packer's pay."

"Thanks for your side of the story," the interviewer talked back. "I think everybody has a stake in this strike," explaining that nobody would have a steak if the strike kept up.

He moved on, stretching the microphone cable as far as it would reach. "Let's hear from a working man. Here's a mighty big one."

"Jivin' at me?"

"What's your name?"

"Loadin' Dock mens calls me Boast."

"What's a loading dock man gonna get out of the strike?"

"Gonna strike it rich!"

"Is money the only benefit you're striking for?"

"Ain't money whole ball-a wax?"

"Working conditions, vacations, seniority?"

"Union say strike, Boast strike."

"Are you working for union, or packers?"

"Workin' fer me!"

"Good luck with yourself," the reporter said, and moved along, put the microphone to a picket. "What's your name, young man?"

"Geno Baranowski, checker at Armour's."

"This young man has a bandage on the forehead," the interviewer told his listeners, and turned to geno, asked if he'd been fighting with police or non-strikers?

"Car accident!"

"Are you a Marxist? Sign you carry says Nothing to Lose but Our Chains."

"Carry sign, don't read it. No chains on me."

"Aren't you chained to wages? How you strikers gonna live without wages?"

"Union gonna jack us up."

"20,000 meat packers on strike in Chicago alone. Union got enough jack?"

"Packers gonna go bust before us!"

"It's a house divided," the reporter told is listeners, and turned his microphone toward a black girl on picket duty. "What's your name, Honey?"

"Rubamalinda McHenry."

"What's a woman's view on the strike?"

"Same as man's, 'cept woman take-home pay ain't as good as a man's!"

"Don't you have a man to look out for you?"

"No steady. Ain't so easy for single gal to keep body and soul together nowadays, an' legs together, too."

"This gal's legs are dancing as we speak," the reporter was quick to inform his listeners.

"Mah feets made for dancin'!"

The reporter wished her "good luck" with her feet," and took his microphone as far as it would reach. "Here's a man of the cloth," and asked the priest what a man of the cloth was doing in the "biggest slaughterhouse of the world?"

"I'm Father Gregory, chaplain at the Cook County School for Boys. God's everywhere."

"In slaughterhouses?"

"World's a slaughter house."

The interviewer asked if God took sides on the strike, and the priest said God takes the "good side," and the reporter said each side thinks it's on the "good side."

"I don't speak for or against the Union, for or against the Packers, only speak for those who are hungry."

"We'll all be hungry if this strike doesn't get settled," the interviewer said, turning away, telling his listeners to "listen up!" He raised his microphone to pick up the chants of angry strikers.

"Nobody shall pass!"

....

"Little girlie not to pass," yelled a picket in an old Navy peacoat and knit cap. "You be dead meats, sister, if ya try to wag pretty ass cross line."

The girl, Marya Nowak, said she was a "desk worker, not union." She kicked a foot, showed hose and heels, pulled herself together in the yellow raincoat that covered most of her tailored outfit. "Can't stop me. Free country."

"Not free to pass!"

"Takin' my freedom away."

"Satin dolly ain't sashayin' cross line! Nobody passes!"

Another picket told her, "Office workers turn down chance to join union, ain't got no office job no more!"

"Marya."

Geno, waving a picket sign, came rushing along the picket line toward the girl of his dreams.

"Get goons off my back!"

"She's my bitch," Geno panted at the pickets.

"I'm nobody's bitch," she snapped back, "belong to myself."

"Belong back of line," a picket roared.

"Lose my job!" Marya cried, almost in tears.

"Call in sick," Geno suggested. "I'm off duty. You an me can get our tongues blessed for Saint Patty's Day!"

World's End was on her way home," Marya said with the shrug of a shoulder, "could use a drink an' a blessin'."

....

World's End was a family bar, not like the saloons lined-up outside the stockyard gates, and it was Geno's new home. Just out of school, working full time, he'd rented the only room in the hallway, back of the barroom. It got him a pad of his own, a life of his own, away from the Uneducated Ones. The barroom, up front, was his livingroom, furnished with chairs and tables, and company. It entertained him with a big radio console, and a newfangled television set. The bar was famous for its beer on tap, bottled booze, pretzels, pickles, and lots of stockyard jive.

World's End had been known as Mack's World in the old days. Some regulars still remembered old Mackowitz in a leather apron strapped round a strapping big belly. Mack's World was a man's world, "no women allowed." When hard liquor wasn't allowed, during Prohibition, Mack's World stayed open with "watered-down beer," peanuts, political talk, and a little "moonshine" in the dark of the back hallway. When "Old Mack" bellied-up and Young Mack took over, his wife was allowed in, but all other wives still had to send little sons inside to fetch dads home on paydays. Young Mack's wife helped tend bar, kept the glasses clean, blew them dry. Sometimes she drew beer, blew off heads, blew kisses to patrons. When Young Mack was called up for war service, Mrs. Mack kept peace in the bar. When Young Mack's ship went down at sea, Mrs. Mack kept the bar on an even keel. Her heart was as big as the rest of her, and she opened the bar to women, if they had an escort.

When the war ended with an atomic bang, the Bomb hovered over the world with threat of total destruction! Mrs. Mack thought her tavern was a good place to get "bombed," and a good place to be when the world ended! The neon sign out front was changed to "World's End," but the place was still Mack's World to some of the old timers, and it was the "Livin' End" to most others.

....

"Sure is great to be livin' in World's End," Geno told Marya as he led her toward the neighborhood bar.

Marya thought it would be better to live in world without end! Geno thought of making love to her without end. When they got to World's End, it was still closed. Geno twirled the key around on a chain, and opened up. Mrs. Mack was behind the bar, wiping it down. Geno told her he just got off picket duty, and nobody got across the line. Mrs. Mack looked up and said no "Geno lady friend" could get past her picket line.

Marya said she wasn't that kind of girl, reminded Mrs. Mack that she was the meat inspector's daughter.

"Just bless our tongues for Saint Paddy," Geno ordered up, swinging a leg over a barstool.

"Geno sure need blessin'," Mrs. Mack joked, flipping the towel over her shoulder. She drew the usual beer for Geno, asked Marya what "big shot inspector girl take?"

"Red wine, any kind of red," Marya said, spinning round on the barstool, unwinding herself out of a yellow raincoat. Geno was excited to see her dolled-up for office work.

"Red's a labor man's color," Mrs. Mack told the girl, popping open a bottle. "Your Pa ain't no labor man." She filled a glass and slid it across the bar.

"Pa's a government man, not management man, not union man!"

"Every livin' body gotta take sides," Mrs. Mack said, pulling the towel from her shoulder and giving the counter-top another shine.

"Pa's on public side, on side of safe meat!"

"V'at side inspector gal be on?"

"She be on customer side of bar," Geno talked for Marya. He'd been circling his eyes around the ropes of golden hair wrapped round Marya's head. She was almost the image of the tintype portrait Mama Stara had framed on her dresser.

"I'm on side of lady barkeep," Marya spoke for herself, raising her glass of red wine in a salute to Mrs. Mack.

Mrs. Mack looked up with a grin that bulged out both cheeks. She squeezed lips together, asked if the "picture-purty gal" would like to have the "picture tube" turned on?" Without waiting for an answer she wiped hands on apron and hustled round the bar.

"Never see much tell-a-vision," Marya said, sliding off the barstool and following Mrs. Mack. "My people call tell-a-vision a boob-tube."

"Shows more than tells," Mrs. Mack said.

The television set had a round screen that began to light up at the touch of Mrs. Mack. She patted the box, fiddled with the antenna ears. A picture began taking form. She said the round screen was a porthole where a body could see the world, "like a sailor man."

"Like a magic carpet, Marya said, settling down at a chair and table.

Geno got down with her, said he never knew he was poor until he saw the way people lived in the "picture-box."

Mrs. Mack said everybody was rich with a picture-box, said she'd leave them to a "soap opera" and waddled off. Customers were gathering at the front door.

Geno struck a match to the cigarette stuck at his lower lip. He shaped smoke rings, blew words through them, asked Marya if she liked the picture box?

"Sometimes I feel like I'm in a box," she said, "can't get out."

"I'm your Genie in a box!" Geno reminded her with a slap at his crotch, "give me a rub, see vat comes out."

Marya looked away, said he was the same horny bull of the stockyards. "Once upon a time, I figured a good man was tryin' to get out of you."

"Outside man counts," Geno said, squaring his shoulders, getting up, strutting toward the television set. He changed channels, tuned in a news report. "Might get update on strike," he said, flipping the curl out of his eyes.

A newsman began reporting fighting in Palestine where a Jewish state was struggling to be born!" Geno didn't like to think of anything struggling to be born, but couldn't find another station. By the time he was back at the table, the newscaster was throwing out the news of a treaty signed in Brussels to line up European allies against the Soviet Union.

"Let us make peace treaty," Geno offered, turning to Marya.

"Got no fight 'gainst you. Got no interest in you, neither!"

"Got interest in some fancy office dude?"

"Got interest in men using brains." She licked a finger and pasting down a loose strand of hair roped round her head.

Geno said brawn is better than brains, and his brawn could make big bucksin the "fight ring."

"Too much fighting," Marya sighed, pointing to the round screen of the television set. The newscaster was reporting the threat of war over a crisis in Berlin!

"No skin off our bones," Geno broke in. "No skin at all if big bomb goes off!"

The newsman came up with a news flash. President Truman would be addressing the nation on the meat strike, "tomorrow."

....

"Dialin' up Mr. Truman talk on talk-box," Mrs. Mack announced to the men huddled together in World's End. "Ain't on picture box."

A blast of radio static shattered the air, settled down to the scratchy voice of the President. His words, in an accent unfamiliar, proclaimed a "national emergency!" He said meat packing is the third largest industry in the country, only behind steel and auto-making! He said the meat strike was putting the whole economy at risk! He warned of injunctions to keep packinghouses open, warned "management" and "labor" that the strike would only keep meat prices going up! The "coal strike" remained unsettled, he reminded the nation, and the meat strike would be adding hunger to the cold!

Speaking in sharp, crisp tones, the president announced the creation of a "Fact Finding Board" to deal with "the inflation-threatening meat strike." As his words kept vibrating through the loudspeaker, the listeners kept pounding tables, talking back to the radio.

"Vat's inflation?"

"Vat's fact findin'?"

"Vat be injunctions?"

The "National economy," the president kept speaking, would spin out of control if meat prices kept spiraling up. "National Security," he spoke more loudly, would be threatened if a shortage of meat added to world hunger. Hunger would drive people to Communism! He said there was a "Cold War" between the

Communist East and Democratic West, and it was "heating up in Berlin." The Soviets were threatening to cut off the German capital from Allied occupation zones!

While men in the barroom began shouting at each other, trying to connect "national economy" and "national security," the president was calling the nation to arms, calling for a peacetime draft of young men, the "eighteen to twenty-five year olds." The "price of peace," he affirmed, is "preparedness for war."

"Vat price-a -peace got to do vit piece-a-meat?"

"Drafted men gonna put bayonet to us strikers?"

Mrs. Mack switched off the radio as the president signed off, and called for Draft Beer, not Draft Boys! She began pumping the tap, filling steins of beer.

Hands tossed coins spinning on the counter, hands reached out for steins of foaming beer. Toasts went up for the "strike," not the "draft."

Arguments began popping up like bottle corks. Talk of war against the Soviet Union got mixed-up with war against the Packers! The talk broke apart, settled down at separate tables.

Way in back, Geno Baranowski was scrunched-up with some of the Forty-Niners at a small table. They'd taken in the president's talk with beers and smokes, and aired their pros and cons. 'Moocher the Mouth" wanted to know what an injunction was? He hardly ever opened his mouthful of rotten teeth except to swish down beer and mooch cigarettes. "Slick," the crafty one of the Forty-Niners, told the "Mooch" an injunction was a "court order" that could outlaw pickets from barricading public streets. "Rabbits, the Bits," said it was only a "piece of paper" the union could wipe ass on! Moocher said he wanted an injunction to keep from getting drafted, and asked for a smoke. Geno said he wanted an injunction to keep Moocher from bumming cigarettes. The Mooch got up, witout a word, and took off to look for another table.

Slick got up with him, said he had to work on a "deal."

Ricky Koczur, Kozy's big brother, turned up, grabbed Slick's empty chair and slapped it under him."Let a Vet join ya," he sputtered. He was just out of the army, squared-up in his Eisenhower jacket, garrison cap cocked to one side.

"Good to see ya back to Yards," Bits said with a friendly punch at the newcomer.

Ricky Koczur stretched out his legs, showed off his army boots, squirmed around to get comfortable. "Army goona get your asses," he predicted, "make men outa youse."

"Can't be no better men! Ain't gonna be no draft in peacetime," Bits said. "Free country ain't it?"

"Us strikers see more fight on picket line," Geno sputtered through his beer, "than Ricky- Boy ever see on occupation duty in Germany."

"Got guard duty at Nuremberg trials," Ricky Koczur bragged, "kept Nazi big shots in line, an' got to drive American and British brass round." He stuck out his chin and pushed back his garrison cap. "Army taught me to drive a truck. Geno can't keep car on road!"

"Livie took my eye off road," Geno snapped. "Keep eye off Liv," her brother shot back.

"Don't make bull of stockyards see red," Bits warned. He wanted to see a fight between him and Geno.

"Gun make all men same size," Ricky Koczur slurred, slapped at his hip.

Everyone knew he sneaked a souvenir Lugar out of occupied West Germany, and could use it. Geno only feared the Koczurs would find out about the Kozy condition.

"Got no eye on Cousin Livie," Geno shot back. "Only givin' cousin a joy ride."

"No blood cousin!"

"Oughta be no bad blood between us relatives," Geno said with a shrug. "Only got bad blood fer Packers."

Kozy's brother cupped hands around his lighted match, lit up, blew out smoke and cusses. "No more Packers fer me," he said, getting up, "college on G.I. Bill gonna be my ticket uptown." He scraped his feet on the floor, waved his cigarette, said he was going to scrape the stockyard crud off his boots.

As soon as he was out of earshot, Geno told Bits to keep his mouth shut about Kozy.

"She sure got ya down fer long count."

"Ya didn't get me up. Black pills got no punch, car-bump a bust."

"Army do ya."

"Army lock me up like marriage ball an' chain."

"Army tour, two years. Marriage, lifetime."

"Army make me pay child support, maybe make me marry-up. Checked it out at recruitin' office, uptown!"

"Got final solution fer ya," Bits said, blowing his words and smoke in Geno's ear. "Back alley Roto-Rooter job get ya unscrewed! Got lowdown on crooked sawbones. Couple Century bills get Geno back to good times."

"Can't shell-out so many clams!"

"Get married to a bank loan!"

"Bank not gonna marry a kid like me to a loan."

"Mob make ya a deal."

"Ain't gonna put my balls in a sling!"

"Got big enough balls fer scabbin'? Packers gearin' up fer production. A scab could get big bonus, overtime, double time, make a killin'!"

"Geno ain't no Judas?"

"Union ain't no Jesus!"

Their muffled talk had been swallowed up in the chatter of the barroom, but was blasted away by the sound of Mrs. Mack at the loudspeaker.

"Listen up! Gonna turn up tube, see if it got picture of strike news."

"Tube beats books," Bits told Geno as a picture took shape in the round hole of the television set. "Body don't need no readin' no more."

A reporter on the screen reported that "meat packers" stopped negotiating with strikers! Hisses spread around the barroom. When the voice of the newscaster came back through the noise, men got word the "packers are cranking-up production with non-union labor." The barroom got shook up with stamping feet.

Mrs. Mack had to switch off the television before men ripped it off the stand. "Trim fat off scabs, not me," she yelled, and reminded the strikers of her Strike Benefit. "Money go to union," she proclaimed, "put meat in soup kitchen." She held up a roll of raffle tickets and said the prize-winning drawing was coming up on Saturday night.

....

The Saturday Strike Benefit at World's End was about to get swinging, but Geno was hung-up with thoughts of scabbing, not dancing. He'd lived a union life, but had to break with it to save his life! How could he get away with it? He kept thinking about it as he brushed back his hair, except for the corkscrew curl that hung down and obscured the bandage left over from the car "scrape." Slicked-up in his Sunday suit with the sharkskin pants pressed to a razor's edge, he slowly dragged himself up the steps to the decked-out dance hall. It was strung with paper streamers and colored lights. Tables were pushed back to make room for dancing. He was early, only one girl was spinning round on the dance floor, dancing with herself, twirling around and round. Skirt sailing high, breasts rolling loose in a sailor-jumper, her long yellow hair was streaming under a sailor's white hat. She was a fully packed seabag, Geno thought, until the body turned round into Kozy!

"Daddy-O," she shrieked at sight of him.

Geno didn't want to be seen with her, had to acknowledged her, keep on her good side until he got her to go under the knife.

"Missed every little inch of ya," Kozy said, shaking herself out of jive time, coming to a standstill, letting her skirt drop anchor. She caught her breath, asked why he'd been keeping himself scarce?

"Figured my Kozy was grounded!"

"Off leash!"

The jukebox started stirring-up the hall with Z Brooklyna Dzieczyna, drawing dancers on the floor.

"Man alive," Kozy belted out, "got G.I. Jive, man alive!" She caught Geno in both arms. "Give Kozy a drive round dance floor, no crackups!"

Geno held back, blamed the crash on her for taking his eyes off the road. She snuggled up, told him to keep his eye on her from now on, snapped her fingers, put her hips in gear. "Show your stuff, show me off."

Showing her off was exactly what he didn't want to do, but had to keep her in line until he got the bastard kid off line. As he let himself be drawn onto the dance floor, he caught sight of his mother and sister at a woman's table with Kozy's mother. Did they see him? Were they putting him down for the crackup, putting him up for marriage?

He took Kozy to the hop, bounced her out of their sight. Kozy squealed at the spark of his touch, kept up with him until the last beat of the jukebox. Dancers stood in pairs for the next platter to drop. It came up with a singer's voice. "People will say we're in love!"

Kozy squealed, swung Geno into the rhythm. He didn't want people to think they were in love. "Too slow," he snapped, holding back.

"Song come from Oklahoma," Kozy shot back. "Broadway show comin' to Chicago! Show me off!"

He said she'd be showing in a broad- way, if she didn't get fixed-up.

"Done all I be told," she protested, "tubs of smelly kerosene an' mustard, mouth fulls of rotten pills."

"Got me a card up sleeve," he said, leading her off the dance floor,"could give ya a royal flush!"

"Deal me in."

"Ain't easy to get in game, gotta ante-up lotta chips. Got any cash?"

"Ain't got lunch money no more."

He looked over Kozy's shoulder, caught the eye of his mother sitting with Teresa and Kozy's old lady. He knew what they were getting at.

....

"Geno-boy got good intentions," Kozy's mother was asking Mama Stara, "or just takin' Liv fer ride?"

"Boy live on own," Mama Stara said, with a lick of the lips, "got own mind," and she took a paper cup of beer to her pouting lips.

"Boy don't got mind on road," Mrs. Koczur raised her voice, "put Liv in stitches." She folded puffy arms across a sloping chest. "Girl get crash-bang-bang from Geno-boy, still got crash-bang crush on your Geno-boy."

"Crash bang accident!" Teresa spoke up.

"Love ain't no accident. Liv talk 'bout gettin' married-up."

"Too young for talk like that," Teresa broke in again.

"Not too young in Old Country."

"Not in Old Country."

"Not easy to bring up girl in new country. Girl too free."

"Boy not easy to bring up," Mama Stara intervened. "Boy in America got no right to job til almost man, free to get in troubles."

"Girl should be free," Teresa spoke up.

"Free to get in troubles?"

"Free to be."

"Most gals free to marry, all free to make babies!"

Teresa talked back to her mother, said "babies keep a girl down, keep a girl from getting up in business."

"Babies be woman business."

"Keepin' my man in school, my business," Teresa kept talking back, knowing her mother wanted her to quit work and start making babies.

"Babies be too much cost in America," Mrs. Koczur mumbled in her beer, "an' don't payoff like in Old Country."

....

"Baby cost bundle to get rid of," Geno was telling Kozy when the music from Oklahoma sounded off. "Takes lotsa dough-re-mi-dough."

"Beer Barrel Polka on tap," Kozy squealed as the sounds of concertina, drum, and tuba came roaring out of the jukebox. "Gimme barrel-a-fun."

"Gotta roll out barrel-a bucks," he told her as he jerked away, headed across the dance floor. He'd just gotten sight of the rich dude, Jamie Delaney and Doc Godfrey on the other side of the dance hall. The rich dude hadn't put the screws on him for car repair, might be a pushover for a loan!

....

Figuring schemes for getting money out of Delaney, Geno parted his way through the polka line, hailed the rich dude when he got to the other side. "Good to see ya stickin' up fer union!"

"Union sticks up for working man," Jamie Delaney greeted Geno in turn.

His companion, Doc Godfrey, said the union backs the Community and the Community Settlement House backs the union.

"Hang out with us," Jamie Delaney offered, waving Geno to one of the empty chairs at their square table. He took a pitcher, slopped beer into a paper cup for Geno.

Geno slapped a chair under him, raised the cup with a word of "Cheers."

"Cheers for you," Jamie Delaney said, raising a beer with a toast of his own. "Good to see you up and around, after smash-up."

"And up and around the dance floor," Dr. Godfrey noted, "with a sailor girl in tow."

"Cousin by marriage," Geno slobbered with his mouth bubbling in the head of his beer.

He lowered the paper cup to ask Delaney if his car was up and around?

"Fender-bender straightened up," Delaney assured him. Suds at his lips, he sputtered that the Insurance Company was paying off "like a slot-machine," but wouldn't pay off anymore if he wasn't the one at the wheel.

"No more drivin' fer me! Droppin' Driver's Ed! Learned my lesson."

Dr. Godfrey said the world was a "classroom for learning how to live together." Geno said the world was more like "a boxin' ring, a fight fer life."

"Missing you in the ring," Jamie Delaney brought up, raising his voice over the sound of the jukebox coming up with another polka.

"Missing Geno at the Settlement," Dr, Godfrey piped up, with a smile, and offer of a cigarette. "Toothpick Nick was afraid you hurt your hands, not worried about your head."

Fitting a cigarette in the side of his mouth, Geno said his fists were ready to hit leather, "soon as union fight's over."

"Union's got Packers by the meatballs," Jamie Delaney declared, mouth foaming with beer.

"I hear the packers are hitting below the belt," Dr. Godfrey mentioned, "calling up scabs, tooling-up for production."

"Low blow," Geno said with a blast of smoke, even as he simmered inside with thought of scabbing. His words were carried off by the loudspeaker tuning up.

The voice of Mrs. Mack filled-up the dance hall with the announcement of one more chance to buy "fistful of lottery tickets to sock it to Packers!"

Geno looked up at the bandstand to see Mrs. Mack supporting an Armour Star Ham in both hands. Shaped-up in a formal gown, she surveyed the dance hall and said the lucky winner would get "best end of pig, an' Union Relief Fund get best end of profits." She announced the drawing "after another round or two of "polka hoppin'!"

At her signal, strobe lights began exploding, bursting into slivers of light. A mirrored ball hanging overhead started turning, flashing around and around, scattering jewels of light in all directions.

"Polka going to everybody's feet," Jamie Delaney noted through the music that began shaking the walls, "and beer going to everybody's head."

"Pick yourself a dancin'gal," Geno suggested to him. He pointed at tables of young women ready to spring into the dance.

"No good with girls, or polka," Jamie Delaney excused himself, "but good with lottery tickets." He held up a string of them.

Geno leaned over and promised to win him a "piece." He knew the rich kid had never been down with a woman, claimed the women on his side of town used their bodies as collateral for marriage.

The rich kid shook off the proposal. "No gambler," he said, worrying about morality and venereal disease, "and it's against my way of life." He went on to say he envied people living free and easy with unmarried sex. He lit a cigarette, sucked in the smoke and let it out with his thought that men didn't have much in common anymore, except sex, and he felt left out!

"Get vit it, join men's club!"

"Waiting for right girl."

Geno thought he should have waited for the right girl, but never liked to wait for what he wanted. Now he wanted out of trouble, bent over, whispered that he was in "sex trouble," needed his "good buddy" to set him up with a "good loan."

"Car trouble got my bank account out of commission," his friend confessed in a breath of smoke, "folks put my finances in a bind." Raising his voice he asked if he could help in some other way.

Doc Godfrey picked up the last words, wondered what was wrong, asked if he could help. "Strike got me flyin' low on Uncle Sam's green eagles!"

"Can give you a few bucks," Doc Godfrey offered, pulling out his wallet, "but I'm one payday away from the poorhouse." He slapped a few dollars on the table.

Geno thanked him and scooped up the bills, said it would keep him on the feedbag for awhile, and assured him he'd get paid back as soon as the union won higher wages.

"Soup kitchen at the Settlement's running low, too," Doc Godfrey kept up the union talk, slipping his wallet back in place.

"Everybody's runnin' low!"

The men looked up to see Geno's brother-in-law, Cas Koczur.

"Sit yourself down," Doc Godfrey said to the man who worked for him at the Settlement. "Sittin's all I can do," he said. "The little woman's not up to swinging the light fantastic." He let himself drop in a chair, stretched legs out, almost tripped a man looking for a place to sit. The man was Marya's father, the meat inspector, Boris Nowak.

"Take meat off feet," Geno welcomed the meat inspector, waved him to the last empty chair.

"Boris Nowak, U.S. Meat Inspector," Marya's father introduced himself as he slumped down.

Cas Koczur grinned and asked if the meat inspector was "checking us out for trichinosis, or pig-rot?"

"See plenty beer bellies," the meat inspector answered with the trace of a smile, "but no rotgut."

Geno asked if "Miss Marya" would be "showin' up?"

"Girl not union," her father explained, spinning a dime on the table and pouring himself a paper cup of beer.

Cas Koczur asked if the meat inspector was on the union side?

"Meat Inspector not on union or company side," Boris Nowak talked back with foam of beer bubbling on his lips. "Inspectors work both sides of fence." He reached into his pocket and pulled out a roll of lottery tickets, "but takin' a lotta chances on union."

"I'm now a college man," Cas Koczur brought up, "but got my start in meat business. Inspectors made more work for us laboring men."

"Packers more interested in profits than safety," the meat inspector talked back. "Public safety, my business. Safe streets oughta be union business."

"Union got to close streets to Yards," Jamie Delaney spoke up, "to win living wage for workers."

"My daughter got office job, pickets don't let her in," Marya's father countered. "Public streets should be open."

"My woman's a desk jokey, too," Cas Koczur contributed. "Packers be setting up living quarters inside the plant to keep office workers from goin' in and out."

The meat inspector confessed that his daughter was already on the inside, and he'd been called back. "Meat gotta be safe."

Doc Godfrey said there was a city ordinance against workers sleeping where food was prepared.

The meat inspector said living quarters were set up in "Pullman cars, Soap Shed, Cooper Shop, Wool House."

Cas Koczur admitted that his wife might have to get bedded-down inside the plant, and he'd have to be a bachelor on the outside.

Doc Godfrey bet the office people would be put to meat packing work. Geno said Packers can't make "pig stickers outa chair sitters."

The meat inspector suggested that Packers could recruit the "D.P.s." He said displaced persons from Nazis "Konzentrationslagers" could do all kinds of work.

Jamie Delaney claimedthey wouldn't scab, not after being slave labor in Hitler's Europe, "branded like cattle." He said he taught them English at the Settlement and they taught him about the horrors of concentration camps.

"They know 'bout Molotov Cocktails," Geno said, fearing he might get a taste of one if he scabbed. His words, and thoughts, were shattered by the blast of a loudspeaker.

"Time fer ticket draw!"

Dancers and table sitters started gathering around the bandstand. Kozy caught up to Geno, squeezed-up next to him, said she had a winning number for him, "me fer prize." He wished someone else could win her in a raffle, looked up, got surprised and embarrassed to see Mama Stara standing on the bandstand, her toes bulging out of slits in high- button shoes.

"Our own Mrs. Baranowski gonna draw lucky ticket," Mrs. Mack proclaimed, and got a clap of hands for her announcement. Mama Stara only pouted, pulled a ticket out of the box.

Mrs. Mack read the name of the winner, "Joe Josowski."

An undertone of disappointment swept through the hall. Everybody knew Joe Josowski lived high on he hog, didn't need the best part of a pig.

"Donatin' piece of meat to union soup kitchen," he announced at the microphone.

One-armed Malivek jumped up, flapped his empty sleeve, led all the shouting and arm waving. Mrs. Mack tried to hold back the shouting with both hands uplifted, managed to announce another "big winner!" She said the Wojciechowski songbird, and Antanas widow, won an audition for a chorus job in Broadway's Oklahoma coming to town, said the songbird was going to sing them with a show-stopper. A whoop went up.

Slinky in a black gown, plumed with black feathers, Marie Wojciechowski Antanas came out of the wings. As the applause and shouts settled down, she began to fondle the microphone, purring her thanks into it, announcing, "Big Zur Koczur gonna be pumpin' accordion, and Bruno Koczur gonna tickle ivories."

As she spoke, Big Zur was swinging into accordion straps, and his nephew, Bruno, was getting settled at the piano.

Kozy elbowed Geno, said her old man was a good squeeze-box man. Geno hoped he wouldn't put the squeeze on him, hoped the songbird would get him introduced to long-legged chorus girls in the Broadway show. He was thinking of choice meat on the hoof while the songbird was telling her audience that her name would be in lights someday. "Not Antanas," she said, "surely not Where's your house key," she slowly pronounced her maiden name. "Need name to fit Broadway billboards. "Gonna be a star, gonna name myself Marie Starski."

"Starski, Starski" came roaring back to her.

While cheers for the girl in plumes were sounding, Geno was picturing her without plumes, or anything, remembering her in straps and garters when her bedroom shade was halfway up. Now he thought the curtain was going up on a Broadway star and he might get in the limelight. A piano chord stifled his thoughts, got the songbird going. A big note flew out of her little body, like hundred proof whiskey coming out of a pop bottle, Geno thought.

"Many a new love will find me," she was singing out. Geno remembered her as a widow finding love with him. He gave her something to sing about!

Her song was over before his thoughts ran out. The songbird was getting a standing ovation, gathering kisses from the audience with both hands, tossing them back with both hands.

As the clapping hands struck less and less, the songbird took the pianist's hand and flew off stage with him.

"Piano man only Koczur man not makin' livin'in meat," Kozy told Geno. "Bruno be good catch for Starski songbird."

"Marie's a somebody," Geno talked back. "Bruno's a nobody."

"Bet songbird got a somebody inside!" Kozy popped gum and words at the same time. "Girl like me can see signs."

"Showgirl don't show none!" Geno said with shiver, starting to count the months since his one-night stand. He counted himself out of trouble, wondered why a lay was called a stand. "Gotta call it a night," he told Kozy, "got picket duty at ass-crack-a day."

"Could ya sneak me in?"

"Can't take no more chances."

....

Down to his last chance at getting Kozy unscrewed, Geno plotted scabbing, all the way down to his room. He slammed himself inside, slipped out of clothes, down to his skivvies, squatted on the side of his bed, pulled off a sock, figured on disguising himself and getting through the picket line. A knock rattled his door, and mind. He figured it was a drunk looking for the latrine. He shot off a salvo of cusses.

"It's Cas, need a man to man talk."

Geno threw a sock against the wall, ground his teeth together, feared his brother-in-law got word of his little cousin's pregnancy!

"Gimme a break! In bed, got early picket duty."

"Only take a minute," the older man's voice came through the door.

Geno squared himself, pulled open the door, saw his red-headed brother-in-law filling up the doorway. His red hair brushed against the ceiling.

"Sit yourself down," Geno offered, pointing to the only chair in the room. "Ain't Teresa showin' up?"

"She's still in gossip at the women's table." The brother-in-law squinted through the glare of a bare light bulb hanging on a wire. "Digs only big as a foxhole," the old soldier spoke up, dropping in the lumpy armchair, squirming to get comfortable.

"Big enough fer a sleep."

"Your Sis and me," Cas got around to gearing up his voice, "might be needing a bigger place. Room for a kid!" He ran both hands through bushy red hair, clasped hands behind his head, sat back. "Not good time for a kid!"

Geno stopped holding his breath, relieved that Cas was only concerned about his own trouble. It didn't seem like trouble to Geno! Cas was long married, past due for a kid. "Ya make a good livin'," he said, "make good old man."

"Bad time to lose Teresa's paycheck! Can't stay in college without it." Hecrossed his legs, swung a foot up and down at a frantic pace.

"Should used rubbers," Geno said, giving the advice he'd gotten.

"Accidents happen. You ought to know," and Cas pointed at the bandage on Geno's forehead. "Accidents can take a life, and make a life."

Geno nodded, asked how he could help.

"Forty-Niners got a lead on some medical doc on the take?"

Geno shook his head, didn't want Cas to know he was in the same bind, or know about the sawbones he could hire-up.

"Teresa's pregnancy not a sure thing," Cas mentioned, leaning forward. "Don't let on about it. Bad luck to speak of a pregnancy before it's certain."

Geno never heard of that kind of bad luck, wondered if he got bad luck for leaking his troubles to the gang! He promised Cas he'd keep his "trap shut."

"Might have screwed myself out of a better life," Cas sighed, mostly to himself. He sat back, let his crossed legs separate, and tap the floor. "Was a good writer," he said. "Pen got me in college. Penis taking me out!"

Geno didn't know what to make of that?

His brother-in-law kept talking, said the pen is mightier than the sword, but the penis is mightier than the pen!

"Penis sure is better," Geno said, not knowing what Cas was talking about, "but penis can cost a man's freedom. Too bad sex ain't free."

"In some cultures, men share women, and all kids are raised in common."

"Got a hankerin' fer dat kinda place."

"Maybe no love with free sex?"

"Ain't sex love?"

"Not in my book."

"Got a book on sex?"

"The Sexual Behavior in the Human Male. It just came out, a sensation in college."

"A man don't need a book to make out."

"You'd be surprised," Cas said, leaning back. "There are more kinds of sex than a man can shake a dick at!"

"Maybe I could teach author a t'ing or two."

"Doc Godfrey knows the author, an entomologist at Indiana University."

"Entomologist?"

"Scientist of insects."

"In-sex?"

"Well, yes," Cas laughed. "Kinsey made sex a scientific study."

"Kinsey got Superman eyes to see into every bedroom?"

"He had lots of interviewer's eyes, made plenty of surveys."

"Men don't talk sex to strangers."

"Men talk sex all the time!"

"Men tell lies about sex."

"Kinsey put together lots of corroborations. In my course on interview and polling techniques, I learned Kinsey's research methods are reliable."

"Didn't use me, best authority on sex."

"You brag a lot about sex!"

"One time vit me, an' bitch carry mattress on back!"

"Men talk big when feel small," Cas kept making his point. He cocked his head in thought. "It's a theory I made up for one of my class assignments. Men don't kill lions anymore to catch eye of women, need to be sexy killers in bed. Sex is the way to feel manly today!"

Geno remembered the Delaney dude telling him that sex is the only thing men have in common these days, and brought it up. His brother-in-law agreed, explained that the word as become too complex and specialized, but the only real he-men nowadays, he emphasized, had to be big at sex. They didn't kill lions anymore or drag big animals home to eat.

"Men kill big animals in slaughter house," Geno brought up.

"Animals don't fight back."

"Ain't army men big killers?"

"Solders nowadays are only little cogs in a killing machine!"

"Take football players! Ain't our Chicago Bears tough as Cavemen?"

"Football, only a game."

"Ain't sex a game? I'm good at it!"

"Keep provin' my point. All men need to feel big in sex, feel small in big companies, big unions, big cities."

"OK if ay say so."

"Got any big ideas about little cousin, Livie?"

"Livie an' me just cousins, ain't kissin' cousins."

"You danced her up tonight," Cas said with a smile, "but don't see no mattress on girl's back."

"Mattress time fer me, got me picket duty at crack-a day."

....
——

The pickets were out in force when Geno turned up for duty in the morning, but police were opening up the picket line for scabs. He was told the Packers got an injunction against the union, made pickets open up the streets to Stockyards.

Still open to thoughts of scabbing, Geno figured it would be easy to get through the lines, but he'd be seen, be dead to the neighborhood! He hung on to his picket sign, and schemes, kept linked-up with the chain of pickets at the barriers. Scabs were getting through, but getting insults and warnings about being followed after work.

It was the seventh day of the strike.

Geno recognized the voice of the Moses Man rising above the pickets' threats and chants. "Awake ye to ram's horn! On Seventh Day, walls tumble down."

Geno saw the old ribber moving up and down the line, shouting, and singing. "Oh, Precious Lawd. Sing, Brothers, an' walls come tumblin' down."

Geno caught up with the Moses Man, complained about the little black pills that didn't take him to the "Promised Land." Moses Hamilton, singing to the strikers, and to the Lord, tried to shake Geno off. Finally, he stopped raising his hands to the sky and reached into both pockets, paid Geno off.

"Precious Lawd want precious chile to come into precious world. Lawd Boss Man be praised!" He went back to calling on the Lord to make the walls come tumbling down!

Behind the walls, the packing plants were heating up. Smokestacks were beginning to spew smoke and cinders. Police were escorting scabs through the lines. They didn't have to come out. The Big Four Packers were setting up living quarters inside their plants.

It was the eighth day of the strike.

"An' when eight days be accomplished," Moses Hamilton was preaching, "baby Jesus got hisself circumcised in flesh."

"Cut 'em off," strikers were yelling at the "scabs."

Police let them through. Strikers told the scabs they'd be followed one day, their homes fire-bombed. The union Axe and Cleaver featured a formula for the "Molotov Cocktail, couple of jiggers of gas and dab of oil." Geno didn't want to get a taste of that, but he was getting desperate! The strikers were getting desperate. The Stock Handler's Union had not gone out on strike, and meat critters were hauled in, their meat hauled out. Pickets could hear the clang of freight cars switching back and forth in the Yards, and the bellowing of cattle, squealing of hogs.

Geno was told that Company meat trucks were making deliveries to local butcher shops, and union Rolling Squads were tailing them, threatening butchers about "scab meat."

....

"Scab meat ain't good fer ya," Geno warned old man, Diener, proprietor of Diener's Meat and Treat Market. He'd run the neighborhood butcher shop as long as anyone could remember. It was around the corner from World's End, and Geno got assigned to warn the old butcher.

Geno didn't like the assignment, but liked taking himself in the butcher shop. Diener's was a good place to get away from the stink of the Yards, catch the scent of pine sawdust on the floor, fresh meat on the hook, garlic hanging in bunches, oranges mellowing in bushel baskets, coffee beans in the grinder. He remembered Diener's in the "Dark Days." Diener gave scraps of meat to the hungry, and credit to old customers. In the War, he reserved scarce meat for his regular customers. Geno didn't want to make trouble for the old man, but the union was on his back. He told Diener that scab meat wasn't good for him.

The old butcher wanted to know if his "young friend" was going to beat him up, or sell him "protection?"

Geno said he was no rat racketeer, only fighting for a living wage.

"Diener make no livin' if got no meat to sell."

"Diener can make out," Geno said, thinking the butcher must be rich enough to live in hog heaven.

"Baranowski boy make out" Diener said with a snap of his suspenders. "Female meat not on strike."

....

The strikers who started on St. Patrick's Day were still swinging picket signs by Easter time. They were used to going without meat during Lent, but didn't want to fast on Easter Sunday. Men at World's End grumbled about Wigilia, said they'd only get a Holy Wafer for Easter dinner. The Church offered soup for the hungry, but it was watered down, "weak as Holy Water." Charities and Community Services were all running out of relief funds. Landlords were running renters out. There were men sleeping on the streets, and in doorways. Mrs. Mack put Geno on her tab, "live now, pay later." She thought the world was not coming to an end, not yet, and allowed her "regulars" half a buck credit every day. Whenever she could lay hands on pork sausages or chicken livers she made snacks to go with her nickle beer.

The Church served communion everyday. Everyday Geno kept wondering how he could get around God and Union, play the Judus scab. He was on picket duty at the Racine Street Gate when a meat truck tried to inch its way out of the Yards.

"Stop scab truck!"

Pickets broke the law, rallied round the refrigerator truck, stopped it. Police were waving it through. Pickets were refusing to give way. Geno dropped his picket sign, felt himself straining against the pressure of pickets pushing from behind. He got slam-dunked against the truck fender. The eight-wheeler began moving, shaking strikers off. Geno sensed himself on the running board, sliding off. He was yelling, couldn't hear his own voice. Through the window he could see the driver's look of panic, began feeling himself slipping off. It seemed like a long time before he hit the bricks, got a look up at a fuzzy-haired man in bib-overalls. He was slipping under the slowly rolling truck wheels, disappearing under the back fender. It was Old Nate, the steamer man. He reappeared after the wheels had moved on. Nate's mouth was slack, gold tooth missing. He had the look of surprise in the white of his eyes.

Everything went into slow motion for Geno. He viewed Nate getting slowly lifted, every limb of him dangling. Geno felt himself getting helped up, couldn't get rid of the image of Nate going under the wheels. The picture in Geno's mind appeared in black and white on the front page of morning newspapers. Some papers headlined Nate an "accident victim!" Some papers called him a "crucified martyr!"

Geno was branded with a bandage on his backside to go with the bandage on his forehead. That evening, the Union observed a memorial for Nate. The new president praised "Brother Nate," said he died for "our salvation!" He went on to tell the packinghouse workers they were slave laborers before the UWPA. Before the union, he raved on, some foremen made men fork over money to stay on the payroll, and women had to get laid, or laid off. They all had to work ten hour days for whatever the Packers offered. "Job security? Forget it! Seniority? Forget it! Overtime pay? Forget it! Paid vacation? Forget it! Pension? Forget it!" He raised his hands as if in prayer.

In Protestant churches on the "Black Side of State Street," sermons paid tribute to Nate, and collections were picked up for his family. In Catholic churches, Back of the Yards, candles were lit for Nate. Geno followed pickets to the Stations of the Cross, mumbling "I Crucify," at every stop!

....

"Crucify trucker scab!"

"Stick it to Packer Pigs!"

Curses rang round Geno in the street outside Union Hall. He was waiting with the overflow crowd for the union to take action. Anger hung in the misty air, with the scent of thawing earth promising Spring, lilacs to come. Geno was only thinking about the bastard kid to be, and how he could put an end to it.

The double doors of union headquarters burst open, let out an explosion of noise, let out one of the union muscle men, "Stash!"

"Gonna get us some scab meat fer supper," Stash yelled, and asked for "volunteers!" Without waiting for a hand to go up, he motioned at Geno and two huskies around him, ordered them to pile in the backseat of the Oldsmobile idling at the curb. The sedan went into gear as soon as the three "volunteers" scrunched together in the back seat, and the car got cheered off by the men left standing in front of Union headquarters.

Geno sat upright, sandwiched between two strangers. It seemed he only had room to move his eyes. Sights of Ashland Street were swishing back and forth between the swipes of the windshield wipers. Storefronts, gas stations, and movie house marquees were swishing past. Darker streets of row houses swished into view. Back and forth the windshield wipers brushed away one scene after another. The car radio was in swing of Glenn Miller, but didn't get Geno in the mood. A few blocks later the melody of Moonlight Cocktail put him in mind of a Molotov Cocktail.

The Oldsmobile was rounding corners to the swing of the Big Bands while big Stash was humming and checking house numbers. He called for the driver to "pull up," looked over his shoulder at the three men in back. "Time to give trucker fucker a truckload of bruises."

....

Geno rubbed his bruised hands together when he got back to the barroom at World's End.

He swung himself around on a barstool, told Mrs. Mack he needed a "pissin' good brew."

Mrs. Mack said he looked piss poor, pushed aside a loose strand of hair dangling over an eye.

Geno held up bruised knuckles, said he handed the killer truck driver a knuckle sandwich. Mrs. Mack said it should have been his last bite to eat, told Geno that "suds be free."

Drawing him a beer, she went on to say a "good man died for us today," and she pointed to a plate of Easter Eggs. "Take Babka, blessed by priest."

"Ain't gonna be no blessed Easter," Geno said through a gulp of beer and bite of egg. "Maybe Geno-boy get Easter dinner at Koczur table," Mrs. Mack said. "Livie girl been tryin to get through to you on the "wire line."

....

"Talk ain't gonna do me no good, gotta see ya!"

Kozy's voice set the wire vibrating when Geno got connected to her through the public phone back of the bar. Kozy said her breasts were budding out, swollen and sore, and her belly button was pushing out!

Geno promised to meet her at their usual hangout, hung up the phone, headed out the back door, met her in the shadows of the street lamp on 49th. Loosely wrapped in her brother's old Eisenhower jacket, she flipped it open it to show bare breasts, one hanging lower than the other, and whipped it shut.

"Swole - up," she cried as a streetcar clanged in the next block and carried her voice away with it.

"Be growin' up, female style," Geno assured her, but couldn't lie to himself, and knew the cost of surgery would go up if a pregnant body had gotten too far along. "Get ya fixed up," he assured her, "get my ass in plant, get chips to get in doctor game." He told her to keep her mouth shut, and work on their plan to get away from home for a night, left her in the light of the street lamp, returned to the dark of his room, didn't bother to pull the light cord. There was no shade on his slit of a window, and a beam of streetlight was all he needed to see his way out of clothes and into bed. How could he see his way out of the neighborhood and into the plant without anyone knowing? It came to him that a disguise would do it, and he could take the elevated train, get off at the end of the stockyard line, find the gate where pickets didn't know him. He'd tell Mrs. Mack he got a "fight gig" at a club in Gary, Indiana, and would be out of town for a few weeks. The time had come, he told himself as he sank heavily into the mattress, and his thoughts. This is it!

....

"This is it," Geno was still thinking, "this is it," and the wheels of the elevated train were answering him back, clickity-click, this is it, this is it, this is it. He knew each click was taking him closer to the end of the line, and the end of his labor union life, clickity-click-click! His elbow on the window sill was jiggling, clicity-click. His thoughts about scabbing were jiggling in his mind, clickity-click. Slouched under the bill of his baseball cap, he sneaked looks out the window. The backsides of apartment buildings were showing-up in the window, clickity-click, wooden back stairways, junky back yards, clickity-click. Second story windows at eye level gave dollhouse views of inner rooms. Flower pots and milk bottles on window sills were flying by, laundry snapping like flags on back porch clotheslines. A flicker of billboards alerted him to the last stop on the transit system's Stockyard Spur. This...is...it, click, click, click. The blur of billboards along the station platform was slowing into separate frames, one frame after another, stopping in front of the billboard picturing a surrey with the fringe on top, and the name of Oklahoma! It was the show his songbird neighbor would soon be in! No picture of her on the billboard. He saw a good show of her in a window of his memory.

Passengers were getting up, grabbing straps. He waited his turn instead of pushing ahead, dreaded every step on his way out, heard the jeers of pickets at the far end of the platform. When the elevated train took off, the second story level of the besieged packing plants began showing up on the other side of the tracks. He saw a few men in white frocks taking a smoke on fire escapes. He saw the roofs of redbrick buildings, all strung together by covered bridges and open walkways. There were two prominent smokestacks standing guard over the redbrick backdrop. Rows of overflow brine tanks stood in line like soldiers. His mind was taking him back, step by step, to the fury days of getting the union off the ground. Now he was putting it down, step by step. His eyes took aim at union pickets roped around the turnstile exit. Police had opened up the line to let through. He couldn't believe he was one of them, glad to see no one he knew. Strangers threatened him with raised fists, regarded him with plug-ugly faces. Their chants and cusses got louder as he got closer. A burly picket in stocking cap and Navy peacoat brushed against him, told him to "ship off!" Geno shrugged by, twisted through the turnstile. Down the steps he hopped, two at a time, tearing off a false mustache as he went. His shoes scraped the gritty bricks of Packer's Avenue. His eyes went up to the bars of sunlight split by the grill of overhead elevated tracks. He thought of prison bars.

Thoughts were driven out of mind by the sudden clop of hoofs, and he had to get out of the way of a horse and wagon whipping bits of manure out of cracks between bricks. The boney horse was pulling a Cripple Cart with a stricken cow lying on her side. Geno knew the cow's destiny had been changed from hamburger to fertilizer, wondered if the horse knew what he was doing? Men in Sheep Kill were sure the "Judas-Goat" knew he was leading sheep to slaughter.

Horse and cart t raced out of sight, and out of mind. Geno only thought about what lay ahead as he lined up with other scabs. They were received by guards, picked up passes, checked into the Personnel Office, got badges, work assignments, and living quarters. Geno hoped to get work in the Hide Cellars with the sweet smell of leather, and expected to get berthed in a Pullman Car. He got assigned a work station in Beef Kill, living quarters in the Cooper Shop, and dreaded the life to come! He'd lived a life in Beef Kill when he got his work-papers.

....

Geno was waiting for the elevator that would take him up to Beef Kill. The cattle got slaughtered up high, and gravity helped bring their meat down. He was in line with scumbags, standing between a jazzed-up punk in a shredded zoot-suit, and a young buck decked-out in a sweatshirt, tuxedo pants, gym shoes.

A familiar voice, with his name in it, struck him from behind, and he swung round to catch the eye of his sparing partner, the street kid calling himself "Ski." The big kid was pushing his way through the crowd of scrounges.

"Don't lip-off on me," Geno greeted him, "an' Geno don't squeal on ye!"

"Ain't no squealin' pig," Ski shot back, and brushed a friendly punch off Geno's shoulder. "Surprised to find a good neighborhood man on bad side of picket line?"

"Good side of pay line, same side as Ski."

"In pay line to get me a ring an' a marriage."

"Marriage ring like ring in bull's nose," Geno said, realizing he was scabbing for the opposite reason. "Gonna get ya led around."

"Gonna get me a better life."

Ski's words ended with a bang. The shaft-elevator hit down, and Geno recognized the elevator operator. It was Old Mal, the legendary one-armed doorman who pulled the lever to open mechanical doors in the Beef House. Now his one arm was put to use on the elevator.

"Don't bad mout' Old Mal," he said when he saw Geno. "Gotta feed mout'!"

"Don't lip off on me!"

Old Mal wiped his mouth, as if to seal it.

As soon as the elevator was packed full, Old Mal put it in gear, got it slowly limping up, one floor after another. The air kept getting hotter. The noise kept getting louder.

"Guess Hell's way up, not way down," someone was muttering at the back of the elevator.

Another voice thought they were lucky to be riding up. "Bulls gotta walk."

'Only gotta come up once!"

The elevator bumped to a stop, not quite level with the fifth floor landing. "Vatch step," Old Mal slurred, and slid open the wire door, got out of the way. The men pushed out, got met by guards who handed out assignments. Geno and Ski got the same work station, the Knocking Pen.

In their own silent thoughts they followed the crowd to the locker room, dug up dungarees that fit, found empty lockers for storing street clothes.

Geno planted a foot on a bench and tore at his shoelaces. His hands seemed to have a mind of their own, worked without thinking. He wished he could keep his mind from thinking. "Good duds," Ski was saying, already down to skivvies and stocking feet, and holding up a pair of overalls for inspection.

Geno said scabs don't fit so well in working men's "duds."

"Stickin'union in back ain't good," Ski agreed, hoisting work pants, belting up. "Dressed to kill," Geno grumbled, pulling himself together.

....

The Killing Floor was shut down when Geno and Ski got directed to their work station, the Knocking Pen overlooking the empty cattle chute. They were told of a temporary problem up the line, ordered to wait for the foreman to check them out.

"Only room fer one critter at a time," Ski said, looking down at the chute.

Geno said it was going to be tough to keep knocking heads when the cattle started getting pushed through. He said six hundred head got slaughtered every hour when he worked the Killing Floor.

"Got no belly fer killin'on Good Friday," Ski thought out-loud.

"Knockin' only take kick outa critters, make 'em easy fer Knife Man."

"No more killin' time," a voice growled at them from behind. Geno turned to see their foreman, an old-time company man he vaguely remembered.

"Crew boss, Wieczprick," the foreman called himself. "Hope ya ain't desk jockeys. Had my full of 'em."

"No sittin' marks on my ass," Geno talked back at Wieczprick, remembering him as a foreman always getting written up in the Axe and Cleaver. He was a "company man," called Wise Prick, charged with working his men too hard. The union Grievance Committee was always on his case.

"Monkey see, monkey do," Wieczprick yelled over the grind of machinery, showing his men how to do their work. He raised a sledgehammer at the bull getting pushed into the chute below, struck him between the eyes. The bull went down in a heap, one leg slipping out of a sliding door. The leg was shackled to a chain. The door opened all the way up and the bull was swung off in the air, hoofs still kicking.

Another bull was snorting right behind him, struggling to get out. "Bulls-Eye," Geno cracked, dropping it with a single swing.

The foreman told them to keep swinging, and left them to it.

"Blood fer blood," Ski said in resignation, and heaved a sledgehammer up, and down.

Blood for blood didn't make sense to Geno. The sledge didn't draw blood. He stopped thinking, kept swinging. Snorting cattle kept heading his way, hour after hour, until a steam whistle blew them to a stop. The foreman showed up, told his men to "knock it off," and take their ten minute break.

Geno and Ski dropped the weight of their sledgehammers and dragged the weight of their bodies to a platform outside. They sucked-up a breath of cool, smelly air, let out sighs and curses.

"Dead tired," Ski admitted, flicking a flame out of his Zippo lighter and giving the breath of life to his cigarette. "Plenty live meats left to knock off," he said through a ring of smoke, and pointed to the cattle bumping into each other in the Holding Pen below.

"Dyin' to make love," Geno cracked at the sight of a bull trying to mount one cow after another, no cow holding still.

"Dyin' to make life," Ski said.

The horny bull with a brass ring in his snorting nostrils gave up trying to mount cows, tried to hump a steer, slid off, looked up, caught Ski's eye.

"Bull's eye on me," Ski sputtered through his smoke, and wondered what the bull thought of him?

His thoughts were blown off by a steam whistle announcing the end of the break, and he snapped his cigarette into the cattle pen where a man with a shockstick was beginning to flick cattle flanks, probing them into the Catch Pen.

Geno and Ski trailed back to their stations, got set up, looked down on the head of the next target. Geno dropped the bull with a single swing, and the trap door slid open and the animal, still kicking, was swung off.

Taking up his sledge, in turn, Ski looked down on the bull with the golden ring in his moist nostrils, the bull who had caught his eye in the outside pen. The snorting bull was looking up with a glint of recognition in the blue of his eyes. Ski couldn't swing, let Geno take the shot at him.

When Geno's sledge was in the air, the bull's eyes were targeted on him. The sledge hit, and the eyes had the same look of surprise that Old Nate had when the truck rolled over him.

The blue of the bull's eyes began draining away, turning very white.

....

Opening his eyes to the white of his hospital room, Eugene Baran got sight of the old boy who'd assisted him at the Knocking Pen. Ski lay in the bed across the way, reminding Geno of the time they bunked together in the besieged packing plant. They'd been assigned billets in the Cooper Shop, converted from barrel-making to sleep-making. Cots and bunks replaced the barrels. Sweat and cigarette smoke replaced the barrel smell of pine and oak. He remembered how good a lower bunk felt after a shift at the Knocking Pen, closed his eyes again, saw himself as Geno again, waking up in the Cooper Shop at the sound of a whistle. It was the dawn of Holy Saturday, and men were cussing and crashing out of bunks, except for Ski. He was already dressed, squatting on the floor, reading his Lenen Missal.

"The Saturday Psalm's all about David," he spoke up to Geno, "and David's prayers for good judgments!" He asked Geno if their scabbing was good judgement?

"Ain't Judgment Time," Geno said, skinning out of his skivvies and heading for the makeshift washroom. "Baptism time."

When he came back, Ski was still at prayers, now sitting on Geno's lower bunk. Geno thanked him for making up his bunk, asked if he'd made up his mind about judgment? He got no answer as he pulled on his work clothes. He shrugged and took off for the plant cafeteria, a high vaulted space with rows of tables and chairs under a high overhead of pipes and girders. He scanned the wide open space for sight of Marya, gave up, got in line for a slop of grub. The white-frocked woman in front of him turned round, turned into Teresa! She gasped at sight of her little brother, said she couldn't believe he was a scab! He put it to her that she was not dressed for office work.

"Office girls got no choice," Teresa protested, swinging a tin tray off the pile. "Got put to work in Chipped Beef, get canned if I don't do my job!"

Geno confessed that he had to scab to save his "ass," promised, while scrambled eggs and hash browns were slapped on his tin tray, that he'd give her the "scoop" as soon as they found a secluded place to sit.

When they settled down at the far end of a long table, Geno served up his "mess!" The sister, who'd been more of a mother to him than Mama Stara, gave him sympathy, agreed he was too young and wild to settle down, and "Livie" was much too young to mother a "kiddo!" She promised to give him a little money for the "dirty deed," and promised not to give his shame away. As she loaded her mouth, she saw a neighborhood man at the next table. Swallowing hard she told Geno to hide his face. "I see Old One-Arm Mal," she warned.

The old neighborhood man was humped over his tray, false teeth clamped to his white cooler frock. Gumming his food, he kept sticking a slice of bread in the pit of his arm stub, tearing the bread apart, dropping the pieces for his good hand to feed-up to his mouth.

"One-armed Mal ain't gonna finger me," Geno said with a swing of his fork. "Old boy in same bed as me."

"Guess all us be in same bed!"

Geno asked where Marya got "bedded down."

"Visior's Entrance. Same as me. She gonna be freaked-out to get sight of her old boyfriend!"

....

Geno surprised his old girlfriend in the Cafeteria during the lunch break, found Marya benched-up by herself in a far corner table. Her coils of golden hair were squashed under a white cap. She was as stiff in her well-starched uniform as she was stiff inside. She looked away when he hailed her as "Marya, full-a Grace!"

"Figured I'd be gettin' a scab on my hands," she told him with a toss of the head. "Teresa said you'd turned scab."

"Teresa let on 'bout reason I need blood money?"

"Lookin' out for Number One, as usual, I figured."

Relieved that she didn't know about the kid to be, Geno told her she was Number One in his book.

Marya said he didn't read books, and needed to come up with a shave.

He said he was keeping a low profile, hiding behind whiskers, told her she looked like she slept on her face.

"No place in Visitor's Entrance to pretty up!"

Geno said he'd like to visit her at night. She said Visitor's Entrance was out of bounds for men. He said he could find an empty freight elevator for them to go up and down together in. She said she was too busy in Sweet Sausage, stuffing pig guts all day. He asked if she'd like him to stuff her all night.

"Genie never gonna get mind outa meat barrel!"

"Give ya a barrel of fun."

"Always got mind in a bunghole."

"Livin' in barrel shop."

"No good man comin' outa my Genie," Marya sighed, spooning her untouched egg salad onto his tin tray. "It be Holy Saturday," she said, 'an' no priest to bless eggs."

"Ain't it custom fer Polska girl to give Easter Egg to man she like?"

"Egg salad, no Easter Egg. Savin' my eggs to give to good man."

"Don't find no gooder man than me."

"Maybe I find rich office man?"

"Big shot office man only gonna bag office clerk fer a one-night-stand."

"Office man a good man."

"Only one good man," Geno said, knowing she was a devout Christian. "Only Jesus man."

"Holy Saturday Mass in Cafeteria tonight," Marya brought up. "Genie could take Communion if he's ready to let his good self out."

....

Geno let himself go to Communion with Marya in the Cafeteria, night of Holy Saturday. A priest had been allowed in the plant. Geno and Marya joined the body of strike breakers for the breaking of bread, and pouring of wine. He and Marya stayed on for the holy word. The priest challenged everyone to reflect on their own resurrection.

After the time of prayer, Marya said she'd always stayed up for the Easter sunrise, asked Geno if he'd wait-up with her. They sought privacy on the outside platform overlooking the cattle Holding Pen, sat together for the long wait to sunrise. Marya said the dark before Easter dawn was the sin of the world, the dark before the light of Jesus.

Geno thought the dark was a chance to get his hands on Marya, but she shook him off. As they sat without talking, they heard the snorting and scraping of cattle in the pen below. Marya said it was a sin to kill.

Geno got thought of Ski's life for life, figured it would impress Marya! He told her animals sacrificed themselves for the higher life, like the "animal sacrifices to God in the Good Book."

Marya leaned over and whispered that there really was something good trying to come out of him.

....

___

On Easter, all white workers were led out of the Cooper Shop and resettled in the Wool House. The scabs were being segregated according to race, and the Wool House was cleaned out of sheepskins and bales of wool to make room for them. There was a space at the far end where men could get down on knees and roll the bones. Geno thought he might make as much throwing the dice as swinging the sledge.

The make-shift barracks was well-lighted and furnished with a radio to keep the men tuned into the outside world. Between shifts, the radio blared out news about the national meat strike, and the international crisis in Berlin. There was even a strike threatened at the atomic plant in nearby Oak Ridge. One night there was breaking news about the meat packing plant in St.Paul. The strikers broke in the besieged plant, killed a scab in the skirmish, took over. The Minnesota National Guard was called up.

The news unnerved the men in the Wool House, and Geno took off to work off his sweat in the Company Gym.

....

The Company Gymnasium offered a swimming pool, handball courts, exercise rooms, lockers and showers. Before the strike, it was reserved for company executives, except for special occasions, like boxing exhibitions on Father and Son Nights. Geno remembered sitting at ringside with his old man and a crew of big brothers, close enough to the ropes to feel the splash of sweat and blood. He grew up dreaming of getting in the ring, fighting for money. Now he was in the gym with company executives and strawbosses. He'd always felt inferior to men in suits, but equal to any man in shorts or trunks, superior to any man in the showers.

That night, while keeping the punching bag in a blur with fists and elbows, he caught the eye of an older man pulling weights. The weight-puller said he wished he could punch the bag with such authority. He let the weights drop, introduced himself as

"Harry S. Snook, office manager." He laughed and said he "pulled a lot of weight" in the company.

Geno let up on the punching bag, let himself be known as "Eugene Baronowski, Industrial Engineering." He asked if "Mr. Snook" might be related to Baby Snooks on the radio? The Snook man came up with a smile and confession that he was a different "Snook," with "two baby Snooks of his own."

Geno went on to ask what management thought about strikers taking over the Minnesota packing plant? The Snook man said it couldn't happen in Chicago, the police were too strong, and the company had its own protective force.

Geno changed the subject, said he was getting set up in the "fight racket," lied about scabbing to get money for coaching. The office manager told him he looked like he had a lot of promise, and asked where he was "camping in?" Geno said he was "stashed-up" in the Wool House," joked about "counting sheep to go to sleep."

The office manager laughed about being "berthed in a Pullman Car, going nowhere." He asked if Geno came from "Back of the Yards?"

Geno nodded, wondered if the way he talked gave him away?

Later, in the hiss of the showers, the office manger said one of his office girls, from Back of the Yards, was single, but starting to eat for two. He wondered if that was a "big deal, Back of the Yards?"

Geno said that a "broad drawin' a pregnant card," had to have a man bid for her, or play the "slut game fer life!" He was thinking of Kozy. The blast of hot water was needling his conscience.

"You look like a young man who'd turn any girl's head," the older man sputtered in the showering water. "What would it cost to get you to take the office girl off my hands?"

Geno cocked his head and shook the water out of ear, thought he wasn't hearing right. Then he heard the office manager say the office girl was worth a million!

Geno knew he couldn't take on another woman, not until he got rid of the one on hand, but asked the office manager to give him a call, after the strike.

....

Geno kept counting the strike days, day after day, and and the strike money, dollar after dollar. Next payday would get him the payoff. He got a hand on the phone in the foreman's shack, got through to Kozy, told her he had the chips to get in the game. He got an earful of squeal. Kozy could hardly wait to get her "body back," and his "body!"

He told her she'd have her fill of him next Friday, told her to put their plan in action, get lined up for a night out.

"Be all set. Don't get off line, talk to me."

He asked if anyone knew he was on the inside?

She said everyone thought he was prizefighting in Gary. He asked what was new on the outside.

She said it was the same old thing, no money, no nothing, but plenty of buzz about the Minnesota packing plant.

"Any talk 'bout Flyin' Squads breakin' in on us?"

"Not a word. Mostly talk 'bout songbird Marie not showin' up fer big show practice!"

"Not like the old songbird."

"Bet she's gettin' a clean out job, like me."

"Your time's come."

III

The Great Unborn

Geno was set to get it over with when the Five o'clock whistle blew an end of the workday. He sneaked through the picket line in disguise, made sure he wasn't followed, got a streetcar to the Five an' Ten Cent Store in the old neighborhood. Kozy was leaning over a straw at the soda fountain. Bits was hanging out next to her, swinging on a swivel stool, sniffing his big nose and twitching ears.

"Go time," Bits spit out at sight of Geno, and swung off the stool, led the way out. Geno didn't know where they were going, grabbed Kozy and followed him. They waited at the corner for the Halsted trolley, hopped aboard when it came to a grinding stop with a shower of cable sparks. Geno and Kozy squeezed together on one side of the aisle, Bits took a seat on the other.

Geno squirmed round, couldn't get comfortable in body or mind. His life seemed to be on tracks, no will of its own. Steel wheels on steel tracks kept grating at his nerves, shaking his mind. The familiar sights were disappearing in the window. Halsted was getting walled-in by unfamiliar rows of storefronts, Auto Repair, Rooms to Let, Dime a Dance, Fortune Telling, Funeral Home. He got a momentary glimpse of an old women at a second story window. She was leaning on the windowsill, watching the world go by. She went in and out of mind, with boarding houses and apartments. The dusty buildings had sculptured facades, cornices with rounded and fluted masonry. He lifted his eyes to the castle-like turrets. Gargoyles, weathered beyond recognition, were looking down. They must have looked down on horses and carriages. Metal rings for tethering horses were now useless relics, rusted to iron posts along the sidewalks. He thought Halsted must have harbored the rich, once upon a time, and was abandoned to the poor. Time passed in Geno's mind, places passed in his window.

"Next stop," Bits called out from his seat across the aisle.

In the screech of the streetcar wheels, they swung from strap to strap and hopped off, got together on the sidewalk.

"Couple blocks to go," Bits directed, taking the lead. He didn't tell them the doctor operated in a rigged-up room in a condemned flophouse.

Kozy seemed to have a premonition, started to hold back. Geno pulled her along. Night was following them, starting to catch up. Bits held up, pointed out the house where he said the sawbones hid out. It was an unpainted frame house, the only house of wood in a neighborhood of brick and steel. The shabby two-story building seemed to be squatting on its haunches, stuck between the paws of steel girders holding up elevated tracks.

Kozy said it looked like a Spook Joint, didn't want to take another step.

"Only scary outside," Bits explained between sniffs. "City condemn it, inspectors scared to go in."

"Spooks me out," Kozy said with handkerchief clapped to her eyes.

"Sure looks like a dump," Geno agreed.

"Inside, it be snug as old shoe," Bits assured his companions, "lived in by old woman who got so many freeloaders she don't know what to do!" He didn't tell him that the old woman looked like a hag-bag, and had no control over the street people crowded-up inside.

Kozy said she wasn't going to set foot inside. "Snug as old shoe," Bits repeated.

"Get yourself put to sleep," Geno said, "feel no nothin'!"

Kozy let him pull her along, as if she already had been put to sleep. When they reached the front door, Bits gave it a bang with a fist, and the house seemed to quiver, but the door stood firm.

"It sticks," Bits said, shouldering it open.

Loud music burst out the opening door, and the scent of urine and alcohol. Their eyes looked straight down a dimly lit hallway to a rickety staircase in back.

Bits twitched his bulbous nose at the smell, closed his pink eyes. Geno caught his breath, figured the smell of alcohol was hospital disinfectant, thought the loud radio or phonograph music masked screams. He had to push Kozy inside.

"Nobody around," Kozy gasped with a shake of her head and swish of her ponytail. "Let's split."

"Lady Shelbourne gonna pop up," Bits foretold, pointing to closed doors along the hallway. "Lady look like sack-a dirty laundry," he warned, "but real lady under pile of duds."

"No lady live in Dump Joint!"

Bits told her that the house was a grand mansion in "olden days." He said the lady of the house, Lady Shelbourne, told him she was born in it, back when Chicago was a long way off. "Chicago sneak up on it," he kept explaining, "and took over!"

Out of the shadows, a body took shape, as if by magic. It appeared as an old woman bulging in layers of clothes. She greeted them as "Lady Shelbourne," asked if they were the "guests" with the "reservation?" Her voice was in such pure English, it sounded foreign to the guests.

Bits gave her a nod, and a "yeah," and she told him "arrangements are made."

She wrapped at the first door on their left, swung it open to an explosion of light and sight of the wreck of a room. Wallpaper was cracking, buckling, peeling off the walls. The floor was littered around a brass bed with an old women pasted between the stiff and brownish sheets. Paper plates and pie tins with hardened remnants of food lay scattered among the bedclothes. Under the bed, a slop pan and tiny pointed shoes peeked out.

"Got company, Gert," Lady Shelbourne announced to the scrawny body in the live-in bed.

"Woulda baked a cake if knowed you was a-comin'," the witch of a woman cackled with a toothless grin. Her head was wreathed in half-gray braids of hair that were coming undone. A spider's web of gray was spun around her face.

Geno felt his shoes grating on the linoleum floor, and his heart pound as he forced himself inside Lady Shelbourne introduced the bedridden woman as "Lady Gertrude Muldoon," and the bed-ridden woman pointed to the kitchen chairs lined up against the wall, told her "guests" to "put butts to rest, and pass time with Gert whilst waiting for your pretty one."

Lady Shelbourned told the "pretty girl-child" to follow her.

"Ain't goin' no place 'less I got my man!"

"Man not allowed," Lady Shelbourne raised her voice, and hands. Kozy tried to open her mouth but words wouldn't come out. "Sleep medicine take Kozy to dreamland," Geno promised her.

The girl already seemed to be in a dream, let herself be led away. The door closed her and most of the loud music out! Geno and Bits were left with the hag in the live-in bed. She reached for her crutches, said her four legs could take them on a dance, but the men sat down without a word.

"Got me a two-legged maiden lady for a daughter," the witch-woman sputtered in another gasp of breath. She stuck the bone of a finger at the shadowy corner where a woman was cowering like an alley cat. She was shrouded in the threadbare remnants of a formal gown that looked lived-in.

"That critter be Miss Maggie," the mother cackled, "unclaimed blessed! Interested?" Both men looked away, but couldn't help seeing the cat-like woman arched-up in the corner. They shook their heads, stuck cigarettes to their lips.

"Gert all fired-up for a bit of smoke," the bedridden woman spoke up as she brushed the cobwebs of hair from her face and reached out a hand of bent and knotty fingers.

Both men blew smoke her way, offered no cigarettes. A tin pan fell off the bed, banged around the floor. Nobody picked it up. The young men stayed seated, backs to the wall, eyes to the front, smoking and flicking ashes on the floor.

Bits finally tossed his scrunched pack of cigarettes at the bed. Gert found one cigarette, fumbled in the brownish bedclothes for a box of matches, scratched up a light, lay back in her shroud of smoke.

Geno didn't know what to do with his eyes, but couldn't help sneaking a look at the "maiden lady" cornered in his edge of vision. Her hair was uncombed and stringy, lips twisted in a knot. Her eyes had a vacant stare. No one seemed at home in her body.

Gert followed Geno's eyes, said, "Maggie a-feared of men. Guess it come natural, her coming from a man who took me by force."

Geno tried to hide behind a cigarette smoke screen, hoped time would pass as swiftly as his breaths of smoke. The bedridden woman ran out of smoke, called for "Miss Maggie" to "fetch Mama her bottle."

The "maiden lady" edged toward her mother's bed. She held an uncorked bottle of red wine in two trembling hands, poured unsteadily into her mother's tin cup. Barefooted, her toes were clawing the floor. She backed into the shadows as soon as her mother's lips smacked.

"Girl better off not born," the mother screeched, words echoing in the tin cup.

Better not born stuck in Geno's mind as an elevated train was approaching. The train shook the house, and his thoughts, as it roared overhead. When the house settled down, he was relieved to think it was a good thing to keep the bastard kid from getting born! He fished a flask of whiskey out of his back pocket and took a swig, passed it to Bits. The flask went back and forth until it was empty, but not Geno's mind. He let himself go down in dreams.

....

A wooden cross was going up. Geno was ringside at the Crucifixion! Vendors were peddling cans of beer and bags of peanuts. Kozy was selling silver crosses at a concession stand. Jesuswas looking down on him!

Geno awakened at a blast of music, looked up at the lightbulb glare of a hellish room, got sight of Kozy in the opened doorway, thought he heard the womb is empty!

....

Empty of mind, Eugene Baran woke to the white of a tomb-like room. His mind filled up with memories of a hospital room, and the man he shared it with. The curtain between beds was parted and the man sitting up in the opposite bed looked across the way and told him he'd been mumbling in his sleep.

"Been having bad dreams!"

"Old men shall dream dreams," the man in the opposite bed said with a tap at the bible he was holding in lap, "and God shall pour out his Spirit."

"Had me bad spirit dreams."

"Dreamed yourself through your helpmeet's visit."

"Did the old girl look mad?"

"Why'd she be mad?"

"Cracked -up our new Caddy."

"She looked worried, didn't want to disturb your rest, said she'd be back after consulting your doctor."

"Did you recognize her?"

"Should I? She didn't recognize me. She's still a good looker, after all these years."

"Keeps herself up, at a price."

"Was she the woman carrying the kid you didn't want?"

"That's a whole different story."

"What became of the girl in the different story?"

"Book closed!"

"Your wife left a book," Ski was reminded, and pointed at the photo album on a bedside stand.

Geno cranked up his bed, reached for the album.

"I'll leave you to it," Ski said, looking down at his bible again.

The photo album weighed heavily in Eugene Baran's hands, opened up a load of memories. He got a look at the wedding reception of Teresa and Cas, and wished he'd kept up with them, but when they moved downstate to Trinitarian University they lived in a different world.

The Kozy kid showed up in a photo at Teresa's Choosing Party. Her cheeks were dimpled by a wide-lipped smile, ear to ear. Her hair was parted in the middle, tied-up in back. She was better looking in the photo than in memory.

The album slid out of hands, but Kozy hung on, in memory. He began picturing her in the doorway of that witch-woman's hell-hole. Half-drugged, she was a rag doll, hardly able to talk or walk. He got her out of the condemned house, but had to hail a cab to get her to the apartment of Teresa and Cas. Kozy's parents gave her permission to spend the night with Cousin Cas, but Cas spent the night at the Southtown YMCA. Teresa stayed holed-up in the packing plant. Geno and Kozy had the one-room apartment to themselves.

The folding bed came down in memory, but Kozy wouldn't go down with him. She wanted the hot water bottle instead of his body, and he had to get through the night scrunched down in an easy chair. When memory flashed up the next day, Kozy said she was sick of him, didn't want him anymore! He was off the hook with Kozy, but got hung up on another hook. His union settled with the Packers, settled for the original nine-cents an hour company offer, but didn't settle with scabs. Word got out that he was one of them, and he had to take off in the Air Force. His memory had come full circle, filled in all the empty spaces, but he still wished he knew what happened to the Kozy kid!

He picked up the photo album in search of her, got a look at himself in Air Force fatigues. He was posed in front of the Flying Dumpster that carried him to West Berlin, and back. He never liked flying, or life in the Air Force, but looking back, it didn't seem so bad. Turning a page, he got a snapshot of Kozy standing next to Jamie Delaney's four-door Frazier sedan. It reminded him of the accident that failed to end the bastard kid to be, and the accident that caused the bastard kid to be, the time he got Kozy in the back seat, gave her the line that she wouldn't get pregnant if she kept her clothes on. She lost a shoe when she kicked the ceiling!

He flipped the page, whipped up a newspaper clipping with the headline, Local Girl In Chorus of Broadway's Oklahoma. It opened back windows in his mind. He saw the neighbor girl in stages of undress in one window, saw her toe-tagged body in another window! He remembered her lying on a slab in the morgue, had to help identify the body. It was cut down the brisket, all the way down, found in a suitcase alongside Bubbly Creek. The autopsy reported she was over four months pregnant, cut-up with a surgeon's precision, the probable victim of a botched-up abortion. The police investigation never found the butcher, or the father who might have been. He was lucky Kozy made it through the knifing, quickly turned the page, put down the bloody memory.

He came to another picture of himself in uniform, corkscrew curl unscrewing out of his garrison cap. He put down the album, began flying through a break in the clouds of memory, back to the Berlin Airlift. He remembered the Milk Runs to the German capital in the creaking C-47. The Flying Dumpster was hardly ever hassled by a Soviet MIG, but he was always tensed-up. Cheers of West Berliners eased him up when his plane landed with supplies. He remembered the crowds of happy children getting candy handouts.

The American Airlift was called the Air Bridge to Berliners. He'd joined the Air Force to get away from home, but was now wanting a bridge back home. Airmail was his bridge. He got word that Teresa was "expecting," and Cas was working full time at the Settlement by day, carrying on at the university by night. A letter from Teresa carried word about his dream girl, "Marya." Gossip had her pregnant! She'd given up her plushy secretarial job in the General Office to stay a few months with relatives in Buffalo, way off in New York. Marya squashed the rumor in answering one of his letters, spelling out her need for a special course in shorthand, and showing him how his name looked in shorthand. He took up correspondence with her in longhand.

Memory was now his bridge over the years to the Airlift. He saw himself in the cold steel Quonset hut where he bunked on the far side of the potbellied stove, billeted with three other airmen. He remembered their faces, not their names. Off base with them, he noted that spoken German didn't ring in his ears like the German his "Pruski Old Man" sputtered round the house. Mama Stara said he had the heart of a "Pole, stingy!" The Old Man said she had the heart of a "Ruski, cold!" Everybody knew they were both Poles from the German and Russian sides. He knew Poland had been split up in the time of his parents, the way Germany, in his time, was divided.

Life in the American occupation zone came into focus when he looked down at snapshots of himself and friends in various German cities. The cities were war-torn graveyards. Skeleton remains of buildings were lined up and down every street. He could see the moon through most of the buildings along the avenues at night. It seemed that every other building was almost completely taken down, corresponding, he thought, to the space between bombs in a bomb-bay. He paged through snapshots of German streets with staircases going up to nowhere, bathtubs hanging on pipes in midair. The gutted streets were haunted by the absence of young German men, as noticeable as the missing walls of buildings. The flower of German manhood was dead, he was told. Flowers of the field were for sale, everywhere, in leftover artillery shell casings.

Only women were working in street and field. Fraternization with them was against regulations, not always obeyed. At first he didn't think the women were worth a court martial, later learned they hid their bodies in baggy clothes, rubbed faces with coal dust to look old and dirty to soldiers. The only stimulant he got off base was in dug-out beer halls that lay under mountains of debris. He got beer in reused U.S. Army bottles, served-up by women in reused bodies.

Up came his picture in dress uniform, the time he flew back home for his wedding! He hadn't planned to get hitched-up, not for awhile, but marriage got him a furlough, a bridge home. Wedding pictures fluttered through the pages. In one of the photos he thought Mama Stara looked like a babushka-head. He saw himself frowning in every photo, pouting like Mama Stara. He remembered the moment he got married in "the mystery of the bread and the wine," but got a mystery when he lifted the bride's veil. Her face was like wax, melting in tears. Was she unhappy about marriage? His best man, Max, the oldest brother, told him a bride's tears were a good omen. He should keep her in tears! One of his ushers, Jamie Delaney, told him a bride's tears were for joy. The dude with the rhyming name showed up in a photo, looked as golden in body as in wealth. A photo of his other usher, Bits, showed him in a tuxedo that made him look more like a penguin than a rabbit. Bits said a bride's tears didn't mean "dick," but Eugene Baran was never sure. Was the wife happy with him? Throughout their marriage she always tried to "make something" out of him.

Pages of wedding pictures kept turning up. The wedding reception was in the upper hall of World's End. Mrs. Mack was leading a congo line in one of the photos, one leg forever lifted in a kick, a forgotten word sealed on her opened lips. He remembered she gave him use of the hall for free, and he collected a bagful of coins and dollar bills from all the men buying dances with the bride.

He turned up pages peopled with familiar and unfamiliar faces, tables full of sausages and pressed meats, potato salad and dill pickles, cakes and honey for the "sweet life" to come. A postcard of the Edgewater Beach Hotel fell out of the album. He spent the honeymoon night there in lush luxury and lust. One night at the Edgewater Beach cost as much as an airman's monthly paycheck, but it really paid off!

The next set of photos pictured him in West Germany again, without his bride. He couldn't afford to keep up a wife off base, and privates weren't eligible to get military housing for dependents, but the Airlift was soon over, and his enlistment was running out. Flying was limited, workloads lightened. He got recreation flights around Western Europe, got a look at himself in Paris, the Eiffel Tower towering behind him. In dress uniform he saw himself next to the nude statue of David in the old square of Florence. He didn't remember where some of the photos were taken, but the wreckage of war was in every background. The photo album slipped out of hands, memories out of mind. Sleep was flying him into darkness.

....

In the light of day, Eugene Baran opened his eyes to the white curtain separating the hospital beds, dividing the room like the Iron Curtain had divided the world! Someone was parting the curtain, a man of the cloth. A priest! Last Rites?

"I'm Father Christian," the priest introduced himself, "son of your roommate."

His father, Ski, was wobbling on crutches right behind him. "He's a doctor of the soul," he said, "and his mother was a cousin of "Cas Koczur, that big red-headed trainer we knew at the Settlement Gym."

The doctor's words hit Eugene Baran with a knockout blow.

....

Eugene Baran thought he'd been down for the long count when he opened eyes to a man he thought was the referee. The referee turned into Ski, the husband of Kozy!

In the grip of thought, Eugene Baran knew the man's wife would show up. He knew he'd get to the end of the story, and his own story would get opened up.

"What's my roofer been up to!" Nurse Rose followed her voice into the room, checked the monitors, and her patient's blood pressure. She pronounced his "vital signs in good order." She thought he might need a change of medications.

Eugene Baran thought he only needed a change of scenery before the Kozy of nightmare turned into flesh. His nurse gave him a pat, and a shake, and twisted round to the priest.

"Old roofer's not ready to go up to heaven!"

"Priest's my son," Ski informed her. "He's not here for last rites."

"How's it feel to have a Father for a son?"

"How's it feel to be my Mama Hen?"

"Only gave you a couple eggs for breakfast," she said with a gold tooth shining in her smile, "but I'll keep you under my wing," and she nodded and waved off.

"She nurses our sense of humor," Ski told his smiling son.

Eugene Baran managed to ask Ski when his good wife would be turning up? "Only in spirit," Ski sighed, looking down.

"My good mother died, when I was born," the priest explained. "Dad raised me from scratch."

"I wasn't his real father," Ski confessed to his old friend. "My son's mother was abandoned when I met her, and you know I needed help." We clicked, helped each other."

It came to Eugene Baran that Kozy skipped out of the abortion, and he was the priests biological father! He was relieved that the real story would never come out.

"His mother gave her life for him," Ski told Eugene Baran. "Priest-son's my ticket to heaven."

"And you're my ticket to Dad's past," Father Christian told his father's friend. "Dad never talked about his life, Back of the Yards. I only know he was abandoned at birth."

"I only remembered your old man in the boxing ring and slaughter house," Eugene Baran volunteered. "We grew up in bad times, Back of the Yards, had to kill for a living."

"Life for life!" Ski came out with his old refrain. "Lower life is sacrificed for higher life."

The priest said his mother was a higher life sacrificed for him, and Christ was a higher life sacrificed for a lower life.

Ski said exception proved the law.

Eugene Baran asked why life needs to be sacrificed.

Father Christian spoke right up, said life and death were two sides of the same coin. "It's how we spend the life we're given that matters. Dad invested his life in me."

"My life just got spent," Eugene Baran laughed, feeling obliged to comment, knowing he only spent his life on himself. "Out of pocket, out of mind," he finished.

"A lot of life is spent, and forgotten," Ski pointed out. "We all need a memory stick to plug in our brains."

Father Christian said the computer is a modern miracle.

Ski said it opened up the windows to all his patients' records, might open the window to God, "if we knew the right keys to punch."

"Christ is the key," Father Christian proclaimed, "and the computer simulates body and spirit. Spirit's the software. It can exist in or out of the hardware."

....

In and out of sleep and dreams, Eugene Baran opened eyes to his dream girl. Her yellow hair, wrapped in ropes around her head, looked like a halo.

"Marya!"

"You gave me another gray hair," Marya told him, even though no gray was in the yellow tint of her hair.

"And I put another dent in my bones."

"Never had a good bone in your body," Marya said with a smile and a gentle stroke at the top of his head.

Her husband admitted going off the wagon, going off the road, wrecking the car. Marya said it was good he didn't cash in all his chips.

"Would you bet," he challenged her, "that a kid I hung out with, Back of the Yards, is on the other side of the curtain?"

"Nobody's on other side."

"He's got crutches, must be on the go with his son, a priest."

"Who is the old boy?"

"Don't think you knew him, a street kid known as Ski."

His wife laughed and asked if he might be the ski "you dropped off your name?"

"Old boy looks a little like me."

"Bet you'd never guess who your old wife ran into? Remember the crippled girl behind the Candy Counter at the Corner Store? She's a retired nursing nun, helping out in Admissions, didn't know you without the ski on your name."

"Would you believe," Eugene Baran interrupted with a gasp, "the man who wanted to marry her's my roommate?"

"Didn't know any man wanted to marry her.

"Can't believe," a voice sounded from the outside, "that the bull of the stockyards is corralled in my hospital!"

A nun appeared in the doorway, under the crucifix. She limped into the room.

"Have I got a surprise for you! The street kid who wanted to marry you is here at the Good Samaritan."

"Nobody but Jesus wanted to marry me."

"Street kid called Ski sure did! Man's on other side of curtain."

"Nobody's on other side. You always had this room to yourself!"

The nun drew back the curtain. The bed on the other side was all made-up, piled high with folded linens.

AFTERWORD

At thought of his past, Eugene Baran got thought of fathering a new self. He had the conception of the world as a womb where the spirit is conceived in every physical self. It needed to be nourished with love for others, developed for the spiritual world to come. He panicked at thought of aborting the self he might have been!

THE BORROWED
PLUMES

I grew up in a dream, woke up in a nightmare! Dreams of fame as a concert pianist blacked-out in the pit of a North Korean prisoner-of -war-camp! My Chopin fingers, drafted to hit the butt and barrel of a rifle, were clinging to life in a death camp, and to the remembered touch of my bride. The present was dark, dark of my future unforeseen! I could only look back. Not far back, my fingers grew to the reach of an octave and touch of a Chopin. I came into wide shoulders and narrow hips, sported the body of an athlete, never went out for sports, or girls. My body, given to music, was taken by the army!

A divided country on the other side of the world had gone to war with itself in the middle year of the century, in the middle of my summer vacation between high school and college. The United Nations called my country to the defense of South Korea, and my country called me to an army physical. In a lineup of raw and raunchy bodies, my body was seen fit for the uniform, but I slipped into college before the army could suit me up. Deferred for the academic year at Trinitarian University, downstate Illinois, I kept growing in my dream world.

While the war was running up and down the peninsula of Korea, I was running fingers up and down the keyboard. When the fighting in Korea came to a standstill, I was at the piano, but keeping a coloratura soprano on key. "Nicki" opened-up my heart! I wanted to accompany her for the rest of my life, but my deferment ran out, the army took me away, all but the heart.

I can tell you my body was really out of step with close-order drill and close-ordered life, but it got me through Basic. A weekend pass got my body and heart back together, in marriage. After a moment musical with my coloratura soprano, I had to face the music in Korea. Overtures of peace were in the air when I hit the pits on the Main Line of Defense, but the instruments of war kept playing, turning the music in me to noise! One shrill note left me in dead silence!

Dead? I rose up. Ghost? I felt pain. Alive, my body was a prisoner of war, forced to drag itself across country to a hut behind barbed-wire. Penned-up with a pack of fellow prisoners, my body was shoulder to shoulder with them by day, head to foot with them by night. I lost touch with my own body. It was another prison, holding me in the constant grip of fear and hunger. The North Koreans had taken my wristwatch, taken me out of time. They'd taken my wedding ring, couldn't take me out of love. The spirit of Nicki stayed with me, kept me immune to the "give-up-itis" that weakened and sickened and carried off so many bodies around me.

Nicki's face was mirrored in memory, her coloratura voice echoing in mind, but only a few of her letters got through the barbed wire. They were the notes of a Requiem. My mother died. Nicki gave premature births, and deaths, to twin girls. I didn't know my mother was failing. I didn't know I'd left a pregnant wife behind. I couldn't write back! No paper, no pencil, no permission, no Red Cross.

My days kept going round and round in a rut, like the screech of a broken record, around and around and around. All the while I had to learn how to take care of myself. The only son of an only son, and the only son of a mother estranged from her family, I'd grown up without rivals or competition. Now, at Nineteen, I had to learn how to fight with fellow prisoners by day to keep from starving, share body heat with them by night to keep from freezing!

Nicki's spirit kept my body clinging to life, all the way to the "Cease fire," and "Operation Big Switch!" Repatriated, I was free again, free as an enlisted man can be. In Freedom Village, I got debugged, debriefed, and beefed-up for discharge. Returned to my land of dreams, I woke up in another nightmare! Would you believe I came home to a stranger pretending to be my wife!

The Botticelli Venus I'd left behind was no longer in the picture, a poor reproduction in her place! Where was Nicki? Who was the pretender? What did she want?" What could I do? The imposter fooled everyone but me! I raised an outcry, but my missing bride had no family to back me up. Nicki never knew her biological parents, had been passed from foster home to foster home. The only foster parents to be found only knew her as a child, weren't sure who she was as an adult. The few acquaintances we had at the university were gone. I knew her landlord, but none of her roommates by name. My letter to the landlord came back, undelivered. I knew the name of Nicki's employer at the University Bookstore, but he thought the imposter's photo resembled the girl who worked for him. He didn't remember very well, or got paid-off!

I was sure of a conspiracy! While penned-up in North Korea, I had the good fortune of coming into a fortune! My mother's estranged and prominent brother died childless, and forgiving. The Leighton Plantation in Louisiana was willed to my mother, and on to me. I don't think the arrangement set too well with my stepfather! He'd never been a father to me, always held me at a distance. I suspected he conspired with the pretender to share half my estate in a divorce settlement!

My theory didn't pass police inspection. No proof! The marriage license only documented my name, Leighton d'Arcy, and the name stolen by the imposter, Nicki Laishen. The minister who'd given us a "quickie" marriage, off base at Fort Leonard Wood, had our recorded names but no memory of our appearances. I had no good buddy in Basic, no Best Man to identify me and Nicki, and the only official witness to our marriage was the minister's wife who swore that an army of soldiers marched young women through her parlor. My snapshots of Nicki had disintegrated in my hands during captivity. My mother was no longer in the picture. The imposter had no pictures of the two of us, reported them lost in a stolen wallet! My stepfather, who didn't know Nicki until I was shipped out to Korea, claimed the imposter was my wife, alleged that I'd married in haste, didn't want to share my newfound wealth. He also intimated that I was "brainwashed" in North Korea! I'd never heard that word, thought my brain must have been the only part of me that got washed in North Korea!

I'd been indoctrinated, yes, forced to feed on Communist propaganda, but never did I swallow a shred of it, not even for an extra scrap of gruel. It was true, I'd been forced to speak out against war. Isn't everybody against war? I was never a collaborator, like some of my fellow prisoners. The twenty-one Turncoats who refused reparation after the Armistice brought suspicion on all POWs. We all might have Communist shadows following us back home!

The police didn't accuse me of any Communist sympathies, but thought I might be wounded in the mind. I was called a "hidden casualty," suffering from wounds that didn't show, and the police went along with the imposter's story, corroborated by my stepfather. On top of that, I was considered a "spoiled only child," wanting my own way, wanting out of marriage responsibility. Case dismissed! I was threatened with legal action for making "false accusations!"

The False One had played her role well! Only I could know she got details of our courtship and marriage mixed-up, or "forgotten." She blamed her "memory," said she only remembered how much she loved me, how much she wanted me. She kept offering herself to me as my wife, but my morals hadn't been taken away with my wedding ring. Adultery was wrong! Stealing and lying were wrong! I knew the imposter had stolen Nicki's name, and was lying. I didn't want to think of anything worse, thought Nicki was restrained somewhere, or living in amnesia.

While held down at the Separation Center, I'd feared making a scene. An army investigation would delay my discharge, get me fouled-up in military chickenshit. While confined to base, waiting for the walking papers that would set me free to run down the truth, I hung out with another POW, Dick Kreutzer. He liked to be called Big Dick, but was no bigger than me. We hadn't been in the same prison camp, but knew the same mistreatment. We also shared missing wives, but his wife gave warning, left a note. She was going into hiding with their infant son, didn't want to live with him, didn't want to live with the disgrace of divorce! He never found her, or his son. Unlike me, he got over it. I had no son to lose, but thought I'd lost myself as well as my wife.

After discharge, I joined up with Big Dick to share an apartment and the readjustment to civilian life. I couldn't adjust to life without my "Cinderella," couldn't imagine living happily ever after without her. The false one stayed on with my stepfather, in the family home. Were they having an affair? I knew she couldn't keep up the pretense forever, planned to wait her out, and took time to settle my inheritance in Louisiana. The Plantation Leighton Line had come to an end, and the d'Arcy Line was beginning, but I felt at the end of the line without Nicki, sold out, went back to Trinitarian University, put my hands to the piano, put my mind to the search for my coloratura soprano. I only found my own Voice, a talent for musical invention. I had my music again, and Nicki was music to me, but I kept looking for my muse.

A piano sonata was coming out of me with the counterpoint of true and false, missing wife and her imposter. In time, I called it the Borrowed Plumes, a term for "false colors, false pretenses." My music-theory professor thought it suggested a "pretense of Schoenberg!"

While my sonata was taking wings, the woman of the "false colors" kept hovering round me, following me to the university, taking up voice training at my stepfather's expense. I finally got the idea of playing along with her game, getting a look at her hand. You won't believe what turned up! Let me tell my story as objectively as I can, in the third person.

Let me know what you think.

I

The Hidden Life

Leighton "Lee" d'Arcy only loved music until he went to Trinitarian University and music materialized in the body of a coloratura soprano. Her voice was her "instrument," and it was as lyrical as her body that used it. His piano helped keep her "instrument" on key, and one note led to another, and another, and the harmony of romance! He always knew the piano had a physical touch, never knew the touch of a woman could be so musical!

Before Lee and "Nicki" got completely in tune, he was drafted for service in the Korean War! He was out of rhythm with the cadence of military life, but marched through it, got a pass to marry Nicki before ending up in the dissonance of war! He carried Nicki's memory with him through war, capture, and imprisonment, would have given up the ghost without her spirit. It kept him going all the way to the Armistice and the exchange of prisoners. Restored to the world of shaving, and world of mirrors, he didn't like what he saw when the mask of beard came off. The face was drawn tight and rigid from fear and stress. Looking down, his frame was shrunken by hunger and dysentery, yellow from cholera, scarred from beatings. He remembered his coloratura soprano told him she loved his "well composed" face and body. What would she think of his face and body now? She'd fallen in love with him at "first sight." Would she fall out of love with him at second sight?

"I'm afraid my wife won't know me, won't love me," Lee opened-up to the lieutenant assigned to his debriefing in South Korea's Freedom Village. "I hardly know myself."

"You are a different person!" The lieutenant addressed him from the other side of the desk, looking up from Lee's service record. "I'm Lieutenant Delaney, here to help you get acquainted with your new self."

"I don't like my new self. How can my wife like it?"

"She'll see the boy she married has turned into a man!"

Lee, still living with the childhood ridicule of "piano sissy," and "girly-boy," liked to be called a man. He liked the officer even more when he said they both came from the same neighborhood in Chicago, Hyde Park. They exchanged recollections, learned they both lived lakeside and spent summers on the same patch of beach between piles of barrier rocks. They went on excursions to nearby Jackson Park, "snow-white in Spring with Japanese cherry blossoms." The Park had remains of the Nineteenth Century Columbian Exposition, and they both remembered touring the old replica of the Sanata Maria that sailed from Spain for the Four Hundredth anniversary of America's discovery. The Park was transformed for another World's Fair, Chicago's Century of Progress, when they were youngsters. The lieutenant was old enough to slide down the Magic Mountain, and go up on the Sky Ride. Lee only remembered people talking about it. There were shaky elevated rides around the Loop for them to remember, walks along State Street, "Marshall Fields," and "the Chicago Theater." Mention of "Michigan Avenue" brought back visions of the Lake Front, fancy shops, the Art Institute, Orchestra Hall. Their reminiscences made them feel at home, away from home, but the officer finally said they had to get down to the "required interrogation." He explained that it was his job to help men adjust from war to peace, from soldier to civilian. It would be as hard, he predicted, "as making the original adjustment to military life."

Lee said he never got adjusted to the military life, and nobody could get adjusted to life in a prison camp!

"Almost half our men couldn't adjust, and died," the lieutenant was quick to agree. He said no one managed to escape, and it was also his job to look into it.

"Something sure was wrong with those prison camps," Lee was quick to bring up.

"Were you put to torture?"

"By captors or fellow prisoners?"

"Give me names of fellow prisoners who abused you."

"Don't remember names. We all fought with each other to stay alive."

"Did your mother overprotect you?"

"What does my mother have to do with it?"

"Momism is the theory that mothers spoiled our generation, brought us all up with permissive child-rearing practices!"

"Should mothers raise children to survive prison camps?"

"Permissiveness doesn't prepare us for a world that's not permissive."

"I wasn't raised to do what I wanted. My mother made me practice the piano, constantly."

"You left our neighborhood school to attend the Francis Parker School," the lieutenant brought up, looking up from Lee's service record. "Isn't that a private, Progressive school? Isn't a Progressive School permissive?"

"Child-centered, not permissive!"

Lee was afraid the interrogator thought progressive meant collaborator, as it did in prison camp. He told the lieutenant that the Parker School permitted him to center his studies around his musical interests, related other subjects to music, worked him hard.

"The world isn't centered around our interests."

"Prison camp sure wasn't," Lee agreed, "but it was permissive. We had no rules or regularities, lived in chaos, didn't know what would happen next."

"They wanted to make you hate each other, and your country, wanted to capture your mind."

"They never had my mind," Lee insisted. "Had my mind full of my wife. Never swallowed a word of Commie drivel." He sat uptight in his folding chair, and it creaked under his weight.

The young lieutenant was quick to remind Lee that he'd confessed to being a "warmonger, and imperialist dog!" He waved a sheet of paper at him.

"Only remember saying I hated war," the ex-prisoner of war managed to explain himself.

"I'm not here to condemn you," the young officer insisted, "only want to find out how you were treated as a prisoner."

"Commies treated me like a dog, made me sleep on corn stalks, beg for scraps!"

"Dogs are loyal to those who feed them"

"Are you trying to say I might have sold my birthright for a mess of potage? Gooks only had my body."

"Didn't they mix good and bad treatment, keep you off balance, take you over?"

"A few good handouts surprised us."

"Did the Commies let you get any letters from home?"

"Got a couple letters from my dear wife. Nicki lost our twin baby girls, born prematurely!"

"Commies let the bad news get through."

"Got news of my mother's death! She lost my father in the last war, must have thought she'd lost me in the new one. She probably grieved herself to death."

"A man can have many wives, only one mother."

"A man can have only one wife like Nicki."

"Tell me about her?"

"She's an aspiring opera singer."

"I remember you thought she wouldn't love you anymore. Think she wants to be an opera singer more than a wife?"

"We always planned to keep up both our careers."

"Have you always wanted a musical career?"

"I was made for music. I was my mother's career! She had to give up music for marriage, and me."

"She must have doted on you."

"Are you getting at Momism again? Blame Commies for so many deaths in prison camp. Blame God, if you want, not mothers."

"Do you blame God?"

"Thought God abandoned me. Lonely universe without God."

"You still believe in God?"

"I believe music's the language of God."

"You're a Baptist, I see by the record."

"Baptist on my mother's side, Catholic on my father's side, Jewish on my Christ's side."

"A holy trinity," the lieutenant smiled.

"My mother's family disowned her for marrying a Catholic. My father gave up his religion to let my mother raise me in her faith."

"Tell me about your Catholic father."

"He was killed in the war, the big war."

"What did he do with his life?"

"He was an athletic director for the Chicago Park District."

"You must have inherited your athletic build from him."

"Didn't inherit athletic interest!"

"Your record shows you have a stepfather, Ashley Newton. What's he like?"

"Are you looking for some kind of Freudian hangup?"

"I'm a sociologist, not a psychologist. As an officer, I only want to help you fit back into your fatherland."

"My stepfather also worked for the Chicago Park District, but had a 4-F body the army didn't want. He got my mother to want it after my father was gone. He always took me for some kind of rival." Lee ran out of breath, caught it, asked what all this had to do with his discharge?

"Army wants to make sure you're sound of mind, and body, wants to make sure the Communists didn't grind you up in their propaganda mill. We're still in a Cold War!"

"Think Commies gonna start another hot war?" Lee feared getting called up for another tour of war duty.

"Massive Soviet armies have taken over Eastern Europe, threaten the West. Red China endangers Southeast Asia. Only thing stopping them is fear of the atom bomb."

"We all fear the atom bomb! Guess I shouldn't fear facing my wife."

....

Facing himself in the mirror was getting easier for Lee d'Arcy as days passed. His body was getting patched and prepped for discharge. Letters and newspapers helped fill-in the blanks in his life. Nicki's letters brought love, and news of his inheritance! Newspapers let him know the Soviet Union had the big bomb, and there were thousands of American soldiers unaccounted for in North Korea. His favorite pianist, "Horowitz," had celebrated his silver jubilee with the New York Philharmonic. Lee only wanted to get back in time with Nicki and music.

It was a long ocean voyage from Korea to the States, but he had few work details. Days and nights made their rounds, turned up the Golden Gate Bridge. It reconnected him to his dreamworld. He was "processed" for a few days in San Francisco, got a first class train ticket for Fort Sheridan, Illinois, shared the ride with another soldier, a square-jawed private leaning on a cane. When he met him, the old boy said the cane was only a "sympathy stick." When looking for their reserved seats in the Pullman car, Lee mentioned to his companion that no one gave them any notice, even though they were in uniform. "In my father's war, homecoming servicemen and women were honored."

"I was old enough to enlist in the last days of the big war," his companion brought up, stowing his gear and slipping into the window seat, "did my time in the States, and inactive Reserves, bitter about getting called back up for Korea!"

"Lots of officers and enlisted men in my outfit were bitter, too," Lee said, fitting into the seat next to him.

"I'm Dick Kreutzer," the man with the cane said, squaring his big jaw and extending a hand, "first class private about to make first class citizen."

"Leighton d'Arcy."

"Fancy moniker!"

"Call me Lee."

"Call me Big Dick!"

"Should call you Big Stick," Lee said, pointing to the cane leaning between seats.

"Really did pick up a little shrapnel, but the cane's for picking up sympathetic females.

You look like you don't need any prop for picking up girls."

"Only one girl for me."

"Lost my woman," Big Dick admitted.

As they both got comfortable in their upright seats, Big Dick told Lee that he'd been called "Big" since he was a "little sprout." He said the letter B is for boisterous, I for insolent, G for groovy.

"My name doesn't mean a thing now," Lee kept up, "but I expect to make it mean a lot in music."

"Big Dick is big in life insurance," Big Dick carried on, "but I gave a lot of my life to the Service, expect to make a lot of money on lives of others." As he talked, he palmed a dime, suggested a flip of the coin for the lower berth at night. He tossed up the dime, called "heads," said he won.

Before Lee could object, the older man shrugged, apologized, said he couldn't take the chance of getting shelved in the upper bunk. "It would freak me out! Had me the panics in Solitary."

They discovered they were both POWs, came out of different camps, didn't want to talk about it.

"Upper's O.K. with me," Lee assured his companion, but didn't know how he'd ever fit in the pull-down shelf above. He told his companion that he could use a private night, never had one as "a private in the army."

Big Dick asked what Lee was going to do with his private life, "beside making music?"

"Making love!"

"You're talking to a lover!"

"Got a bride waiting at home," Lee volunteered as the train wheels began grinding on the tracks, starting to inch him closer to his bride.

"You look a little young to be sporting a wife," Big Dick finally spoke up, as he shook a cigarette out of a pack, popped it in the side of his mouth, offered one to "Lee."

"Too young to smoke," Lee said, forcing a laugh.

"Most men married to tobacco," Big Dick said with both sides of his mouth. "Guys in my outfit would sell out to the Chinks for a smoke."

"Some guys in my camp," Lee brought up, "found weeds on work patrols, smoked 'em in homemade pipes, said it smoked-up visions of home. Never lost vision of home and wife!"

"Had me a wife," Big Dick confided in a breath of smoke, "but she disappeared, like a puff of smoke!"

"What happened?"

"She left me a note, a dear John. Never found her."

"My wife's gonna be waiting for me at Union Station."

"Reunion at Union!"

"Wheels can't turn fast enough," Lee said, starting to count the clicks.

The wheels kept clicking, time kept ticking, and the seats were turned into berths for the night. Lee managed to fit into the upper berth and get out of uniform. When the berths were turned back to seats, next day, mountains were in the window, and after dinner in the diner, mountains had flattened into plains.

The morning finally came when Lee was roused by the Pullman porter's warning that Chicago's Union Station would come up in another hour. Lee squeezed into clothes behind the curtain of the upper berth, climbed down the ladder, shoes and shaving bag in hand. After a wash and shave in the men's lavatory, he sipped coffee in the dining car with his new friend.

The wheels finally screeched to a groan and a stop. Pullman porters brushed-down passengers with whisk brooms, brushed them off to Union Station. The high-vaulted Waiting Room was crowded with people, and memories for Lee. He stopped to look up and around, told Big Dick that he saw his father off to war in this "big hollow space, never saw him again."

"You'll be seeing your wife pretty soon," Big Dick said, trying to cheer him up, "and get another load of me, up at Sheridan." He waved goodbye with his cane.

Lee headed for the scheduled rendezvous with Nicki, rushed up the granite steps to the Jackson Street level. He only sighted his stepfather, Ashley Newton, in coat and tie. They embraced awkwardly. Lee was surprised to see tears in the eyes of the man who'd taken the place of his father.

"Wish your mother could be here for this moment," the stepfather was saying, pulling away to get a better look at his stepson.

The stepson could only ask, "where's Nicki?"

"Poor girl's crying her eyes out at home. Didn't want you to see her with that facial skin outbreak. It just broke out again. Nerves, probably."

"How could pimples and splotches come between us?"

"Maybe you don't know how women feel about their looks."

"Only want looks at her! Loved her looks."

"She wants you to keep loving her, see her at her best."

"How could she wait any longer to get a look at me?"

"She's already waited a long time! How long before you get your separation from the Service?"

"As long as the army wants." Lee hardly knew what he was saying. He was feeling empty, disappointed, a little angry. "Army's a waiting game, one line after another," he said, closing his eyes to see the memorized picture of his bride.

The stepfather said the army could wait for him to get a bite of breakfast! "Let me treat you to a civilian mess at Fred Harvey's."

Lee nodded, swung the bag over his shoulder, kept up with his stepfather as they rushed through Union Station to the restaurant on the far side.

As soon as the waiter took their orders, the stepfather asked Lee about his plans. "Back to the college Ivory Tower, and the piano ivories."

"You have a wife to support."

"We'll make out on the G.I. Bill, and my inheritance."

"You need to make something of yourself, stand on your own two feet."

"My two hands will make something of myself, at the piano."

"Only one in a million makes it to Carnegie Hall."

"I know you don't see me as a Horowitz," Lee conceded, "but music's in my blood, and Nicki's."

"She's going to need a lot of looking after."

"All I need is a look at her!"

....

"Didn't get a look at my wife," Lee told Big Dick when he checked in at Fort Sheridan, got assigned to an adjacent bunk. "She didn't want to face me with her face a mess."

"A woman's face can't launch a thousand ships unless it's shipshape," Big Dick quipped, trying to make his friend smile, "but she can let you hear the sound of her voice."

Lee waited in line for a phone, almost lost his voice when he heard the coloratura tone of Nicki's voice. He choked up, had to wait a moment before bursting out his greetings. She apologized for not meeting him at the station, said she didn't want him to face her red, spotty face. He said her face was always rosy to him. She said he always saw her through rose-colored glasses!

Her voice seemed to sing through the wire. Nicki told him she couldn't hit her High-Cs since the twins took a lot out of her, but she'd hit the high again with him back from overseas!

They kept the wire humming, talked through the operator's three minute warnings, again and again. He kept pumping dimes in the slot, down to his last coin. He was in line next day, at break time, loving the sound of Nicki's voice. All other times, he was lined-up for poking, probing, piercing. When not up for medical examinations, he was put down for lectures. Time stood still, the way it did in captivity, even though he kept looking at his new wristwatch.

All the daytime was bright with Big Dick's company and wisecracks. They bunked together, one up, one down, shaved, showered, messed together, side by side. Lee mostly talked about getting back his wife. Big Dick mostly talked of his life in life insurance. He also liked to talk about his old neighborhood on Chicago's North Side, near the "home of the Cubbies." He wanted to take Lee to a ball game in the "friendly confines of Wrigley Field." Lee didn't think any "confines" could be "friendly." Lee wanted to take "Big Dick" to a concert at Orchestra Hall. Big Dick didn't think he had the ear for that. They both talked about "Visitor's Day."

....

"Visitor's Day" finally turned up on Fort Sheridan's "Plan of the Day!" Lee and Big Dick got shaped-up, faced the same mirror in their same dress uniforms. Lee saw himself brushing back the ringlets of yellow hair coiling all over his head, and Big Dick kept squaring his jaw and shoulders.

"No private place on base for you to get laid," Big Dick cracked as he slanted the garrison cap over one eye.

"Only want to lay eyes on Nicki!"

"Let's get on the stick," and he led the way, swinging his cane.

They headed for the Visitor's Center, walked together in silence across the parade ground. Soldiers and civilians were beginning to mix together, all around them.

"Got a bead on my little old bro, an' stepsister," Big Dick yelled, and ran off.

Lee stood at watch, targeted a woman who wore a wide-brimmed red hat like Nicki wore. She waved, rushed in his direction. He turned around to see who she was running toward, but she was reaching out to him!

"Don't look too close," she said, "cosmetics can't cover everything."

"Do I know you?"

"Are you joking?"

"You're talking up the wrong soldier!"

"Do I look older? You look different, too."

The imposter's words struck Lee dumb, and he began blanking out. He barely remembered getting escorted back to the barracks by the military police.

....

Put on report for "getting out of line at the Visitor's Center," Lee was confined to barracks, and to the turmoil in his mind. He wasn't sure what happened, felt sure a young woman was pretending to be his wife! He rang-up home, rang-up no answer. His body took refuge in his bunk, the only private space in an enormous public space, but he couldn't console himself with making music in his head.. By dinner time he was allowed to draw rations in the mess hall, but dumped a full tray, came back to confinement, and bewilderment. He wondered if Nicki had sent a friend in her place and he misunderstood?

He got in line for another phone call, got connected to his stepfather, got a blast of angry words, got cut off! The phone seemed to shake in Lee's hand, the voice of his stepfather kept ringing in his ears. "You broke Nicki's heart! Have you lost your mind?"

Had he lost it? He only knew for sure he'd lost Nicki, must get off base to look for her. No way, not without a pass! He had to stay confined, kept his problem pent up inside, carried it to the sanctuary of his bunk. It was almost time for Taps when Big Dick turned-up alongside, asked how Lee's reunion worked out.

All Lee could tell his friend was that "Nicki didn't show up, again." He told himself to keep quiet until he got the unbelievable mystery solved.

"Give me the lowdown tomorrow," Big Dick said, stepping out of dress pants, folding them, tucking them in his locker.

Lights went out and Taps sounded in the dark as Lee saw the upper bunk sag down with Big Dick. During the long black of night, Lee couldn't sleep, but thought he might have been dreaming up his wife's imposter!

When Big Dick's feet came crashing down with the sound of reveille, Lee confessed that he was on report for getting in a fight at the Visitor's Center. Big Dick had no time for an explanation, gave him a slap on the back, ran off. In a little while, Lee had the barracks to himself, didn't like a vacuum. When men dribbled back for a morning break, and a smoke, Lee gave Big Dick his story in a couple of breaths.

"Nobody gonna go for that crap," Big Dick told him after a moment's thought. "Don't make a stink. It'll get your discharge fouled up! Army gonna figure you went ape-shit."

"Think I've gone ape?"

"Think your wife, like mine, left you swinging. I'd bet she got a friend to throw you a curve."

"Nicki wouldn't foul me up, no way."

"Somebody has. Give it a rest, hang loose till you get off report, get yourself out of service."

....

Off report, waiting for walking papers, Lee got calls from home, but no explanation, only more frustration and fury. In the evenings he blew off steam with Big Dick, let him keep showing ways to smoke and inhale. Smoking it up, they shared theories about Lee's missing wife. Lee dug up all kinds of plots, never contemplated her death. Big Dick thought the missing wife had a hidden life, faked her disappearance to get on with it! Lee almost believed it, turned it down. Big Dick went on to say women are good at faking it! He reminded Lee of his own wife faking a new life. He let his words fly through smoke rings, began passing out his own story.

"Covered her trail," Big Dick said. "Her folks wouldn't help me. She's dead to me now, has a new life somewhere. You better close the book on your wife, like I did."

Lee said it was harder to close a book in the middle of a mystery, and got ready to turn in. The barracks went dark. Taps settled everyone down with the order to sleep, but Lee couldn't obey, lay awake in the dark of his own mind.

....

In the dark of the barracks, and muffled sounds of heavy breathing, snorts and snores, a scream echoed up and down the rows of bunks, reverberating in Lee's ears. It was his own scream! He opened his eyes to see Big Dick hovering over him.

"Cease fire, old buddy!"

"Nightmare!"

Lee recalled his dream of scanning a musical score, notes strung along the lines. Notes turned into naked bodies hanging on lines of barbed-wire!

....

No longer hung-up in the army, getting away with honorable discharges and a load of back pay, Lee and Big Dick rented a furnished apartment on the North Side, close to the Cubs' Wrigley Field, but Big Dick only wanted to "hit on the women, play the field." Lee only wanted the police to help him find his wife. The "Case of the Missing Bride" was opened and quickly closed. Nothing came up to prove "Nicki's name" on documents wasn't the imposter's. Lee was threatened with trouble for making "false charges." He retreated into himself, and the apartment on the North Side, spent hours sending inquiries to all the local newspapers, reading all the "personal notices."

II

The Private Eye

"You ought to get yourself some professional help," Big Dick insisted one evening when he came home to find Lee's head on the kitchen table. "Get yourself a Private Eye."

Lee tried to laugh, said all eyes are private, "that's why we see things differently."

"You know what I mean, a P.I.'s a private investigator."

"Why didn't you get one of those eyes to look for your wife and son?"

"Didn't have the dough. You're rolling in it."

"I could get a private eye to look for your wife."

Big Dick shrugged, said he didn't want a wife who didn't want him. Lee knew Nicki must want him! He looked through the Yellow Pages, turned up the "Hunter's Detective Agency," and a phone call got him an appointment. When the time came he took off by cab to the Michigan Avenue office building, got a lift all the way up to the twenty-fifth floor. The man who answered to the name of "Hunter" wore a brim hat, in his own office! He greeted Lee from under its shadow. "Private Investigator C.I. Hunter. What can I do ya for?"

Lee briefed him on the "missing wife," and the "false wife." The investigator said he'd tracked down missing wives, but never ran across a wife's imposter! "This one's for the book! Clue me in, chapter and verse."

Lee paged through memory and laid out the whole story. Mr. Hunter asked for the missing wife's picture, but Lee had to let him know there were no pictures, and explained why. The private eye said it was hard to look for an unseen face.

"You can get a look at my false wife," Lee said, writing down her address, "get the lowdown on the imposter."

"You think I can get the truth out of her?"

"You can size her up, pry something loose."

"I figure there's a loose nut around."

"You can get hold of her handwriting, compare it with these two letter I got in Korea from Nicki."

"Stationery's all crumpled up," the investigator said, carefully unfolding one of the letters, "writing's smudged."

"Kept them next to my heart, all through prison camp."

"I'll see what I can get out of the imposter," the investigator promised, pushing back his hat. "Did your musical wife have a sugar-daddy, or a fling before you?"

"She told me I was the only man more than a friend."

"Give me a list of people you knew together, and places where you were together."

"We didn't socialize much," Lee confessed, and worked out a short list of relevant names and places.

The investigator made financial arrangements and went on his way, leaving Lee feeling free to checkout his plantation in Louisiana.

....

Flying, Lee looked down on clouds hiding the earth, tried to think who was hiding Nicki. When he came down to earth, he followed the passengers to the baggage room, looked for his name on a sign held up by a person scheduled to meet him. The sign showed up in the hands of a grayish man in a gray suit and tie.

"Donald John Stanton, Leighton family lawyer," the older man introduced himself, "known by my middle name, John. My condolences for the loss of your mother!"

Lee nodded, didn't want to mention that her family had disowned her long ago! "Call me Lee," he said, swinging his suitcase off the revolving carousel. He heard the lawyer say that Lee was a hallowed name in the War for Southern Independence.

Lee never heard the Civil War called that, only mentioned he wasn't much of a "military man."

The lawyer said he knew about his "wartime sacrifices."

Lee wondered if he knew what sacrifice happened after that, didn't want to get into it, followed the older man to the parking lot. They shared few words during the hour drive into the "back country." Lee thought he was being driven back in time, back into the Old South he'd seen in movies.

"Manor house just down the road a piece," the lawyer spoke up, at last.

A Greek Revival mansion, with white columns, came into view, down a lane of overhanging post oaks streaming with Spanish Moss.

"Old place needs some upkeep," the lawyer mentioned, "but it's a heap of tradition." He parked in front of the front steps where they were greeted by a bent-over man of dark face and cotton-while hair.

"The old man of color goes with the house," the lawyer told Lee.

The old caretaker welcomed them, said he knew "Master Lee's dear Mama," and said she could "spin purty tunes on Spinet pi-ana." He led them through the entrance hall to the adjoining "Morning Room," pointed out a small piano amid heavy furnishings. Lee took seat at the Spinet, spread his fingers over the keys, but frowned at the sounds coming out. The lawyer asked if the piano might be out of tune? Lee said it was the "pianist out of tune."

The caretaker gave them a tour of the house, explaining that most of the rooms were closed off. He opened a few doors, revealed ghostly furniture shrouded in white sheets. He showed off the "birthin' room," told Lee, "your mama got birthed in dat pretty spool bed."

The caretaker kept opening and closing doors until he came to the "Smokin' Room" where big upholstered chairs faced the fireplace. Framed paintings of distinguished looking men were hanging on all four walls.

"Portraits of family heads," Lee was told by the lawyer, "lined up in succession, for your inspection. Your Uncle Lawrence's last one on the right."

Lee looked up at the face peering down, face of the man who willed the plantation to his mother. Lee thought the face bore resemblance to his mother. It had high cheek bones, upturned nose, but the face looked down at him, seemed to be disapproving!

Lee looked away, told the lawyer that the only thing he knew about his mother's family was that it drummed her out of it for taking the wrong step in marriage.

"That's a long story," the lawyer spoke up as he pointed up to another portrait on the wall. "That's your granddaddy Leighton, distinguished in politics and in war."

"He's the one who disowned my mother," Lee said, measuring up the man posed in a World War One uniform, with three medals in a row across the chest.

The lawyer made no comment, waved Lee to an armchair, and fit himself into the chair next to it. He offered Lee a cigar. Lee shook his head, said he was just getting "hooked" on cigarettes, "the nails of my coffin." The lawyer produced a cigarette case, offered a cigarette, and they were soon sitting in smoke and silence, until the caretaker hobbled in and set down a tray with glasses and a bottle. He displayed the handwritten label on the bottle, said it came from the cellar, "Leighton grape wine, 1932."

"Year I was born," Lee said as his glass was being filled.

"Wine is sunshine stored in grapes," the lawyer said, raising a toast to the "sunshine of the time you were born."

Lee took a sip, felt the glow, wondered if the grapes of today would glow as much.

"A vintage year for you," the lawyer toasted again, "but grapes of wrath for our country. Banks closed down, cotton piled up!"

"I lived on music," Lee mentioned."

"No music down here in those days. Your mother went away to find it."

The caretaker shuffled into the room, said the table was set, and showed them to the diningroom. Lee marveled at an oak table that could seat an even dozen. It was now set for two, and the two took their places. Lee had to be told that a slimy vegetable was okra, and that Chicken Friend Steak wasn't chicken. After a heavy meal ending with "Southern Cherry Cobbler," Lawyer John said he was so full he could pop a tick off his belly, and Lee laughed, but thought of scratching bugs in prison camp.

The lawyer said they could let their stomachs settle in the Smoking Room, "with another touch of 1932 sunshine."

After savoring wine by the smouldering fireplace, they both reached for cigarettes and let smoke come between them. The lawyer finally said it was time to look into the legal matters of inheritance. When he reached for his briefcase, Lee came up with the thought of getting legal advice. He spoke up, revealed his missing wife, and her imposter.

After a thoughtful pause, the lawyer said there was no precedent in "his book" for such a case. He said he'd sleep on it, but advised Lee to arrange for an iron clad will.

Bending down to poke the embers in the fireplace, the lawyer sighed, over the shoulder, that it would be better to look over legal papers in the morning, finish the evening with "wine, smoke, and a touch of family history."

"I don't know much about my mother's family," Lee mentioned, with Leighton wine burning at his lips. He only knew, for sure, that his mother was disowned for marrying out of her class and religion. He asked the lawyer how a father could disown his only daughter for marrying a Catholic?

"Don't have a Brief on that," he said through a breath of smoke, "but marriage to someone of a different way of life was a scandal in those days."

"Why did my mother's brother put her in his will?"

The lawyer held up his reply while swallowing a sip of wine and smacked his lips. "Your mother was the only close relation."

"Did you know my mother?"

"Grew up with her! All us neighbor boys fancied her, but she only fancied the piano." The twang of the lawyer's accent tickled Lee as he listened to more talk about the Leighton family history. The Leightons, he learned, were leaders in war and peace, before and after the "War of Northern Aggression," and Lee wondered if his mother might have been expelled for marrying a DamnYankee! The lawyer railed on about railroads coming along and leaving the Leighton Plantation on the wrong side of the tracks. "Times got bad."

Lee came to full attention when the lawyer raised his glass to toast the beginning of the d'Arcy line! Lee asked if there were any other Leightons?

"None, well none except a very distant cousin, Hailey, a divorced lady who took back her maiden name when getting rid of the drunken husband. She has a daughter, Rosa. They made no claims on the estate, but the mother showed interest in meeting you, the son of her childhood playmate."

Lee kept listening and nodding during the rest of the evening, until he was shown to the "master bedroom." It had been one of the closed-off rooms, but was aired-out for his benefit. A three-step ladder led up to a canopied bed. A trundle bed was tucked underneath. He closed his eyes under the canopy, imagined his mother as a child trundled under it. He sank into the featherbed, slept lightly, waking several times to check his watch. By light of day, he washed sleep out of his eyes at the pitcher and bowl by his bedside.

When he showed-up in the kitchen, the old caretaker was preparing a breakfast of "new laid eggs, store-bought pig-links."

John, the lawyer, who'd spent the night in a guestroom, joined Lee for coffee, and then led him around "the grounds," told him the land was worked by descendants of the original Leighton slaves. "These good people of color stayed rooted to the land, lived on as sharecroppers!"

Lee got to talk with some of workers, could hardly understand their dialect. After awhile, the lawyer took him back in the house, set him up at a table and brought out bank accounts, records of expenses and debts, records of farm income, bank investments. Lee hoped the sale of the land would more than cover its debts.

Later, he was driven to the only nearby town, Leighton Corners. The lawyer told him it had a mill for "grinding local grain," and a general store for buying everything a body needed, a station for "gassing up," and a restaurant for "eating out, and a tavern for drinking-up."

They drove past a movie theater the lawyer called the "old Pix." It was boarded up, with a marquee still promoting a movie, Designing Woman! It was a good title, Lee thought, for the story of his wife's imposter.

They parked in back of the General Store where Lee was told the real estate agent had an office. When they got settled down with the agent, they were told the Leighton estate would sell well. The agent said someone from "up North," had already made inquiries. Lee arranged for the agent to put the estate up for sale, with arrangements for the old caretaker to keep his place, and a pension for life.

His last appointment was with his distant relation, Hailey Leighton, "down the road a piece." Lawyer John dropped him off, planned to pick him up later in the hour.

"Miss Hailey," as she called herself, even though still wearing a wedding ring, received Lee in a shaded livingroom, heavy with massive furniture, dark with long hanging drapes. She was dressed in lace and silk, comb in hair, spray of violets at wrist. Her face was half-hidden in the shadows, and Lee thought the drapes were drawn to shade her age, but what he saw of her didn't resembled his mother or any of the portraits in the Leighton Smoking Room.

Miss Hailey pointed out her "baby grand," festooned with tassels and ribbons and "skirts, to hide its "rosewood legs." She told him she, and his dear Mama "were best friends, and turned that "piano ivories to gold."

He asked to give her piano a "touch," got up and let his hands reach for the keys that kept sticking. "Hands out of touch," he said, crunching hands together as he went back to his chair.

Miss Hailey said "the old piana needs a-tunin' up. Ain't put arthritic hands to it for a coon's age."

Lee was thinking that his very distant cousin bore no resemblance to his mother, but she bore plenty of reminiscences. She poured out tea and stories while a roomful of clocks were ticking and striking the quarter hour at different times.

Time chimed away. Lee came to attention when Miss Hailey told about her only daughter going up to "Yankee land" to make music, "like your dear Mama." It occurred to Lee that the daughter might know his story, might be the pretender!

When Lee asked about her daughter, the mother only said she was about Lee's age, and "blessed unmarried." He asked to see her picture, but Miss Hailey shrugged, said she was "out of the picture for now."

Time had ticked away on different clocks, sounded the quarter-hour at different times, and it was soon time for the lawyer to pick him up. While fields and farms were flashing past the car windows, Lee asked about "Miss Hailey's daughter."

The lawyer only knew the mother and daughter were estranged, and the daughter, Rosa, "recently flew off, up North, "to seek her fortune!"

....

Flying b ack North, carrying thought of the Rosa relation, Lee came down to the same world, the empty world without Nicki. The "private eye" had only come up with "blind spots," and Lee put him on the track of his distant cousin, Rosa Leighton.

Big Dick was still in "rest and recreation." The only "news" Big Dick had for Lee was a request for a "home visit!" The stepfather and imposter wanted to see him.

Lee persuaded Big Dick to stand with him in the confrontation! They rode the "el" to the Hyde Park station on the South Side. When the familiar station platform rushed into sight, Lee's mind began catching memories of train rides to the "Loop" for piano lessons. When the train grated to a stop, its sound was music to his ears.

Many steps and minutes took him and Big Dick to the yellow-brick bungalow where he'd grown up in dreams and music. When Lee's stepfather opened the door, he opened up a living room furnished in mahogany, and memories. The polished grand piano stood on one side of the room, as it always stood, and brought music to Lee's mind.

"This is Dick Kreutzer, another POW," Lee introduced his buddy, but gave no greeting to his stepfather.

Everyone was uneasy, avoiding any exchange of words, or looks.

"Nicki will be with us in a moment," the stepfather promised, waving the guests inside, asking if they'd like "a little fine wine time?" Without waiting for an answer he dribbled wine from a crystal decanter into glasses arranged on a mahogany table. "To the resolution of misunderstandings," he toasted.

Lee and Big Dick took up their glasses, but Lee didn't return the toast. Everyone sat down, crossed legs, sipped drinks.

"The magic of memory played tricks on my wife's son," the stepfather finally explained to Lee's friend.

"Somebody sure played tricks on him," Big Dick said with a wave of his glass.

"He tricked himself."

Lee wasn't listening. He made his way to the grand piano, struck a key, waited for the sound to die, but a girl's voice came alive first.

"It's been a long time since you played for me."

Lee turned to get sight of a young woman framed in a doorway. She was the portrait of a lady in blue, draped in a blue flowing gown. When he saw her wearing Nicki's teardrop earrings, he wanted to know where she got the "teardrops."

"From the husband who came home to put teardrops in my eyes."

Lee looked away, put a finger to the keyboard, struck a high note, asked for the imposter to reach it with her voice.

"Can't hit the high notes, not anymore."

"How convenient. You could never imitate Nicki's voice."

"She lost her voice, with the babies," the stepfather intervened, standing up with a wine glass trembling in hand.

Lee banged his fist on the keyboard, scattering a cluster of notes into the air. The imposter reached both hands up to cover her ears. Lee noticed Nicki's pearl engagement ring on her finger! He felt his own fingers at the imposter's neck, felt the gasp of her breath, felt the restraint of a hammerlock at his back.

"Lost control of myself," Lee gasped, letting go of the pretender, and getting released from the hammerlock. It occurred to him, for the first time, he wasn't a gentle soul. There was a killer in the soldier who never fired his weapon in combat!

Big Dick gave him a hand, steered him out of the house, into the street, up steps to the "el" station.

"She asked for it," Big Dick calmed Lee down as they stood on the platform in wait for the next train. "She wants you to lose your cool, act crazy, get shut-up in the booby hatch."

A distant elevated train started to shake Big Dick's voice, and the platform. The train rattled into view, came grinding to a stop in front of them. Doors opened, and quickly closed with everyone on the platform piled-up inside. Lee and Big Dick slumped down together on a double seat, got rolled into each other when the train jerked into motion. The window was featuring the moving picture of the backsides of three-story apartment houses, their back stairs and fire- escapes.

"Our stop's coming up," Big Dick noticed. The moving picture in the window was flickering into slow motion.

"I'm at a dead end," Lee said, trying to pull himself together. "What can I do?"

"Your wife's gonna show up," Big Dick promised as they got off the train, but he didn't think there was a ghost of a chance.

....

"It's like looking for a ghost," the "private eye" reported to Lee. "I'm finding a body of evidence, but not the body of your wife." He lay out several manila folders, and his expense account.

"Couldn't you break down the imposter, get her to talk?"

"She was cooperative, but wouldn't take back a word of her story."

"It's a made-up story, pure fiction!"

The investigator agreed, but said he couldn't find the nonfiction truth! "Records only give names."

"Locate any foster parents?"

"Ran down one, the family that raised her as a child, but they couldn't say if the imposter's adult picture was Nicki. You'll find it in my report. I even checked Cook County hospital records, got her birth certificate, and certificates of her twins. Couldn't run down any patient in the Maternity Ward at that time your wife gave birth. No nurse remembered her."

Turning up another document, he pointed to Nicki's school records. "They only reported grades, heights, weights, and deportment. No high school graduation picture in the school yearbook, only her name. She was pictured in the Music Club, the A Cappella Choir, and the cast of the student production of The Pirates of Penzance. Group pictures, very indistinct. He said he found her music director, but he only remembered the voice."

"How about the Justice of the Peace who married us when I finished up at Fort Leonard Wood?"

"Only line on him was a phone call. He had record of your marriage, no remembrance of you two. Why didn't you have a best man?"

"Didn't buddy-up in basic."

"Looks like you and your wife also kept to yourselves most of the time! Can't check out the few casual friends you and Nicki had at Trinitarian, but we need to drive down there while the trail is hot. I did managed to run down the list of people the imposter knew in Chicago. Those I found were satisfied that the imposter's picture was "Nicki."

"The imposter gave you the list! What about the handwriting analysis of Nicki's letters?"

"Inconclusive! Letters you got in prison camp were mostly smudged, but seemed to match the imposter's handwriting."

"Could she tell you what she wrote in those letters?"

"She couldn't remember. You might be interested to know that a graphology expert thought your wife's handwriting revealed an introvert with a flare for creativity."

"That's Nicki!"

"Imposter's writing showed the same characteristics, but so would a million others! Trip to Trinitarian's our last resort."

"What about my very distant cousin in Louisiana, Rosa Leighton?"

"Her mother told me she could be anywhere up North. How's that for a clue?

"When can we hit the road for Trinitarian?"

"Got an opening in my schedule, Monday next." Arrangements were made.

Lee contemplated the mystery he'd married, and carried into bed.

....

The distant sound of music began rousing Lee out of sleep. Why was the radio on? Why was there a crack of light in the hallway? He began recognizing the somber tones of Mussorgski's Night on Bare Mountain, and burst into full wakefulness! Big Dick was gone for the weekend! Who was in the livingroom? His heart was in beat with Night on Bare Mountain, skipped a beat when the music stopped and a voice sounded, "we interrupt this program now in progress to announce the escape of a hospitalized state criminal!"

Moussorgski's music began creeping down the hall again, got cut off again.

"We interrupt this program once again to warn listeners about a criminal now at large. Keep doors locked!"

Lee knew the hospital was nearby, didn't remember if he locked the door, must not have! Moussorgski's music began raising a sweat in him. Through the music, Lee kept feeling the presence of someone down the hall. Almost paralyzed, he tried to feel his way out of bed, feel for his army revolver. Big Dick must have taken it away! No back door! No way out! Barefooted, he rose up on toes, sneaked down the hall. A Night on Bare Mountain became more shrill with every step. The livingroom light became brighter with every footfall. The music was booming!

A quick glance around the corner gave him a shot at the armchair and back of a man's head! Lee's military training in hand-to-hand combat flashed back, along with the old fear of hurting his musical hands. He had to save his life, flashed round the corner, arms slashing!

The armchair was empty! A sweater looking like a head hung in a hump over its back. He was alone with the music, found the door locked. He must have forgotten to turn off the radio and lights. There was an empty bottle of wine on the table next to his armchair. Did it empty his mind?

Night on Bare Mountain came to an end. A radio voice announced "Caro Nome. from Verdi's Rigoletto." He let himself drop in the chair to hear it out. Caro Nome was the first aria he heard Nicki give voice to. Memory had him opening the door of a practice room in the Music Building at Trinitarian, opening up his first sight and sound of Nicki! He could hardly believe such a full-bodied voice could come out of such a slender body. Thinking he'd made a mistake in his room assignment, he turned to leave, but Nicki's voice dropped from a high C to a low word of apology. She confessed being an "interloper," not a registered student. He said she was too good to be a student, and he'd like to hear more of "Caro Nome." She turned on a smile, asked for his "Dear Name." He said he was Leighton d'Arcy, known as "Lee." She introduced herself as Nicka Laishen, known as "Nicki," and explained that she was saving money for college, had to look for empty practice rooms to vocalize. He asked if he could accompany her at the piano, and at the nod of her head, he was on the piano stool, checking the score, striking a chord. Piano and voice came into accord, all the way to the last note of the Verdi aria.

Nicki told him his fingers held the keys to the Kingdom!

He told her she had a well trained coloratura voice. She told him that coloraturas are "a little crazy, have an "empty space in the head for resonance."

Memory faded at thought of craziness. Could Nicki's mind have come to an empty space for him?

Caro Nome came to an end. A radio voice announced Chopin's Ballade No..3 in A Flat Major. He knew the music came with a narrative, the story of a sailor who fell in love with a mist that took the shape of a beautiful woman. It now seemed to him that Nicki had disappeared like a mist! Was she a mist? Chopin's music was delicate, like a mist, always carried him into the candlelight of a Parisian salon. He used to imagine himself as the reincarnation of Chopin, down to the fingertips. How else could he have come into the world so well programmed for the piano? How else could he have the same delicate fingers? He'd seen a picture of the cast of Chopin's left hand, and it matched his own.

Reincarnation! He'd learned in school that everything in the physical world is recycled. Why not people? Sometimes he imagined knowing Nicki in a former life. He began thinking Trinitarian University was in a former life, tried to relive it, found himself walking with Nicki, under the canopy of trees on Maple Avenue. She lived on that street, in a room high up in what she called the "house of many mansions."

"It's no college dormitory," she told him when he took her home for the first time, "but my room has a dormer window, way up there." She said she had no roommate in the one room with the dormer window, but shared the top floor with other girls.

Young men were not allowed in the upper regions, he remembered. The landlord, a graybeard widower by name of Magruger, made sure of that! He kept boyfriends waiting with him and his two Giant Briards, "Big Boy" and "Little Boy." Big Boy, a prize-winning best of breed, sired Little Boy. His offspring was bigger, but undisciplined, jumped up and pawed the shoulders of visitors.

A veteran of the Spanish-American War, Mr. Magruder regaled the "callers" with war stories while they waited for their girls to descend. The old man served in the Philippines, claimed the Filipinos were the best warriors in the world, "couldn't be felled by a single bullet."

He'd roll up his sleeves, show tattoos, his "barbaric war souvenirs," and tell and retell war stories. He remembered every detail, but often forgot to zip his fly.

Unlike her landlord, Nicki never had much to say about herself, except she came into the world as an orphan, a "love child, unloved!" He began loving to be with her, began taking her out for dinners after musical sessions. Saving money for school, she lived on a 35-cent breakfast, a soup for lunch at work, a quart of milk and crackers in her room at night.

One night he took her to a university concert that honored Henry Cowell, "guest speaker and renown composer." He made fists and pounded the piano keys to make "tone clusters," climbed into the piano to pluck different sounds out of it. On their way back to the Magruder mansion that night, they laughed at Cowell's "musical gymnastics."

At her door, Nicki joked that the only place where they could be alone would be in Cowell's piano. She thanked him for a night of "musical magic," and her lips reached up to give Lee a magical kiss! He was left at the door, thinking her kiss was as musical as her voice. He went back to his dorm room, kept imagining all the way that he was accompanying her, inside the piano. At their next musical session, in the Music Building, he accompanying her rendition of Flowers that bloom in the Spring, asked if she'd like to accompany him on a picnic along the town creek. She agreed with a trill in her voice, suggested the next warm Saturday.

When the day came, Nicki appeared in full bloom, a flowery scarf twisted around her neck, breasts well arranged, deeply divided by the strap of her picnic basket. Her sculptured feet in Grecian sandals took tiny steps along the winding creek that led them out of town. The path was under the bare branches of trees twisted like roots in the sky. She was humming the Jewel Song from Gounod's Faust, swinging now and then. When she sang "is this some bewitching dream," he said she was a dream, and and asked if she'd sell her soul to the devil, like Faust, in exchange for love and wealth?" She said she couldn't sell her soul. It was given to music.

Lee was already measuring the worth of her body, and the worth of his soul! As an adolescent, when he heard Faust for the first time, he was traumatized, associated unmarried sex with damnation! Now he was facing the victim of unmarried sex. He stopped thinking. She stopped humming!

At the curve of the creek she said it was a good place to put music and bodies to a rest, and swung down her basket, spread a blanket over the bare earth, dropped down on her knees. Lee let himself down beside her.

"Finger food for your piano fingers," she said, nesting beside him. "Peanut butter or tuna fish?"

Lee chose "peanut butter," said he didn't want to eat anything that had to be killed."

"How will you face war?"

"Won't think about it. My father was killed in the war."

"My father was always dead to me!"

"He must have died before you were born. No man would abandon you."

"Wouldn't know about that," she said with a tuna sandwich at her lips. "Beginnings are unknown to us, like the beginning, and end, of this creek."

"Life is a stream," he sang out, then asked how a mother could set her adrift.

"Only know she left me with a voice, and a name."

"Great voice, strange name, Nicki!"

"My birth certificate only named me Nickalaishen. First foster parents broke the name in two, called me Nicka Laishen. Named myself Nicki."

"Your name is music."

"Listen to the creek. It makes music. What does the music mean?"

"I think music makes its own meaning," Lee said, taking a slim book out of his coat pocket, reading, "a running brook that sings its melody to the night."

"A lovely thought," Nicki cried out. "Music means love to me."

"Love has no desire but to fulfill itself," Lee read from the book. "So says Gibran in The Prophet. I'd like to set it to music."

"It's already music!" Nicki said. She looked up, paused for thought, suggested that the tree looking down on them should forever be known as their "Poet-Tree."

"Our Poet-Tree!"

"Love the sound and meter of poetry," Nicki said, still looking up at the bare lines of the tree, "but don't always know what the words mean. "How does love fulfill itself?"

Lee thought of filling his arms with her, feared he'd pull a Faust.

Nicki shrugged shoulders and slipped feet out of straps and flats, dipped toes in the creek. "Stream is singing," she sang, shaking up the water with her two feet, making waves of sound. "It's telling me to wade in."

"It's singing for us to stream along together."

....

The stream of memory, and radio music, was turning into static. Lee got himself uncurled from the armchair, turned off the radio, and static, turned himself into bed, kept dreaming of streaming through life with Nicki. He sank into the softness of bed, into the memory of asking Nicki to stream along in life with him. He told her they could stay married to music, become a trio, and she drew him into a hug.

In a shiver, Lee remembered his mother asking him to hold off marriage. She thought marriage would bring his musical career to an end, the way it ended her dreams. He agreed to wait until he'd served his time in the army, asked Nicki to wait for him. She promised to be his "Madama Butterfly," and wait for his return "one fine day." He bought her a pearl engagement ring. Nicki thought a pearl was more pure than a diamond, wanted to glow instead of sparkle. There was no glow to her when waving him off on a troop train. His eyes were watery with sight of her dissolving in the mist of rain. She was trimmed in a trench coat, trying to smile under the flap of a floppy red hat. The train delivered him up to Fort Leonard Wood, known as "Fort-Lost- In-The-Woods," and he was really lost in the woods without music and Nicki.

Lined up in the ranks, he marched to the cadence of the army, but his mind only marched to thoughts of Nicki. He saw her with every forward step, every about face. She was with him at parade rest, and in his dreams, after Taps. Nicki came in person to watch him march in final review, and a local Justice of the Peace married them before the war could tear them apart. When he was shipping out, Nicki told him it was only the end of Act One, but he thought it was the last act of Faust, imagined himself as Faust going down to hell, and Nicki going off to Heaven.

He opened his eyes, realized it was the day for Trinitarian University. He heard Big Dick bang open the front door, announcing his return.

....

The private investigator returned to take Lee downstate. Big Dick decided to tag along, try to "hit it off with a co-ed." The trip took more time than anticipated. The private investigator's Kaiser-Frazier that had two vapor-locks along the way, taking time off to cool down. He excused it as "the first born civilian model after the war."

Big Dick said it was a "miscarriage."

Lee mentioned he never had a car, only put his foot to the pedal of a piano, and the investigator said no one could live without a car nowadays. Big Dick said he drove a second- hand Ford, sold it when he got called up for Korea, couldn't afford a car and garage when he got out of service. Lee didn't want to admit he was afraid of driving, thought his hands were only made for the piano.

Talk gave way to the monotonous tone of humming motor and tires. The car kept plowing along the highway walled-in with cornfields. A road sign finally proclaimed the city of "Vars, home of Trinitarian University." It was only five miles ahead, but seemed a long way back in Lee's memory. The car reached East Gate with its statue of Alma Mater, passed into the walled- in campus, down a street crowded with students strolling or rushing. The car passed the dorm that still held memories for Lee. He had a private room, no private bathroom, had to suffer public facilities. Memory mirrored his face with other soap-lathered faces, brought back naked images in the showers, embarrassment of toilet stalls without doors. What luxuries, he thought, compared to prison camp!

The car slowed down to let students flock across the stree "Where we headed?"

"Administration Building," Lee directed, pointing ahead.

Following Lee's directions, the driver found parking space in front of the Administration Building.

Out of the car, and stretching, the men caught sight of long legged girls with books pressed to their chests. Big Dick waved his "sympathy stick" at them, told Lee he might lay his G.I. Bill on the line for the "co-ed life."

"Books go with education," Lee mentioned, and the private investigator called their attention to the business at hand. Up the steps to the Administration Building they hurried, opened the door to a hallway of many doors. They found the door of the Registrar, got to see him after a short wait. He only recognized the name of Bruno Koczur on Lee's list. Lee remembered Koczur as the piano instructor who helped Nicki find empty practice rooms. The Registrar remembered that Koczur was no longer at the university, had left no forwarding address.

"It was just a long shot," Lee sighed.

"We have a Koczur on the Sociology faculty," the Registrar brought up, paging through the Faculty Catalogue. "Casimir Koczur. I believe he's a relative."

....

"Casimir Koczur, here," the Sociologist, standing tall, introduced himself to Lee and his companions as they were ushered into his office, a foursquare room with two desks, one empty. Koczur's bush of red hair almost brushed the ceiling, but he quickly lowered himself to a commanding position behind his desk, waved visitors into folding chairs. "I'm told you're looking for my cousin, Bruno Koczur. What's he wanted for?"

"We're in search of a missing wife," the investigator spoke up from his chair, "and your cousin befriended her when she was single, might provide the missing link in our chain of investigations."

"I might have known a woman was involved with Bruno," the Sociologist's big voice boomed. "Bruno was a good pianist but put the touch on women, more than the ivories!"

"Know where he can be found?"

"Not a clue. He didn't make tenure, took off in a hurry. We shared the same last name, not much else. Do you think he ran off with your wife?"

"Never thought of it," Lee spoke up, giving it consideration for the first time, "but he looked out for my wife before I knew her, might give us a lead on her disappearance."

"Bruno looked out for a lot of women. He never looked for a long stand." As he talked, the Sociologist pulled an address book out of a desk drawer, said he had the address of Bruno's parents in the Chicago suburbs. He handed off the address, wished them "good hunting."

"Looks like you've been head-hunting," Big Dick spoke up, pointing at the shrunken head hanging on the wall by a string of twisted black hair.

"A war trophy, from New Guinea. Natives carried heads like that strapped to their belts, pedaled them to us grunts for K- rations."

"Not a pretty face."

"It's a prettygood artifact for teaching about exotic human cultures." Lee asked what a shrunken head teaches, "man's inhumanity to man?"

"It teaches that humans see life, and death, differently."

"We know about inhumanity," Big Dick said, "been prisoner of war in North Korea!"

"Must have been inhuman as hell, but let me tell you the cannibals in New Guinea didn't keep prisoners, they eat 'em."

"Time to head out," the private investigator said with a smile. "Thanks for your time and help."

"Might have a lead for you," the sociologist mentioned as his visitors were leaving. "Bruno dated a woman in our music department, an assistant professor, Clara White. She might know where you could contact him?"

"I know that name," Lee spoke right up. "She's in the Music Department, cellist in the orchestra and the University String Quartet."

"You got her number. She's probably in rehearsal now, but you could look her up tonight. She's in the concert, eight o'clock, Auditorium Hall."

The private investigator asked if he could check her out for them. He shook his head. "Wife and I have other plans tonight," he said, standing up with the others. "Music's only a cultural pattern to me."

Lee said he'd remember the cellist, thanked the Sociologist, followed the others out "Somebody left a cane," the sociologist called after them.

"Only a sympathy stick," Big Dick said, coming back. "It's like your shrunken head, a war souvenir."

"Good luck on your wife hunting."

. . . .

"We need to hunt up a place to hang out for the night," the investigator said as he revved- up the car in the parking lot. "Any suggestions, Mr. d'Arcy?"

"The College Inn, straight ahead, just past East Gate."

"College Inn," Big Dick sounded out slowly. "Been thinking of getting in College."

"Students called it The Dropout Inn," Lee told him. "Thinking of dropping in and out?"

"Thinking of majoring in co-eds!"

"No such major."

"Think of majoring in athletics. It's the sporting life for me."

"Need to drop your sympathy stick," Lee advised," but you could pick up ideas for selling life insurance in the Economic Department."

"Never was good at business," Big Dick signed off.

They checked in at the College Inn, got booked in a room with a view of the parking lot. There was a double bed next to the window, and a single bed against the opposite wall. As they began unpacking and dividing closet and drawer space, the "private eye" looked around, tossed a coin to see who'd get the single bed, but Big Dick said he had to have it! He blamed his prison camp experience, said if he woke up in the rack next to another body he might "strike out at it." The investigator said if he woke up with someone in bed he might think the body next to him was his wife. He got the single bed, without a toss of the coin, and the men took off for the motel coffee shop, bunched-up in one of its booths, ordered the "Varsity Home Plate."

Waiting to be served, Lee served himself memories of himself with Nicki in the coffee shop. Memories slipped out of mind when a young waitress dumped plates at their places. When Big Dick tried to pull her apron strings, she told him to keep hands on his "own ass!" He said he hadn't touched a woman since he was a prisoner in North Korea, and pointed to his sympathy stick. She gave him a pinch on the cheek, but said the "Varsity Home Plate" was his, and the ass was her's.

When the men finished eating and got back to their room, the investigator opened-up the telephone directory, looked for names on the imposter's list. He announced that "Magruder, the landlord, isn't in the book!"

Lee thought the old man might be in a nursing home. "He's a veteran of the Spanish- American War, way back at the beginning of the century."

"I'll check it out," the investigator promised as he paged thought the book for more names.

"Time to hit the concert trail," Lee told Big Dick.

"Got no ear for music," Big Dick complained. "Count me out."

"You have an eye for good looking women," Lee said. "Clara White, cellist, is as good for the eyes as the ears."

Big Dick changed his mind. "I'll string along, checkout the cellist."

"We'll compare notes after the concert," the investigator proposed, pulling down the brim of his hat, heading out to look for people on his list.

Lee and Big Dick took off on foot for the nearby campus, found good seats in the Auditorium while the orchestra was tuning up. Lee recognized Clara White on stage, pointed her out, and Big Dick nodded approval, squared his big jaw in hopes she'd get a look at him.

Lights dimmed as the conductor entered. He raised his baton like a magic wand, turned the Auditorium into pure sound, the sound of Paderewski's Fantaisie Polonaise. Lee followed the music in ear and mind. Big Dick followed the movements of Clara White.

As the lights came on for intermission, Lee told his friend he'd never heard the Polonaise arranged for orchestra. Big Dick said he'd like to make an arrangement with the cellist. He'd been fantasizing about being the cello between her legs.

"Great piece of music coming up," Lee told his companion, "I see on the program that my old piano teacher will play Ravel's Piano Concerto for the Left Hand."

"A one-handed pianist," Big Dick gasped with a wink. "I could become a one-legged athlete."

"No joke! French-born, my professor was so shocked when Hitler's army marched into Paris that he suffered a stroke, lost use of right hand. Prominent pianist, he had to become a piano teacher, came to America."

"I'd like to get both hands on the cellist."

Applause shook the disgust out of Lee, and the conductor and soloist, Professor Allard, appeared on stage. In the glow of stage lights, the opening chords of Ravel's Concerto for the Left Hand wrapped Lee in its music. Eyes closed, he seemed to see the music taking shape and color, imagined himself at the piano. He came back to himself at the standing ovation.

As the lights brightened, and the orchestra broke up, Lee led Big Dick backstage where they found Clara White amid an array of tuxedos and evening gowns. In a low cut gown, she was bending over for the cello case, her gown opening up a curving crack of cleavage. Big Dick took note. She stood up, cleavage disappearing. Lee asked if she remembered him, "Lee d'Arcy, former piano student of Professor Allard?" She gave him a smile that rounded both cheeks, deepened the crease in both.

"I think that name was going around the department, last year."

"Professor Allard said I had magic fingers."

"What made you disappear?"

"The war in Korea!"

"We both were prisoners of war," Big Dick butted in. "Low note," she gasped.

"Really off key," Lee agreed, and introduced his friend.

"Kreutzer is a musical name," Clara White noted. "Beethoven dedicated a sonata to Kreutzer."

"Kreutzer's also a German coin with a cross on it,"

Big Dick Kreutzer brought up with a smile, "but I'm not worth a cent on any musical instrument."

"It looks like you could tuck a cello under your chin." Big Dick smiled and squared his jaw for her.

"We're trying to get in touch with somebody you knew," Lee got to the point, "Bruno Koczur."

The rounded cheeks of the cellist flattened. Lee told her his wife's missing, and Bruno knew her, way back, might have a clue to her whereabouts.

"Bruno and I played concerts together, and dated," the cellist admitted, "but we got off key. Sorry, I don't know where he is."

"Can't carry a tune," Big Dick was quick to speak up, "but could carry the cello to your car."

"Music to my ears." She led them to her car, bent over to stow the cello, came up with a recollection. "Bruno mentioned a promising coloratura soprano who reminded him of his sister. You might contact the Bruno family in Downers Grove, near Chicago."

....

"The Bruno we're looking for's not here," Lee was quick to inform the private investigator as soon as he got back to their motel room, "but he'd got a sister, a lookalike of Nicki. She could be the imposter."

"She's our ace in the hole," Big Dick brought up.

"We know somebody's bluffing," the private investigator granted, "but we're not playing poker. I'll check her out. Come up with any other leads?"

"Only memories of Nicki. What did you pick up?"

"Drew a lot of bad hands," the private investigator admitted. "Magruder, the landlord's dead. His big house is up for sale, no more girls in residence. None of the former ones could be located."

Lee choked on his breath of cigarette smoke, managed to say Magruder was their best bet, and let himself wonder out loud what happened to his Giant Briards?

"Not in business of looking for dogs," the investigator spoke right up.

"Not good at finding missing wives," Big Dick complained. "What's on the agenda for tomorrow?"

"Lee should cruise the campus, look for something that triggers a memory."

....

Looking around campus, Lee saw familiar sights that brought back memories, but no insight into Nicki's disappearance. He led Big Dick off campus, down Maple Avenue, past the three-story mansion where Nicki had lived, "way up, behind a dormer window," he said, pointing up.

They walked to the edge of town where Lee waved his hand at the town creek meandering out of sight. He wondered if the Poet-Tree was still somewhere along its banks, wondered if he could ever find it, and Nicki.

"Everything in life passes," Lee mentioned to his friend, "like every ripple in that creek."

"Like to make passes at a few co-eds," Big Dick commented, and Lee took him to the Student Center, left him to his pass-taking, told him he'd meet him back at the room.

In a leisurely walk, Lee took off for the Music Building, Ramsey Hall, found it humming with the muted sounds of pianos in closed-off practice rooms. He found an empty one, and his fingers found a melody his mind had forgotten. He couldn't forget Nicki telling him they were living a melody.

He carried music and memories back to the motel where the investigator was already working on his notes.

"Manager of the University Book Store was no help," he reported, "and I didn't find any good deals, but all cards aren't on the table, not yet."

Big Dick turned up, complaining that his sympathy stick didn't strike sympathy in any co- ed. In poor spirits they all headed back to Chicago, only had one vapor lock to slow them down. The investigator dropped them off and promised to get to them as soon as he made his last investigation.

....

"It's a wrap," the investigator told Lee when he showed up a few days later. "Did all I could. Here's my report and expense account. Sorry I couldn't deliver."

"Did you make contact with Bruno Koczur, and his sister?"

"Checked out his family, saw the sister, and she's not the imposter, no way. Got a line on Bruno, phoned him in New York City. He only remembered a coloratura soprano with a "golden voice.""

"He could be lying."

"Got in touch with a P.I. in New York, got a report that your piano man was living with a woman, not his wife, but she didn't fit Nicki's description, not at all."

"I'll never stop looking," Lee promised himself in a loud and shaky voice. "What if she's in plain sight, like Poe's Purloined Letter?"

"What you getting at?"

"Your wife's in plain sight! The imposter is your wife. You don't recognize her."

"You think I don't know my wife?"

"Memories are encoded. I was a cryptographer in the big war. It doesn't take much to change a code."

Lee, speechless, fumbled for his checkbook, paid-off the investigator, figured he'd already been paid off! From his third floor apartment window he watched the investigator drive away in a flashy new car, a Dodge. It was the "make" his stepfather always bought!

....

Lee began driving himself into oblivion with smoke and drink! One time when Big Dick came back from a night on the town, he caught Lee playing with his army revolver, slipping cartridges in and out. The roommate told him it was time to get "a head shrink!"

"Want to make a shrunken head out of me?"

"Want to get your head screwed back on."

"Don't want one of those shrinks in my head."

"Better than a bullet!"

"A psychologist got me in basic training, only asked if I had a piece of hot tail. I didn't know what it was. He put me down as immature, slightly neurotic."

"Don't sweat it," Big Dick told him. "There's more to life than sex," but knew he was always thinking about it.

Lee wished for a piano, didn't know how it could be hauled up to the third floor. "You got the dough. I got the know."

An upright piano, second hand, was purchased and hauled up by a team of furniture movers. It lifted Lee's spirits for awhile, but didn't have a rich tone, and his fingers couldn't get loosened up as much as he wanted. He feared the loss of his talent, as well as his bride.

One night Big Dick came home from a "night on the town" to find Lee humped over the keyboard. Big Dick gave him a shake, told him to "shape up or ship out!"

Lee agreed to let a psychologist in his head.

III

The Insight

The first name listed in the Yellow Pages under Psychiatry was Dr. Rob Adams, psychiatrist, in private practice. Lee made an appointment, forced himself to keep it, took a cab. The psychiatrist maintained office hours in his own apartment, in a high-rise adjacent to the Lincoln Park Zoo. It made Lee wonder if his patients ever got caged-up.

He was met at the door by a man in the trim of a black beard.

"Dr. Adams," he introduced himself with a growl. Behind him stood a grand piano that brought a gasp from Lee.

"What a magnificent instrument!"

"A monument to my musical past!" Without further comment, the psychiatrist waved Lee into his office, asked what he could do for him.

Lee let himself drop down in the chair facing the psychiatrist's desk. "Haven't lost my mind," he said, "lost my wife."

"Wouldn't the police be more help than a psychiatrist?"

"Police didn't believe me."

"I can help you find your right mind, not your wife."

"Police thought something was wrong with my mind, thought I might be delusional!"

"Don't think police are qualified to make that assessment. Why would they think that?"

"I was a prisoner of war in North Korea, came home to an unknown girl claiming to be my wife!"

"That's one for the book, an imposter wife! How'd she support her claim?"

"Had our wedding license, but no good witnesses. My wife was an orphan, no foster parents to vouch for her, and no friends we had in common."

"I've studied wives with multiple personalities, not multiple bodies." Fingering the trim of his beard, Dr. Adams finally said he'd analyzed Second World War prisoners of war, and they lost parts of themselves, not their wives, except in divorce."

"Could I be delusional? Could I forget what my wife looked like?"

"Couldn't forget unless you had amnesia, forgot everything. Lay your story on me. Take it from the top."

It was always in Lee's thoughts. He lay it out, from love of music to love of a coloratura soprano, from war and captivity to a missing wife and her imposter.

"How did she base her claim?"

"Had our marriage license. I couldn't prove she wasn't the name on it."

"Why would anyone want to impersonate your wife?"

"I came up with a big inheritance, figured the imposter wanted to get in on it, along with my stepfather."

The psychiatrist stroked his beard again. "Your wife must be in on the conspiracy, or under restraint, or worse!"

Lee snapped shut his eyes, pictured all kinds of plots, didn't bury Nicki in any of them.

He asked if his wife could have amnesia?

"She could, but why the imposter?"

"Police think she's not an imposter. Could Commies have brainwashed my wife out of mind?"

"Communists are working on powerful new techniques of brain control, but only want to take over your mind, not take your wife out of it. Could your wife have kept something of her past from you?"

"We didn't share much about our pasts. I knew she was raised in foster homes."

"Could prison camp have put bars on your memory?"

"Why won't anybody believe me!"

"I believe you, but the brain waves of recollection can be redirected, or suppressed. The mind's divided, like Korea, can be at war with itself, can imprison what it doesn't like to remember."

"Why's the mind divided?"

"Intelligence and instinct. Lots of conflicts in life disturb both."

"I only have conflict with the imposter. I'm not hiding anything from myself. It's the imposter hiding something from me."

"We all wear masks," the psychologist kept talking and stroking his beard, "like actors in ancient Greek dramas. We change masks for different scenarios. Sometimes we become the mask! I could unmask the imposter if she'd let me take her into Analysis."

"She didn't let my private eye see though her mask, wouldn't let a psychiatrist have a shot at it."

"Could I try to unmask you with hypnosis, see if you're hiding something from yourself?" Lee agreed, let himself be put under. When he came back up, Dr. Adams said his subconscious was consistent with his consciousness. "You've been telling the truth, as you see it."

"Isn't there more than one truth to see?"

Dr. Adams said some truths are relative, in the eye of the perceiver, and he promised to help him find peace, if not his missing wife.

"Haven't had peace since the war!"

"How was your life before he war?"

"Musical, dreamy. I lived for music."

"Music might be the language for commuting with your subconscious. Let's get you to play the soundtrack of your life?"

He put Lee to the grand piano in the livingroom, asked him to let his fingers do the thinking. Lee's hands came up with a few measures of Chopin's Etude in F Major.

The psychiatrist congratulated him on his touch, said "Chopin couldn't be in better hands, "but what did the music mean to you?"

"Happy childhood at the piano." He let his fingers carry on for a moment.

"Can you strike a note that hits a memory of your wife?"

Lee's fingers came up with the beginning notes of Verdi's Caro Nome. Dr. Adams asked if the notes struck a memory?

"Love," he said, "and loss."

"In your self- narrative, you told me your wife was an aspiring opera singer. Might she have wanted to pursue her career more than her marriage. Might she have arranged her disappearance?"

Lee shook his head, said they planned to pursue their careers "side by side."

"I was married to music," Dr. Adams revealed himself, fondling his beard again, "and music got away from me, like your wife got away from you."

"Your music hasn't come back. Are you telling me my wife will never come back?"

"Let me tell you my story. Like you, I was a piano prodigy. At fifteen I soloed with the Chicago Symphony, aged a thousand years when my hands froze in the middle of Grieg's piano concerto. The orchestra couldn't carry me. I had to carry myself off stage, in front of a stunned audience in Orchestra Hall. My hands wouldn't touch the keys again." He paused to let his words find their target.

"My wife's a musical person, not my talent for music."

"Your mind may have lost a memory, like I lost my talent. A good psychiatrist has to have his own problems to empathize with patients. I've kept myself in Analysis for years."

"It hasn't helped you get back into music?"

"It got me in touch with my inner self, got me interested in the mind, made me a maestro of the mind. You can lose something and find something better!"

"Couldn't find a better wife."

"How did you find her?"

Dr. Adams didn't wait for the answer. "You said she grew up with foster parents. Did she every run away?"

"Don't know."

"Was she satisfied with your sex life?"

"Do you psychologists only have a mind for hot tail?"

"Hot tail? People don't think with the tail, but the tail can wag their minds around. Tell me about your sex life."

"Tha's private, behind bedroom doors."

"Nothing should be kept hidden from your therapist, and you should know sex is natural. All living things, plant and animal, are made for reproduction!"

At the sound or "reproduction," a child's shrill voice began vibrating through the wall. "My son's home from school," Dr. Adams sighed in the middle of a thought. "He's the pure distillation of sound."

The door opened with a bang, and a grade school boy shot in. The young Adams had a huge Adams Apple to go with his name, and it raced up and down as he lay claim to "A-Plus in Language Arts."

Dr. Adams congratulated him, asked him to play for a little while. A motherly woman appeared and led the child away with promise of a hot chocolate.

"We never outgrow our self-centered childhood," Dr. Adams explained, as if to make a psychological point as well as an apology for the interruption. "Children used to be treated as small adults, but now we treat them like children. Would you like to have children?"

"My wife gave birth to premature twins, lost them when I was overseas."

Dr. Adams stroked his beard, said a new mother could slip out of reality, and a grieving mother could lose her mind, at least for a time.

"Lose love for her husband?"

"Lose love for herself, and life."

"Never thought of looking for my wife in hospitals and mental wards!"

"Her imposter might be a friend trying to shield her, and you?"

"Something new to go on."

"You need to get on with your life, not lose it looking for your wife all the time."

"Time's only worth looking for her."

It's good you know what you're looking for. Most of my patients are looking for something, don't know what!" He took to his feet. "Time's up for now."

"Maybe time's up for our time together. Seems you've looked through me as far as you can. Let me settle my account, get on with my life."

"It would be good to get on with your life, stop reliving it."

....

"Got to get on with my life, back at Trinitarian," Lee told Big Dick that night. "Want to head downstate with me, let college get you up in life?"

"Might give it a college try, could make a better life for for some lucky girl."

"Get your application in," Lee advised, thinking it would be good to have a friend on campus. "In the meantime, help me check hospitals for Nicki."

In the days that sped by with their hurried search of hospitals and rest homes, they came across no trace of the missing wife, but Lee got word that he was needed at his Louisiana plantation. Big Dick wanted to join him for a change of pace, and they took flight, rented a car at flight's end, and Big Dick drove them to Lee's backwater plantation. They found it under the bare tree limbs of winter. Lee said it would soon be "gone with the wind."

"I'd keep my cotton-picking hands on a joint like this," Big Dick said as he took a look at the homestead. He didn't change his mind, not after one night in a bedroom with only "a pot to piss in," and only a pitcher of water and bowl to "tidy up in."

They met with the Leighton family lawyer, learned there was a "potential buyer," and a "good offer." The deal was closed with a lawyer for an "unknown party."

"Sorry to see you give up your family heritage," the family lawyer said sadly after the details of the sale were worked out. "The land was in your family before Louisiana was in the States."

"Can't find my wife down here," Lee had to tell him, "and there's no music in the land."

"Your mother didn't find music here, either," the lawyer let on with a nod of agreement.

"Wish I could have seen her, one more time."

One more time. Lee wished for one more time, let himself think of his mother's time running out when he was away, a prisoner.

"Miss Hailey would like to see you one more time," the lawyer broke into his thoughts. Lee wanted to see her, too, find out if the daughter looked like the imposter.

Arrangements were made. Miss Hailey greeted Lee and Big Dick in the same flowing dress Lee remembered from the last time, and she led the two of them into the shady livingroom with all the ticking clocks. She waved them into the snugness of upholstered armchairs.

"My plantation's sold!"

"Good piece-a-land," Miss Hailey said with a crack in her voice. "Been in your family a good-piece-a-time."

After a few moments of ticking clocks Lee asked if there was any news about "daughter, "Rosa?"

"Reckon not." Miss Hailey said, fan fluttering. "Rosa be keeping self up in Yankee land, can't make a livin' in music, don't want livin' down here."

"No music in the land, down here."

"Most my land lost to whiskey," Miss Hailey sputtered with another flutter of fan. "Rosa's daddy drank it up, left me with nothing but my old family house, not a thing from him, even gave back his name."

"He left you with a daughter. Could I see her picture?"

Miss Hailey folded her fan, stood up, gathered her skirts together, said she'd "fetch one," and came back with a framed photograph. "Rosa's high school graduation picture," she said. "Ain't she a purty one?"

Lee strained his eyes in the drape-darkened room to get a good look. The girl in a low-cut graduation dress didn't bear any resemblance to the imposter, as far as he could see in the dim of the light.

Clocks started striking the hour, clock after clock. Lee said it was time to leave the family land.

....

It was time for the Spring Semester to begin at Trinitarian University. Lee and Big Dick drove downstate, Big Dick at the wheel. They registered, got settled in Trinity Hall, the men's dorm where Lee had a private room the year before. He now shared a double room with his friend, but the friends went their separate ways.

Big Dick took up sociology, liked the sociology professor, Dr. Koczur, thought the study of social life would help him sell life insurance to all levels of society. He soon learned, in class, he'd always been a prisoner, a prisoner of culture! He began escaping classes, making himself "big man on campus!" Older than average, he had the gift of getting down to the level of younger classmates and making them look up to him. He dropped his "sympathy stick," picked up the play of intermural sports. He made the Trinity Hall basketball team, told Lee he had the best "hands" on the team, and by far "the best looking legs." While running round on court and campus, he got interested in Clara White, his teacher of the required Music Appreciation course. He'd admired her in concert, and in class, but when he made his move, she said she never took up with students.

While Big Dick was getting in the swing of college life, Lee was getting back in tune with music. In prison camp he'd made music in his head, tapped it out with his foot, and his music was now coming out on the piano, in a piano sonata. His composition professor said he had a gift, and didn't need much instruction, let him go with his own Muse. Lee shaped his musical ideas around the tensions of his own life, tried to tell his story in music, wished there were musical notations that represent ideas as well as sounds.

While Lee's sonata was taking form, his roommate was shaping his life around the Old King Coal Bin, a student "den" for "eating out," and "making out." The Old King Coal Bin, in the basement of the Student Center, had been a real coal bin in the steam-heat days. It served no beer or hard drinks, but steamed-up the place with "progressive jazz" and "hard rock."

Big Dick went for the "Jazz Trio" that featured his music appreciation teacher, Clara White. He learned she had a lot of "pop" in her cello, carried the word back to Lee, told him the cello player set the "Old Coal Bin on fire!"

Lee couldn't believe a member of the Trinitarian Orchestra and the String Quartet could let herself down in a jazz Trio. He agreed to check her out next time she was scheduled at the Bin.

"Joint's rocking an' rolling," Big Dick shouted over the noise as they showed up at the Bin. Music and dancing feet shook the walls and floor. Lee didn't like the cacophony of meaningless noise, or the sight of Clara White sawing and chopping at strings, spinning the cello between her legs in Toreador pants! A lady in pants was as disturbing to him as a classical musician in pop.

"Jungle music," Lee told Big Dick as they looked for an unoccupied booth. "Our civilization is going primitive."

"Going natural," Big Dick talked back with a sniff at the sizzling grill mixing hamburger aromas with cigarette smoke. "Got myself a primitive hunger."

"Hamburgers on me," Lee offered, knowing his roommate was strapped for money.

Hands full of burgers, and fries, they found an empty booth, settled down in privacy. Lee was beginning to get in rhythm with the beat and off- beat of the Trio, considered a little syncopation might be good for his Borrowed Plumes.

At the final beat of a jazz number, Clara White rose up to the microphone and announced, "a change of pace, a song, Getting to Know You, from the new Rogers and Hammerstein musical, The King and I." She went on to say that it didn't rock and roll, "but, if it's good enough for Broadway's King and I, it's good enough for the Old King Coal Bin and you!"

She waited for the strike of a piano key and drum, let her voice fly all the way up to clouds of cigarette smoke hanging from the beamed ceiling. It didn't go as high as his coloratura soprano could send a note, Lee thought, but he always liked the sounds of Rogers and Hammerstein.

After a polite applause, Clara White gave voice to "Break Time!"

Big Dick turned to Lee, said, "White's got more blue in her eyes than Gershwin's got blues in his Rhapsody. Can't believe she's not married."

"She's married to music," Lee said, thinking of Nicki.

"Having a love affair with pop music," Big Dick said with a leaping jump out of the booth, and run to the bandstand. He asked the singer to give him a "break," and try "getting to know me!"

"Been getting to know you as a student," Clara White laughed. "You're the student who called the opera, Salame, salami."

"Wasn't it a meaty work?"

"Shouldn't give you a break for that," Clara White laughed again, "but should get to know you a little better," and she let herself be escorted to the booth where Lee was in wait.

"We me at the Allard concert," she said in greeting Lee, sliding next to him in the booth. "Professor Allard thinks a real work of art's in you?"

"He's full of it," Big Dick interrupted, swinging in, at the other side of the table.

"Professor Allard's giving me a free hand," Lee mentioned. "I'm trying to make music that comes from the beat of my heart, and love of my life."

"It's been said that art imitates nature," Clara White said, as if teaching a class, "but I don't find musical forms in nature, except the circular principle of nature in the recurring themes of a sonata."

Lee liked what he heard and made more room for her in the booth, said "Rock and Roll imitates the chaos of modern life!"

"It doesn't follow the rules," she said. "Maybe there's more freedom in music when there's more freedom in society,"

"Do you think there's more beauty in rocking and rolling?"

"Maybe the old world needs the New Sound," she said with a smile. "Rock's not my style, but I've got a soft spot for it."

"It's got rhythm," Lee admitted, "hell of a beat."

"I may prefer Bach's Suites for Solo Cello, but keep my mind open to new musical ideas and new sounds."

"Shouldn't we be taking a musical break," Big Dick broke in. "How does a coke sound, for a break?"

"Sounds good. I'll drink to that."

"Only eight beats to the bar," Big Dick laughed as he took to his feet.

When he ran off to the Snack Bar, Clara White turned to Lee, asked if he ever found his wife.

"Thanks for your good memory," Lee said, making more room for her. "Only found your piano friend. He's in New York City."

"He's no longer my friend."

"Would you believe I found a woman masquerading as my wife?"

"You're making this up, composing a comic opera with lovers in disguise."

"It's no Mozart skirt changer."

"Got the police on it?"

"Police gave up on it!"

"A masquerade can't keep up forever."

"That thought, and music, keep me going."

"Coke time," Big Dick announced, appearing with three bottles held against his chest. Crashing down, he passed out the bottles, raised a coke to toast "the Trio's First Lady!"

Lee raised his bottle, said she was putting herself down. She raised her bottle, said she had a taste for all kinds of music, and the world needed a new sound.

"I hope the world will need my kind of sound."

"Would you play a few themes from your music for our listeners tonight?"

"Do you think a few bars of my music would hold them?"

"Let's give it a go," she said, getting up to go.

....

"Break's over," Clara White broadcast over the intercom. "Put your feet to the beat of swing and jazz again, and in a little time, the tempo will go to your head instead of your feet."

Piano, drum, and cello put dancers back in time to dancing, jazzed-up the Bin until time was running out.

"Surprise time," Clara White announced at the end of a dance. "One of your classmates, Leighton d'Arcy, will treat you to a measure of his own composition." She called him to the bandstand, introduced him, and his sonata, "The Borrowed Plumes."

As Lee took his place at the piano, and dancers gathered round it, a joker asked if the Borrowed Plumes was burlesque music for the fan dancer, Sally Rand. He said he'd like to borrow her plumes.

Another voice asked if the Borrowed Plumes was based on the Aesop fable. Lee shook his head, felt like giving up.

"Aesop's fable's about falseness," the questioner explained. "A jaybird borrowed a peacock's plume to look like a peacock, but the jaybird didn't pass. Moral, you can't be something you aren't."

"My music fits that moral," Lee piped up, surprised to learn that the term, borrowed plumes, might be derived from an Aesop fable.

"Let the music speak for itself," Clara White intervened.

Lee nodded, let his fingers define the opening theme of The Borrowed Plumes. As he developed it, he sensed a loss of audience. "It's unfinished," he said, stopping in the middle of a passage, raising both hands. "It's my unfinished sonata."

"All our lives are works in progress," Clara White spoke up as the group around the piano began dispersing without a hand of applause.

Lights flickered, dimmed. The Bin was closing-up for the night.

Gathering up her music, Clara White congratulated Lee. "Your sonata carried me away."

"And most of the audience."

"Denizens of the Bin don't have a trained ear, and most are not in college for truth and beauty, only for getting tailored for the blue-flannel business suit."

....

At his next composition lesson, Lee asked Professor Allard if music had become a business for making money, not beauty?

"The fine arts always need support!"

"Students at the Old King Coal Bin didn't buy my music last night."

"You're writing for a different audience. I'd like to feature your sonata at our Spring Music Festival, see how well it goes with our music students."

"It would be an honor, but having trouble bringing closure. I seem up in the air without my wife."

"Beethoven composed music without his hearing. I play piano without my right hand."

"Does music come out of pain?"

....

The pain of prison camp came back to Lee when he and Big Dick were summoned by the sociologist, Dr. Koczur, to be interviewed about their homecoming experiences. Lee didn't want to relive it. Big Dick thought they ought to obey his professor.

On schedule, they both showed up at the professor's home, met by a heavyset woman who introduced herself as the "professor's wife." She escorted them through the living room to "the professor's den," walled-in with book shelves. Dr. Koczur, and an unknown man, stood up at their entrance.

"This is Mr. Jamie Delaney," Dr. Koczur introduced the unknown man. "He was an officer in the Korean Conflict, now a civilian working on his dissertation, a study of returning prisoners of war."

Lee remembered the rhyming name, Jamie Delaney, but not the man wearing a smile and suit instead of a frown and uniform.

"Researching the homecoming experiences of POW's," the man with the rhyming name explained, extending a hand to both Lee and Big Dick.

Recognition of the man with the rhyming name came to Lee in the shake of a hand. "Believe it or not," he said, "I think you're the officer who debriefed me in Freedom Village!"

"Unbelievable," the former officer said, with a laugh, and another handshake, "but too brief a debriefing encounter for me to remember you."

"We both came from Hyde Park," Lee reminded him, and carried on about Jackson Park, World Fairs, Momism.

"I'm from Hyde Park," snapped the former officer, "and Momism was a big theory back then. Give me a moment to research my memory."

"Both you boys lived high up on lakeside," the big sociologist spoke up. "I grew up on the shady side of Chicago, Back of the Yards." He told his guests to "sit," explaining that "Delaney" is no longer an officer, and "we enlisted men don't have to stand in his presence."

As they all sat down, the former officer came up with a grin, said the sociologist was always "over me, a World War Two hero, athletic instructor at the Settlement where I volunteered, now established as a college professor here at Trinitarian."

"Delaney got me interested in sociology," Cas Koczur volunteered.

"I was studying the people, Back of the Yards for one of my sociology assignments," Delaney explained. "Now, researching postwar adjustments of POWs for publication."

"And a publication will help him get lined up for a college appointment," Cas Koczur added.

"I just need you men to give a little time and thought to my research," Jamie Delaney instructed his interviewees. "I'll give you some questionnaires to fill out at your convenience. Your input's anonymous."

"You might find it interesting," Lee brought up, "that I returned to a missing wife."

"Many wives walked out on their imprisoned husbands," Delaney said with a tone of sympathy, and he put a pencil to his notepad.

"My wife didn't walk out on me! She's missing, and some imposter's in her place!"

"An imposter in her place?"

"An imposter in her place!"

....

"Would you believe I saw the woman who claims to be your wife," Big Dick told Lee when he came back from class, next day.

"Got a letter from the step-dad," Lee replied, looking up from his side of the desk, "got told to give the poor girl a break."

"She already broke you up!"

"Got a hunch it would be good to play her game, play along, see if she'd show her hand."\

....

Hands at the piano, day after day, Lee kept playing out the Borrowed Plumes, kept searching for closure, the right coda. One day he ran into Nicki's impersonator in the hallway of Ramsey Hall. They acknowledged each other. She let him know she was a full time student, asked if he'd found what he was looking for.

He tried to compose himself, said he only found a talent for musical composition. He tried to turn his frown into a smile.

She said it must be sublime to make-up music. "I can only follow the notes others make up. Lee knew she was making up the life of Nicki, but had to be friendly, get inside her head. He asked if her voice was coming back.

"It's on its way. Is your memory coming back?"

"I'm leaving the past behind."

"Life must go on, like a stream."

Her words brought to mind that picnic beside the creek. Nicki must have known the impersonator, must have spoken to her of life as a stream! He told the pretender he could help her stream along, offered to give her a hand at the piano, hoped to sound her out.

She told him she was assigned Practice Room twenty-three, everyday from two to three.

....

From two to three, everyday, Lee accompanied the imposter at the piano, but only got music out of her. She told him she was possessed by music!

One time, he put the main theme of Borrowed Plumes to her, and she said his music would sing, if it had words.

One time he jazzed up the aria she was trying to learn. She only wanted the real music, but never let him know anything about her real life.

He began thinking she was playing the role his stepfather gave her, but only played along to further her career. All the while he played for her, he found the inspiration to work out the end of his sonata.

....

When Lee bowed to the audience of fellow students at the Spring Music Festival, he was living the dream of his youth. He announced his "Borrowed Plumes," and put his Chopin hands to the opening measures, played through one movement after another, ended on an unresolved coda, a note that seemed to hang forever in the air. At the sound of applause, he rose up, as in a dream, bowed himself off stage, took refuge in one of the practice rooms down the hall. He was unhappy with the finale, hoped his love for Nicki wasn't final. His fingers were searching for a better resolution to the sonata, and his life, when he caught the scent of lilac. It was Nicki's favorite perfume. He sensed another person in the room, heard a voice congratulate him on the Borrowed Plumes.

"It's a feather in your cap."

He turned round to see his wife's imposter! She stood like a solitary note of music, thin and straight, black and white in a black and white evening gown. He saw her as a false note. He stood up in anger, but only told her, "you're really dressed for a professional concert."

"Dressed in borrowed plumes!"

"You admit trying to be someone you're not!"

"You dressed me up in borrowed plumes, all the while you were in the nightmare of a prison camp! You dreamed up a Cinderella, gave her a glass slipper no girl could fit."

She lost balance, fell into Lee's arms, a perfect fit.

AFTERWORD

What do you think?

I think the flesh of my arms remembered the touch of my soul-mate!

THE
DISCONNECTED

I

Separate Ways

In the ending was the word, "out," and the word was from the professor's wife. The love of his life wanted him out of her life! His marriage was ending, but he didn't know why. Lil wanted him out of his house! Students were wanting out of his classes, but he did know why. They wanted out of the study of social ideals, out of the social Establishment, out of its war in Vietnam! "Head" of the Philosophy Department at Trinitarian University, the professor almost went out of mind. He could face life with disaffected students, not half a life without his wife, or an empty life without his little girl and boy.

Professor Ayres Morrissee was known as "A.M," to wife and colleagues, "Morrissee of Philosophy" to students. He was a specialist in Knowledge Theory, but had no knowledge of discord in his marriage, not until he tried to kiss his wife, and missed! "Miss America," slipped out of his mouth with a smile, but didn't get him a laugh or kiss. He began missing more of her. His wife began serving dinners without a word, turning her back to him in bed. Afraid of failure in the middle of his course of life, the professor let it pass, didn't try to discuss it. He'd become a philosopher afraid of the truth!

When the truth was out, he was out. He knew every divorce had two sides, but didn't know either side of his own. Was there a third side? Had "Lil" set up an unholy trinity of husband, wife, other man? Who was the other man?

He only knew his marriage was ending with the Nineteen-Sixties, a decade of conflict between men and women over equal rights, but no such conflict with Lil. She gave no word of explanation, no hope of reconciliation, kept him in the dark. He went away without a word. What word would bring light out of darkness?

When he told Joy and Jeremy he had to go away, the children wanted to die! So did he! They wanted to know where he was going. So did he! He told them he'd only be a prayer away, but where? His parents were gone. He had not brothers or sisters. He had to find temporary refuge in the College Inn, just outside the East Gate of campus.

With not much more than the clothes on his back, until final arrangements could be made, he got living quarters in the four-cornered world of a motel room. With only a cigarette for company, he drifted off in smoke and thought. What would he do with the rest of his life? What would happen to the children? Shrouded in smoke, he wished Lil put him in the grave instead of a motel.

He rose up, caught sight of his mirrored self with that streak of gray running down the middle of his reddish hair. Had he grown too old for Lil? Book-bound for years of doctoral study, before and after naval service in the Second World War, he had a dozen years on Lil. She'd told him he was "ageless," like the "marble of Greek Philosophy!" When the swath of gray began to run down the middle of his red hair, she said it marked the "parting of the Red Sea," his passage to middle age. Now, he thought it marked his parting from Lil!

He let himself back down in the armchair, bent over, head between knees, mind between love and hate. Why had Lil closed the book on their marriage, set him on the shelf between the bookends of divorce and death? Had she taken up the Woman's

Liberation Movement, blamed him for the original sin of male domination? She must know he never dominated her! Did she want him to play the traditional male gender role? Had he been too passive, like a book in her hands?

The "Head" of the Philosophy Department couldn't stop thinking, but couldn't think his way into Lil's mind. There was no female Socrates to help him look within the female mind. Hardly any female philosophers came to mind! Women give life, he thought. Their bodies are sacred, but don't give the meaning of life. There was no meaning to his life without Lil and the children.

It came to him as he fought sleep that birth comes with separation! Lil was pushing him out, giving him a new life! He was going through the travail of birth, coming into the world alone and uncertain.

....

Alone, washing up on the shore of consciousness, Professor Morrissee's teaching assistant didn't know where he was, or who he was. Hart Benedict came to him. Light was seeping in his eyes, tearing them up. Memory was slowly coming up, like the tide. He'd left his wife and child to find his Existential Self. He'd only found another woman.

Looking up, he squinted at the slant of a beamed ceiling that was beginning to take shape in mind. Looking down, he saw feet without shoes, socks askew, like his mind. He eased himself up on one elbow, looked round. Love beads tugged at his neck, broke loose, scurried noisily across the hardwood floor. Pieces of reality started stringing together, one piece at time—the slanted ceiling, the cushions scattered round the hardwood floor, the walls hung with posters. He was in the Snake Pit, headquarters of the Student Action Committee! He was strung-out, unwinding from his first Hipfest, beginning to tremble. He caught sight of untied army boots stamping around his edge of vision, looked up to full sight of the Snake, Harry Snook, Student Action Committee chairman. He was as hairy as his first name.

"Time for you ass-holes to rise up," the student leader hissed, "and shut down the shit- house!"

The cushions on the floor turned into bodies, male and female, all rising up together in different stages of undress. Hart Benedict knew it was time to demonstrate against the university, its support of the Establishment and the war in Vietnam. He knew it was the first day of his new life, but he couldn't get the picture of his old life, and Alma, out of mind.

....

Framed in a four-poster bed, Alma Benedict was posed with a bare arm clutching the empty pillow beside her. A street lamp was brushing strokes of light through the curtain, dabbing flesh tones to uncovered body parts. A bare breast rolled over amid the ruffled covers, like the swelling of a white-capped wave.

Hart, why have you forsaken me?

Alma, startled by her own voice, woke in alarm, couldn't believe Hart left her, remembered him saying he was running out on his old self, as well as her. She said she loved his old self. He said she loved God more than him. As his words echoed in memory, she wondered if she really loved God more than her dear Hart? He was in the image of God! Marriage was a holy trinity of husband, wife, and God! She'd asked her dear Hart why he was running out on Little Hart? She knew their son loved his daddy more than God, but a curtain was coming down on the scene.

She knew the curtain would go up in the daylight, and she'd be playing a new role. How could she act the part of an abandoned wife? She closed her eyes, and a curtain was going up on the Student Center, University of Illinois, the scene of meeting her Sweet Hart. With a bowl haircut, he was boyish looking in a man's body. He introduced himself as "Hart Benedict, Hart as in Hartvig, one of my Viking ancestors, and Benedict as the Latin for blessing." He asked if she'd bless him with a dance, and she let him swing her off to the whirl of a jukebox platter, a song she didn't remember. In a dip, he whispered that his name, Hart

Benedict, had twelve letters, one letter for each hour of the clock, making him "a man for all time!" She thought he was coming on too strong, but she liked the feel of his arms.

When they sat out a dance, she learned the man for all time was majoring in history, "the study of all time," minoring in Secondary Education to make a living. History was his love, but he really was a Poet Pedagogue! She learned he was working on his "Sophomore Sonnets, quatrains and couplets of love." Without giving her a chance to talk, he confessed that he knew more about sonnets than love, and she began thinking she was getting in rhyme with him. They began dating and she thought he was her man for all time. They married at graduation time.

A Home Economics major, she gave him a good home, and he gave her a good life, and the precious life of Little Hart, but the teaching of high school history was taking the poetry out of him. He had to prepare five classes a day, go through a hundred homework papers a night, and get complaints from students not wanting to claim their rich historic heritage. In time, he got interested in the history of ideas, wanted to teach college students, needed a higher degree. With a scholarship at Trinitarian University, he lifted her out of a house with a picture-window, and a picture perfect life, dropped her and Little Hart in a Student Housing Project, a two-room apartment with no view at all. She didn't care where she lived as long as it was with Hart, but he got so high up in the branches of philosophy she couldn't reach him anymore. He dropped out of Church, and the Campus Crusade for Christ, fell in with a mangey lot of rebels who altered their minds with drugs instead of books. They altered Hart, got him to turn against his own historic heritage. When he let his curly hair curl down over the shoulders, she thought he looked like Jesus, but knew the long hair was his protest against the "crewcut world!"

She drew up the covers, tried to hide from the coming of a new day, and a new life.

....

—

In the light of a new day, Professor Morrissee was opening his eyes to the dark of a new life! He felt like ashes in the morning! His mind, like an ashtray, was littered with half- remembered events of the night before. He knew he was cut off from home, separated. The whole world was separated! The generations were separating like the genders, and the races were still painfully separated! The whole world was separated, East and West, divorced by Communism. Vietnam was separated, North and South, America defending the South against the Communist North. He had no quarrel with Civil Rights, only with violence, no quarrel with North Vietnam, only with Communism. He had no quarrel with Lil, only with separation.

She had condemned him to be free, an Existential refrain, a protest against uncertain existence in an uncertain world. "Existential" was a camp word on campus, but only a word to his radicalized students! They didn't pursue the nature of Being, only wanted to protest the absurdity of an alien school and society.

Mr. Benedict, his teaching assistant, was an exception, a sincere student of the new Existential craze. A former high school teacher, he found similarities between Progressive Education and the Existential philosophical craze. Both focused on the individual, opposed forcing the existent into a preexisting mold. Both promoted freedom to think in school, and religion. Mr. Benedict proposed a comparative analysis for his dissertation, but was advised that the movements were so diverse he should limit the comparison to their "fathers," Dewey's Progressive Education, Kierkegaard's Existentialism.

As the professor lay in thought of Benedict's dissertation, Existential Contributions to Progressive Education, he'd been getting concerned about the subjectivity of Existentialism, and the objectivity needed in teaching. Now he began fearing he was becoming too subjective. He could only think of himself, and his loss of fatherhood. He didn't think philosophical or educational fathers could love their creations as much as biological fathers!

As he rolled over in bed, and thought, his marriage bed turned up in mind. He hadn't made love to Lil in a long time. Had he been afraid of failure, like the last time?

....

Failure in marriage came back to Alma Benedict with her awakening in a messed-up bed. She could get out of the messed-up bed, but not out of a messed-up life. She strapped and snapped herself together, parted the curtain of long black hair, saw her way into the livingroom where Little Hart was still asleep in a makeshift bed on the sofa. She hoped he wouldn't wake up with memory of his father storming out.

Mechanically, she whipped-up scrambled eggs on the hot plate, and gently stirred her little boy awake, fed and dressed him, took him to the apartment next door. Alma greeted her neighbor, Cheryl, asked if she'd take Little Hart to nursery school. Cheryl's daughter and Little Hart were classmates and playmates.

Alma couldn't find words to explain her husband's absence, only told Cheryl that "Big Hart" had taken the car. Cheryl waved mother and child into her living room cluttered with playpen, blocks, stuffed animals, asked if "your Hart's attacking the university with all the undergraduates?"

Alma said she didn't know, but he'd gotten a little radical, a little mixed-up.

Cheryl said her husband was already at research in the library, but supposed the radicals will close it down! Alma said she was disappointed that Hart got sidelined, involved in the Student Action Committee. She was afraid of crying if she said another word.

Cheryl mentioned that the Student Action Committee seemed more interested in the "hippy life than college reform." She was trying to hold her wiggling daughter long enough to fasten a ribbon in her hair. "Hope your man doesn't study-up on hippie free love," she said, giving her child's ribbon a final twist.

"Free love isn't free!" The words leaped out of Alma's mouth. "Free love costs a body's soul!"

"Free love's gonna cost good women their wedding rings," Cheryl managed to speak out, still trying to hold her little girl still. "Men won't ring the marriage bell if they can get a bang for nothing!"

She turned her daughter loose at the same time Alma was trying to straighten Little Hart's coat. He squirmed out of her hands, his baby voice telling her to be nice to him, or he'd "run away, too."

....

Thoughts of his children were running through Professor Morrissee's mind as he looked in the mirror and took a razor to his whiskers. He remembering how the children loved to watch him shave. Now, he only saw himself, seemed to be falling through the looking glass into an unknown world. He wondered how he'd survive, wondered if the children missed him, or blamed him for going away? He wondered how he'd face colleagues and students with his feeling of disgrace? Divorce was almost unheard of on campus, and it meant failure. Failure was a sin on campus. He wondered if his radical students would look on his divorce as proof of social degeneration?

Briefcase in hand, dread in mind, he headed on foot to the nearby campus. The familiar stone arch of East Gate came into view, made him wish for a wall to hide behind. As he passed through the gate, students aimed looks of hate at him. Teachers now seemed to be their natural enemies!

Looking away, and up, he thought the sky was holding the world in prison. Clouds were on guard, breathing gently, inhaling and exhaling the recycled breaths of every breathing being who ever lived. Some of the clouds carried the breath of his own lectures, and the breaths of Socrates and Jesus!

Clouds in his head, he made his way to the Academic Building, and to his office on the fourth floor, halfway down the hall.

....

A.M. hesitated to open his office door, dreaded showing up on the other side, showing up as a failure in life. When the door opened, his office looked the same as any other day. Did he look the same? He knew he'd have to give himself away.

His secretary, Mrs. Bagley, rose from her desk, as usual, filled his coffee cup to the rim, as usual. She was dressed, as usual, in high collar and tailored tweeds. Down her front, as usual, hung the gold ballpoint pen at the end of a pink ribbon. He'd always viewed her as the Essential Bagley, essential to the running of the office, and essential in name. William Bagley was an educational Essentialist, no relation to her, except in name.

He let himself down in the chair next to his Essential Bagley, sipped his coffee, but couldn't pour himself out to her. He had to let her know of his change of address, and change of life, feared he'd break down. Over the top of his cup he began seeing Mrs. Bagley as a woman, not the essential fixture in his office. She'd kept his professional life in order for years, but he'd never kept up with her personal life. He knew she had the given name of "Grace." He knew she was a graduate of the Trinitarian School of Business. He knew she was a war widow with a son grown up by now. On a Memorial Day, she'd let him know that her husband was "rusting at the bottom of Ironbottom Sound, off Guadalcanal." He remembered telling the widow that her husband helped win the war, confessed that his naval service hardly made an impression on the war, not even "a dent in the sea!" He remembered the Essential Bagley telling him that the war made a dent in everyone. Now, he couldn't face her with the big dent in his life, excused himself, sought refuge behind the door of his inner office, slumped down in his swivel chair with hate for the wife he loved. She'd put more than a dent in his life. She'd broken the chain of life! Divorce would change their children's lives, and the lives of their children. In his chain of thought he linked his children with his students, suddenly realized he had a class to meet within the hour! Morality in the Modern World was a difficult class to teach, even when he had his mind together and hours to prepare. Required of all students in Liberal Arts, it was loaded with students who only wanted to do their "own thing," or thought morality was the "shepherd's staff" to herd them round like sheep. He tried to convince them that morality separated them from sheep.

Looking for his class notes, he shuffled through papers, only stirred-up the loss of his family. He thought it was time to let his graduate teaching assistant take over. Lifting the phone, he raised his voice to Mrs. Bagley, asked her to get in touch with "Mr. Benedict." She told him the "young man" hadn't shown up, said she'd called his home and got no answer, not even from his "lovely wife."

A.M. told her to "carry on," hung up, wondered how he'd carry on, wondered if Lil was carrying on? He'd made a list of possible other men. Could it be Cas Koczur, his colleague in Liberal Arts, and neighbor on Faculty Row? Lil liked men with red hair. She liked men who could handle tools. She called on Cas whenever something in the house needed a quick fix.

He swivelled round in his chair, turned thoughts to the Dean of Liberal Arts! He was a widower, kept an eye on Lil at faculty parties. He even asked her to play hostess at several college affairs. Women go for men with power!

The telephone rang the other men out of mind, got him connected to Mrs. Bagley. She let him know that his teaching assistant was "with the student demonstration!" She said the student rally was just getting underway, "take a look out the window."

Student Demonstration! Had he lost his mind as well as his family? He confessed to his secretary that it had slipped his mind.

"You've always been an absent-minded professor," the secretary laughed through the wire, "and will find students absent in mind and body this morning."

Her message brought mixed feelings, a loss of memory and relief he didn't have to teach a class! He told his secretary, in jest, he was paid for teaching, not learning, and would try to fill empty seats with knowledge of morality. He heard Mrs. Bagley laugh at the other end of the line and sign off with the need to get back to earning her living.

He was left hung-up with personal and university breakdowns! He shared many of the student grievances, but not their demand for no negotiations! He was thinking that democracy, and marriage, depended on compromise.

Finding his class notes for Morality in the Modern World, he noted he was up to considering the hierarchy of morals, but didn't think he'd have to get into it. When he got to the vault-like lecture hall he glimpsed a scattering of students in the three levels of seats rising before his eyes. There was a hollow sound in the hall, and an empty space in his mind. It came to him that the hierarchy of morals didn't seem relevant on a day like this, and relevancy was the battle cry of student dissenters.

"Good Morning," he spoke up. Hands on the podium, shoulders squared in a corduroy jacket, he shaped every syllable of his words carefully. "It's not always easy to know the good, but that's why we're here! Would you consider the student demonstration good?"

No hand went up from the handful of students. Did they think he wanted a factual answer?

He had to get them talking, came up with the method of his dialectical duel. He jumped in front of the lectern with the gesture of a rapier's thrust. "En garde," he called out. "Foil my point that the strike is not good!"

No student parried his thrust. He dropped his imaginary fencing foil, returned to the podium, asked for the meaning of dialectics? When no response sounded in the hollow silence of the lecture hall, he had to remind them that it was "a form of logic stressing opposing positions." He asked for their position on the student strike.

A voice cried out from the upper tier. "We're sick of you making us think like you think."

"What," the professor asked, looking to the upper tier, "do I want you to think?" He gripped the lectern until his knuckles whitened. Without looking at the seating chart, he knew the student who aimed the shot at him was the long-haired hipster and peacenick, Harry Snook. He always bragged about attending Woodstock that summer, had predicted the Woodstock Nation would secede form the "Pig Establishment." The professor repeated his question. "What do I want you to think?"

"You want us all to think like the Establishment wants us to think!" The words from the upper tier shot down and echoed around the lecture hall like spent bullets. The voice from the upper tier took a second shot. "Schools are dictatorships. We have to take teacher dictation!"

Snickers sounded up and down the three tiers. The professor feared he was losing the class. He knew it was the worst fear of teachers. Maybe teachers were dictators, afraid of losing control? He stiffened, asked the class if schools could be democratic, if teachers and students were all equal? When he got no response he asked if truth could be proven by majority vote?

"I'd vote against your kind of truth," the protestor's voice came roaring down again from the upper tier. "Schools are gatekeepers for the Establishment, keep dissenters out, and down!"

"How did you get in?"

The hairy one stood up, barelegged in cut-off jeans, waved both hairy arms, promoted the student Speak-Out! "Get the truth," he called out to everyone, "high noon, East Gate!"

The professor heard himself call for the protestor to get "out," and the word, "out," echoed around in his head like that word from Lil! He raised his voice again, apologized, asked the dissenter to "speak out! Tell us what you stand for!"

"I stand against the Establishment that tries to make me a robot, and send me off to war!"

"We know what you're against. What are you for?"

"I'm for Love, Man!"

"I see the opposite of love in you."

"You're too old to get the hang of Love, or the hippie hang of life!"

"On what authority do your opinions stand?"

"I don't stand on any other body's feet."

"I see you don't stand on any social, moral or religious authority!"

"You ain't seen nothing yet!"

The hairy one fingered his belt, sputtered something about Socrates and the unexamined life not being worth living! He yelled, "look within," and stepped out of his cut-off jeans!

Student gasps seemed to suck air out of the classroom. A book fell off a desk and punctuated the silence like an exclamation point.

The protestor reached down and snapped his jockstrap, popped it off. "Examine this!"

""Class dismissed!"

....

"You let your class out," stormed the Dean of Liberal Arts when A.M. made his report. "The Head of Philosophy can't control a body of undergraduates?"

"A student let his pants down," A.M. said with a shrug. "It's a hard act to follow."

"You let your class down, and the university."

Professor Morrissee wasn't surprised at the Dean's hostility. They both had been rivals for the deanship. Both had degrees from the same prominent Eastern university, both published in the same professional journals. A.M. thought they might even be rivals for the same woman!

"My class had a Revelation," the professor brought up in jest. "The Beast appeared!"

"It wasn't the Apocalypse."

The telephone rang like a bell ending the first round of a prizefight. It sent the Dean back to his corner. He picked up the phone, listened for a moment, hung up, came out fighting.

"You got the university shutdown!"

....

"University's shutdown for the day," Mrs. Bagley told Professor Morrissee when he appeared in the office doorway.

The professor dropped into the chair next to his secretary's desk, fumbled for a cigarette, stuck it in the side of his mouth, and "I feel shutdown" came out the other side.

"We heard you had an unregistered male member show up in class," Mrs. Bagley brought up with a laugh

"I see you got the bare facts!"

"Flashed all over campus!"

"Here's another fact. The Dean seems to blame me for the universityshutdown."

"Is he blaming you instead of the Student Action Committee?"

"Blaming me for giving in to the students."

"Why do students come to college to improve their minds," Mrs. Bagley asked, "and lose their heads?"

"They lost a day of academic learning," the professor granted, with a wave of cigarette and smoke, "but are learning they have power."

Mrs. Bagley ventured to say that students only wanted a day off, and the professor said they got it, and she should get the rest of the day off, too.

"I'd really like time off, if you can spare me."

"What do you do with your time off?" The professor was beginning to get interested in the private life of his secretary.

"Read novels. They make me feel like a ghost in the private lives of interesting people."

"I've heard of ghost writers, not ghost readers!"

"Let's say I'm a ghost in the book, like Descartes' ghost in the machine."

"You read Descartes as well as novels?"

"Your thoughts about Descartes go to my fingers, and to the typed pages of your articles."

"Descartes must have gotten printed on your mind, Mrs. Bagley."

"All that about Mind and Body. I got the idea you're the Mind in the office, I'm the body."

"Descartes separated mind and body," the professor said with a blush at the thought of being connected in body to his secretary, but it occurred to him that he might have been the mind in his marriage and Lil the body. Mind and body were separated, and he didn't like it.

"I don't think mind and body are separate," Mrs. Bagley dared to speak her mind. "My mind and hands work together, or I couldn't type."

"Descartes thought of mind as esprit, French for spirit."

"Do you believe we have a spirit?"

"I believe everything has an opposite. Spirit's the opposite of matter."

"Opposites must work together, like inhaling and exhaling."

"I didn't know you were such a thinker?"

"I think, therefore I am. Isn't that Descartes?"

"Cogito Ergo Sum!"

"Why does the mind prove the body?"

"The body's the object of the mind."

"My mind's ready to take my body out," Mrs. Bagley said, bending down to feel for her purse under the desk. Straightening up, she said there was too much separation in the world, "like all this student-teacher separation."

He agreed with her, told her to be careful of students when getting out of the building.

....

Out of classes, and control, students were cavorting around the Quadrangle below A.M.'s office window. He saw them waving placards of Let's Split, and Make Love, not War, felt hate and love in himself! He drew the blinds, shut it all out, fell into his chair, began hearing the sound of a bell ringing. It suggested that students had taken over the chapel, and its bell-rope. The ding and dong of the bell's tongue spoke to him of the bell's opposite sides, and the opposite sides of the students and faculties. The ding and the dong also struck him with the Socratic logic of thesis- antithesis, and the Oriental philosophy of Yin and Yang! He thought there would be no understanding of things without their opposites, no good without evil, no up without down, no light without dark. The bell tolled the truth!

....

The chapel bell was ringing in Alma Benedict's ears as she pedaled her bicycle toward campus in search of Hart. Black hair streaming behind, dark eyes looking ahead, she pumped as hard as she could, thought as hard as she could. What would she say to Hart? Could she get Professor Morrissee to speak for her? Thoughts wheeling in mind, she held course to East Gate, found it too crowded for a chance to see Hart. Her handlebars were grabbed by a college letterman, bulky in his athletic sweater. He wanted her to "join the team." She let him know she was looking for her "husband," and he let her pull away, but she couldn't find Hart in the wreathing student body, took off in the direction of Faculty Row, bent on seeing the Chairman of Hart's doctoral committee. He might be able to put Hart on the moral track.

Wheels were spinning her toward Faculty Row, but her mind was rolling backward, back to the time she met the professor and his wife. Hart had been appointed the professor's teaching assistant, and she and Little Hart accompanied him to the professor's home for dinner. The professor's wife looked plain, and she assumed philosophers looked for "inner beauty," but she was gracious, asked the guests to call her "Lilith." Professor Morrissee told them to call him "A.M.", and Alma thought of God as I AM! Around went the wheels of memory and up came Alma's dinner of beef-upside-down pie. She asked Lilith for the recipe, and it became Hart's favorite dinner treat. Now it seemed that her life was turning upside-down.

She kept pedaling and remembering. After dinner, the professor and Hart took to their pipes and philosophies. The professor's wife took her on a tour of the house. They checked on the children in the "Hobby Room." Little Hart and Jeremy Morrissee were playing with the action figure, "G.I. Joe." Lilith told Alma it was "ironic" that little boys liked to play war, but big boys were protesting against war.

The daughter, Joy Morrissee, was at her doll house, as if living another life in it, and didn't invite them in. Lilith said "Joy" was named for the joy she brought. She said "Jeremy" was named after her father, "Jeremy Clayborne." She often called him "J.C.!" She mentioned that the professor wanted to call him Immanuel, after some philosopher.

Alma said said "Little Hart's named after his daddy," and blushed at saying the obvious. She went on to say her own name meant soul in Spanish.

Lilith said her name was the same as Adam's first wife, and God divorced them! Alma didn't know Adam had a wife before Eve, and Lilith explained that it was only a Jewish legend, something she learned from Jewish friends while growing up in Brooklyn. She went on to say she lived within sight of the Brooklyn Bridge and the Manhattan skyline, lived within range of museums and libraries, in a world of art and beauty, and it was a "letdown" to come to the flat and simple land of Illinois. Alma didn't know how anyone could find Illinois a letdown, but only asked how it felt to be the wife of the "head of philosophy?" Lilith said it depended on whether a wife thought the head was the most important part of a man! Alma said she hoped her man would be the head of a philosophy, someday.

The head of philosophy's wife showed her Jeremy's room, opened a trunk, found some clothes that might fit Little Hart. Alma began wondering if she'd fit Lilith's memory as she braked to a stop in the rough gravel of the Morrissee driveway. Leaning the bike against a tree, she looked up at the two story Colonial house. The eaves were in need of patching, and one of the dormer windows was cracked and taped. She remembered Lilith saying her husband had no mind for practical things. He was "smart in the smart things," and "dumb in the dumb things."

A moment after Alma pushed the bell, the professor's wife was framed in the doorway, the picture of the plain and friendly woman in Alma's memory.

"I'm Alma Benedict."

"I remember you."

"I'd like to speak to the professor, if I may, for just a moment."

"The professor doesn't live here anymore"

....

The professor was holed-up in his office, under the massive dome of the Academic Building. From his window he could look down on a surge of students rising up around his building with only marble columns standing sentry. He saw police in riot helmets lined up on the other side of East Gate, didn't think they had jurisdiction to come on campus, knew the universities were neutral ground eversince the Middle Ages. Even the Russians didn't invade the University of Prague when they took over Czechoslovakia last year. He drew the shades, closed himself off in his inner world.

....

In the outer world, around East Gate, loudspeakers were sputtering commands for the students to "disband." Obscenities were fired back, shocking the pure academic air. The chapel bell kept ringing, more frantically. Fire trucks were pulling up to the East Gate. Hoses were unfurled by men in fire helmets, raincoats and boots. Without further warning, the hoses began spewing water at the chain of students locked hand-in-hand around East Gate. Students dissolved in the spray, reemerged plastered in dripping clothes. They began pouring into the Academic Building.

In precision drill, the police began marching under the arch of East Gate, lining up in front of the Academic Building where the faces of students began popping up in windows. T-shirts were waved like banners. An athletic supporter was whipped into a sling and popped a bottle of ink at the Goliath force confronting the Academic Building.

Looking up at the sound of a scream, the police got sight of a full-bodied young woman on the ledge around the dome. Her statuesque figure stood on tiptoes, stretched bare arms and bare breasts up to the sky. She wavered on the edge.

Cameras flashed.

The police moved back.

....

Behind the window blinds in his office, Professor Morrissee was blind to the standoff outside. High above the storm, he felt like the captain of a ship, safe on the Bridge. He thought ship captains and college professors had much in common. They charted courses. They held command. They stood lonely watches, no equal on ship or classroom. Captains faced changing seas, day after day. Professors faced a sea of changing students, semester after semester. Captains had refuge in home ports. Professors had refuge in home families.

A.M. knew he'd be "at sea" the rest of his life!

A voice jumped into his stream of thought. "You still aboard?"

A.M. looked up at his cigarette smouldering in the ashtray and an ebony dark face showing through the cloud of white smoke.

"Captain's last to abandon ship," A.M. said, greeting Rufus King, a new man in his department, and the only man of color. King was dark as the "King" of the Civil Rights Movement, but no relation.

"It's stormy out there," Rufus King said, sinking into a chair. "Students are rocking and rolling the boat, making their own music."

Professor Morrissee put the smoldering cigarette to lips for a final drag, let it out with the complaint that students were blowing the old social order away.

"You mean the old white man's social order!"

"I mean the shutdown of all social order! We're only one uneducated generation from the caveman."

"The school's not the only teacher," Rufus King spoke up with a smile for his department head. "There's family, church and state, corporations and the market place."

"The schools protect youth from the rat race, prepare them for it."

"Protection segregates them. I think students are in revolt against the school ghetto, want out!"

"Do you think it would be better for children to be in the rough and tumble of coal mines and factories?"

"I'm thinking there can be too much protection. Protection kept women in the home, kept women down!"

His words were picked up by a booming voice in the doorway. "You been keeping woman down?" The red-headed professor of

Sociology, Cas Koczur, began filling the room. Sitting down, he overfilled the chair, asked why the philosophers hadn't gone home?

Professor Morrissee asked why he didn't go home to Teresa? He still considered Cas Koczur a candidate for the "other man."

"I'm hanging on as a sociologist, gathering material for my next book on the Student Movement."

"You're living in your research," A.M. agreed, "an eyewitness."

"I can bear witness to the Student Movement at Columbia," Rufus King volunteered. "I was an instructor there when students took over. Books were burned, faculty research trashed. I left, thought I'd be free to teach here in the Midwest, middle of the heartland."

The sociologist scoffed, told him there were "heart attacks in the heartland when Martin Luther King was assassinated last year!"

"Too bad riots can't right wrongs," Rufus King said with a wave of his cigarette that made a circle of smoke.

"Students think they can wave magic wands," Cas Koczur spoke up in lecture form, "and make the old way of life disappear!"

"Protesters are full of hate," A.M. said. "Hate can't make a better world."

"And ignorance can't make a better world," the sociologist said. "Student protestors don't want to study, afraid of catching the Bright Disease."

"They're not afraid of making noise, and protesting," A.M. said. "What happened to the Silent Generation?"

"Went out with the Beatniks, and hula-hoops," the sociologist answered A.M.'s question as if it had been asked seriously.

Rufus King asked why the police didn't show up, and complained that the "cops were on the spot when riots broke out in the ghettos."

"I've seen badges on the other side of East Gate," Cas Koczur mentioned, "but the university's beyond their jurisdiction."

"The mind of the university should never be policed," A. M. said in agreement. "And a body shouldn't be enslaved," Rufus King made his point.

"Marriage can enslave the mind and the body," Cas Koczur came up with an idea that took A.M. by surprise.

Suspicious of Cas as a rival, A.M. asked him how his marriage was going.

"Only a few skirmishes," the sociologist answered with a smile that creased both cheeks. "Heard there's civil war in the Morrissee union!"

"How'd you get that idea?"

"Your wife told my Teresa that you guys are headed for Splitsville. Can you verify it?" A.M. nodded, almost relieved that his pent-up shame was about to get aired out.

"Thought you and Lilith were close as fingers on the hand!"

"Our marriage got out of hand," A.M. admitted, throwing up his hands, "don't know why?"

"Our students are out of hand," Cas Koczur said, looking up, "and I'm working on the why!" A sudden roar caught their attention. An unshaved youth thrust his hairy face in the doorway. His whole hairy body was only clad in tank-top and cut-off jeans. He was backed-up by other hairy faces and bodies. A.M. recognized Harry Snook, thought he was as scary in pants as without them.

"We changed places with you," the hairy leader proclaimed with outspread arms. "Students now up front, in charge!"

....

"We're up and they're down," Hart Benedict said when he got together with Harry Snook in the abandoned office of the Dean of Liberal Arts. "We've turned the world upside down. What's our next move?"

"It's their move," the student leader replied, swinging round and round in the Dean's swivel chair. He came to a stop and kicked off his surplus army boots, lifted bare feet to the desk, brushed aside the Dean's papers. Rolling a cigar between his fingers he said, "we keep pigs rooting around outside, till we make the national news." He clamped the cigar in his mouth, lit up. "Dean's got good smokes."

"No books," Hart noticed, looking around.

The office was an expanse of blue carpet, wood-paneled walls hung with painted portraits of former deans. Hart let himself down in a chair opposite the desk, threw a leg over its arm, looked up. The bay window behind the Dean's desk framed a scene of bare elm trees arched over the walkway to East Gate. No police were in view. Hart struck a light to his cigarette, asked how long they could hold out?

"Til we get our four and twenty demands."

"Four and twenty blackbirds baked in a pie," Hart Benedict laughed, "a dainty dish to set before the Dean. We ought to get us a few big pieces of the pie, at least student membership in the Faculty Senate and Board of Regents, get equal pay for women professors, fair wages for teaching assistants." He ran out of breath.

"Whole pie! No negotiations?"

"No compromises?" Hart fumbled for another cigarette.

"Did you compromise with your wife bitch?"

"Are we divorcing the university?"

"Never had a good union. University treated us like children!"

"Can't hold off the police forever. They have the upper hand."

"Got us a good hand, three of a kind professors, my sister's ass on dome the ass in the hole. When storm troopers break in, the TV will show the world what kind of society we're up against."

"Heads will get bashed-in."

"A few bashed heads will make headlines in all the newspapers!"

....

"Got breaking news for you," Cas Koczur told his wife on the phone in A.M.'s inner office. "I'm a prisoner of the underclass! No, I mean the underclassmen, not the underclass we came from." He listened in silence "We're up against the under generation," he spoke up, "a War of the Ages!" He began listening again, kept winking at his companions. "I'm safe," he finally sputtered in the phone. "Nobody's messing with me, no hippie girls holding me down!"

A.M. asked Cas to find out if Lil was worried about him.

Cas Koczur relayed the question over the phone, listened, shook his head at A.M., cupped hand over the phone to tell him that Teresa hasn't seen Lilith. Back on the phone he told Teresa he had to hang up before students cut him off. He put down the phone, told his companions that Teresa thought Communists were behind the uprising, and she was afraid students were "messing with my head."

"Your head, or the shrunken head hanging in your office?"

"Can't you guys get it through your heads that the shrunken head's a war souvenir, a cultural artifact, a teaching tool?"

"It's a disgusting souvenir," Rufus King ventured to speak up to a full professor.

"Grabs your attention, a great teaching tool."

"Teaches man's inhumanity to man," A.M. thought out loud.

"One man's inhumanity is another man's humanity. What do you know about the primitives who shrink heads?"

"We professors are headhunters, too," Rufus King looked up with a smile, "but we try to expand heads, not shrink them."

"Seems we have shrunk a lot of heads," the sociologist talked back. "Our students think they have brains to run the university."

"No one ever said no to them," A.M. brought up. "My wife wouldn't let me have a free hand with the children unless I read some book on childcare. The generation we're up against grew up on permissive child-rearing practices."

"Early toilet training would have taught them to do their duty," the sociologist added, with a smile.

"No shit," Rufus King sneered. "You think students are fed up with the compulsive social order because they didn't get early toilet training?"

"There may be more Freud than toilet to it," the sociologist conceded, "sons against the fathers!"

"Sons will take the place of fathers, without war," Professor Morrissee commented, "if they wait."

"This generation has no time to wait," Rufus King argued. "It's way past time to say no to inequality!"

"The kids are saying yes to drugs as much as no to inequality!" Cas Koczur exhaled in a stream of smoke. "They only want to live in a psychedelic state of being."

"They got turned on to social issues," Rufus King professed.

"They want anarchy, no government, no regulations," the sociologist talked back, "want to tear down industry, go back to the simple life."

"We'll all end up in the jungle" A.M. predicted.

"Primitives aren't savages," Rufus King said. "Students want more love and communion in the world."

Crushing out his cigarette, the sociologist took command, said he'd studied the Student Movement for years. "There were over two hundred student demonstrations, rallies, strikes, sit-ins, in the last year alone," he lectured. "The rebels don't agree on what their revolution will accomplish."

"I think these kids are rebels with a cause," Rufus King kept insisting.

"You philosophers don't study things, live in theories of no things

"We philosophers wonder what is real," A.M. spoke up. "Are people only things?"

"Why are we now objects for student hate?"

"We stand betweenthem and the world they want," Cas said. "The Joe College we knew is dead, no more panty-raids. Our students want to make off with the whole university." The sociologist paused to listen. There was a distant roar.

"Some kind of happening's going on."

....

The students were whooping and cavorting in the Academic Building's cavernous rotunda. Shouts of joy and triumph were echoing all the way up to the rounded dome. A makeshift platform had been set up on the main floor. When the student leader mounted it, Harry Snook called for order, and "a session of Sensitivity Training." He commanded "assholes get in touch!"

Students began feeling each other up, getting to know each other, trust each other.

"What's your name," Hart Benedict asked a co-ed when he confronted the girl next to him. "Patty," she said, holding up both hands, asking for the slap of "Patty Cake."

He noticed "Patty" was very bosomy in a tight sweatshirt with Hang Loose across the front. She jerked the sweatshirt over her breasts and back down again. She really was hanging loose, no bra.

"I'm a little uptight about all this Sensitivity Training," Hart admitted, uneasy about touching people in private places. He thought of touching Patty's breasts. Each one would fill two hands, but he held back, didn't know why.

"Touching builds bonds," she was saying, reaching for his crotch.

"Don't think its right," he said, pulling back.

"Got to stop thinking, live it up!"

"Thought college was for thinking?"

"Needs more feeling!"

They began feeling the sound of rock and roll spinning on a phonograph.

"Give me the roll of Elvis the Pelvis," she said, putting her body in motion, "an' dance me up."

Hart confessed he was "square" when it came to dancing, could only do the "box waltz." The Patty girl said he was "square all right," and rocked and rolled away, got in touch with another body.

Hart got in touch with another body, a bump on the back. He turned round to grab the falling weight of a young man. His body was hard as a statue, reminded Hart of a Socratic question. Why did men take pains to make stones look like men, but no pains to keep men from being unlike stones?

"Old boy's stoned," came the opinion of a passing rock and roller. "Psyched out," came another voice.

"Needs a good touch."

Hands reached out to him, and he began warming up. The white marble toned-up to the color of flesh, got animated, rejoined the mass of gyrating bodies at the same time Hart was jarred by the bump of another body.

"Hi, Mr. Teach!"

Hart turned round to face Maxy Snook, Snake's sister, the girl who'd made her bare body the monumental figure on the Academic dome. She was now draped in the folds of a t-shirt with SNAKE stenciled in large letters across the front. It hung down to her knees, dimpled knees, like her dimpled cheeks, Hart thought. Her brassy hair seemed molded to her head, a cut above the ears. It occurred to him that female ears had always been like private parts, hidden by long hair.

"You have beautiful ears," he let her know as they moved out of the way of dancers reeling round them.

"I set my ears free," she explained. "Short hair's a woman's protest, the opposite of a man's. You sure let your hair protest."

"Got my ears imprisoned," Hart said, "until we make the world free!"

"The Age of Aquarius is coming," Maxy sang to him. "Saw Hair on Broadway last summer."

"I was born under the star of Aquarius," Hart mentioned. "Do you figure our fate's in the stars?"

"We're only under the stars. Snake's my star!"

"How'd your brother get called Snake?"

"Snook's the past tense of sneak. He could sneak around all rules and regulations."

"Let's sneak out," Hart proposed, pointing to an alcove at the side of the rotunda.

As she gave him a nod and let him lead her away from the dancers, he asked if she would have jumped from the Academic Building dome if police didn't hold off?

"If I felt like it."

"Feel like falling for me?"

"It's the Fall Semester."

"I fell for you last night, in the Snake Pit."

"I'd have gone down to you, but your dissertation bullshit turned me off."

"My dissertation will kill the sacred cow of traditional education!"

"I'm for dumping all your philosophy bull."

"What do you know about philosophy?"

"I know Plato's Cave, and all that bullshit."

"You must have been in a Morrissee of Philosphy class."

"And you were his assistant, took roll, picked up papers."

"How could I have missed picking up you?"

"Same book, different cover. Cut my hair, changed from dresses to pants."

"I like your new cover, like to know what's inside."

"Body of literature's my other body. I'm an English major."

"Once upon a time I had poetry in me."

"Got a novel in me."

"What's your novel idea?"

"It's a love triangle between a girl and her brother and her boyfriend, all three in love with the brother."

"Platonic love?"

"Physical love."

"Fiction?"

"Can't fiction tell truth?"

"Fiction's made up."

"Isn't Plato's Cave made up? Doesn't it tell the truth?"

"I think it does, but a lot of people think its only fiction."

"I'm fiction, make myself up as I go."

"Like to get a good read on you."

"Got to be alone for reading."

"Everybody's freaking-out down here. We should be alone in Faculty Lounge."

....

"Sure is empty," Hart noted as he led Maxy into the Faculty Lounge reeking with smoke and sweat. Several upholstered chairs and couches were overturned, floor littered with candy and sandwich wrappers.

"Let's get down," Maxy said. "I'm a Horizontalist!"

"Horizontalist? Is that a position or a philosophy?"

"A philosophic position. Horizontalists believe the great things in life come lying down-- birth, sex, death."

"I'm a Horizontalist, too!" He got down to her level.

....

"Can't sleep in the perpendicular," Cas Koczur complained to his companions as he tried to get comfortable. The professors were still confined in the inner office of the Philosophy Department. All three had been languishing there, slipping in and out of talk, sleep, smoke. The phone had been disconnected, guards were shuffling around in the outer office.

"Can't get myself in the shape of this chair," Rufus King groaned in turn.

"Had a dream," A.M. spoke up from his swivel chair. "Dreamt I couldn't remember where I parked my car, didn't know how I'd get home."

"You don't have a home," his former neighbor reminded him, "and your wife's got the car, but you have the best chair to fall asleep in."

....

Alma Benedict, stretched-out on her livingroom sofa, awakened with a story book in hand, Little Hart curled-up in sleep beside her. "Rock-a-bye-baby" was still on her lips, fear of the bough breaking still in mind. She knew her parents were coming to pick up Little Hart, care for him while she got her life back together with Hart. There would be no divorce in their family!

She didn't know how she could get back in rhyme with her poet pedagogue! His poetry was still imprinted in her mind, but he hadn't written poetry for her in a long time. When she gave birth to Little Hart, Hart gave birth to a sonnet that she carried around in her mind.

From humus, human girls are shaped to be the vessels of all Life, eternally.

The first lines gave way to the last lines. So man and woman in one flesh should be as God to man is, symbolically.

She gathered up Little Hart in both arms, put him to rest, remembered the time she was nursing him, and Hart wrote a poem about her breast being the Fountain of Youth!

....

"I could use a drink," Rufus King said, breaking the silence in A.M.'s inner office. The men had gone without supper, shared one concession, a candy bar ripped out of a vending machine by student looters.

"Time to stand up to our students," the sociologist avowed, taking to his feet, raising arms in fists. "We might get roughed-up, but they aren't going to kill us."

"Think we should sit this out," A.M. cautioned, swinging round in his swivel chair. "Time's on our side."

"That's your trouble," Cas snapped back. "You don't stand up for yourself. You should have stood up to the Dean, and to Lilith!"

It occurred to A.M. that "the other man" wouldn't want him to hold on to his wife.

"Marriage's a contract," Rufus King broke into A.M.'s thoughts, "should only be broken by consent of both parties."

"No-fault divorce in this state," A.M. talked back, "only the property settlement can be contested."

"And a wife's not property anymore," Rufus King granted, "no slave."

"But she can take half a man's property," A.M. whispered, "and all his children!"

"Students are divorcing our university," Rufus King brought up, "and may take most academic subjects away.

"How can the university survive without Liberal Arts?" A.M. said it was founded on it! "Liberal arts were for the upper classes," Cas Koczur lectured again. "The liberals in those days were free men, didn't need to work. Modern world can do without leisure studies, only needs to know how to make a living, and live together. We need sociology to live in a well ordered community."

A.M. wanted to know how we could live without beauty, and how sociology could contribute to community! "You can't get people to commune in unity, when sociology seems rooted in cultural relativity."

"You're playing games with words," the sociologist talked back, just as his words were wiped out with a bang at the door!

The professors looked up at the hairy leader of the revolt, backed up by ragged followers. "Games are about to begin," he roared. "Ball's in our court!"

....

"It's their ball and their serve," Cas Koczur mentioned to his academic companions as they were led to the raised platform in the middle of the rotunda, "but they'll be in a legal court one day soon."

When the professors were put down on folding chairs in front of the roaring students, the hairy leader roared to the crowd that he had the "false prophets in the Lion's Den."

The students roared out like young lions.

"Our professors kept us prisoners in the classroom," the hairy leader roared back. "Now we can teach them how it feels."

The young lions roared.

"Schools prolong our infancy," the hairy leader kept roaring, "kept us out of the world, put us to sleep with nursery rhymes and fairy tales."

"Goosey-goosey-gander," roared out one of the students, and it rang around the rotunda, followed by "let's Mother goose 'em!"

"Humpty Dumpty had a great fall," the hairy leader led the protesters into Mother Goose, "and all the university men couldn't put eggs-ucation back together again!"

The young lions roared.

"Once upon a time," the hairy leader took over with a wave of the hand, "there was a young man named Snake. He had to crawl up the beanstalk of education, grade by grade, rung by rung, all the way up the ladder to higher education, way up in the clouds."

When the storyteller paused to clear his throat, the young lions cried out for more Jack and the Beanstock.. He told them Professor Humpty Dumpty of higher eggsucation kicked Snake down the beanstalk, but he tore up the roots, and "Higher Education had a great fall!"

All the young lions roared.

"Let's get groovy with Mother Goosey," the hairy leader called out when the roaring sound tapered off. He flapped his arms like a bird. "Jack and Jill went up the hill to fetch a little pill.

Jack fell down and got a little thrill!"

When the leader's voice broke off, a girl's voice rose up with "Patty cake, Patty cake, baker's man, make me, make me, fast as you can!"

A baritone voice wanted to sing a "ditty" about a pretty little "titty." Another voice popped up with, "hey diddle, diddle, on the pigs let's piddle."

"Dick and Jane of first grade fame, discovered they were not the same. See Dick see Jane."

"Three little co-eds lost their maidenheads. Naughty co-eds! They shall have no pie in the sky, by and by."

"Rub-a-dub-dub, three men in a tub," roared the hairy leader, pointing to the professors, all three, sitting together in a row, "shall we rub 'em out?"

"Dub 'em to Mother Goose us," one of the young lions roared.

"I dub Morrissee of Philosophy," the leader announced, "to lead us down the hole to his wonderland."

The young lions roared.

Professor Morrissee had been escaping in thought, remembering how his little children loved nursery rhymes. His leg was their cock-horse riding them to Banbury Cross. The sound of his name called him away from Banbury Cross. He uncrossed his legs, stood up to the challenge of addressing the students.

"Can't take you to Wonderland," he said, voice circling around the rotunda, and back to him, "but can make you wonder!"

The young lions roared.

"You deserve a Mother Goose Award," he talked through the roar, speaking louder. "Never have I seen so many happy faces on campus."

The young lions roared.

A.M. knew he couldn't keep Mother Goose on the wing, or tell the students their cause was a gone goose, but he could try to make them wonder and think. "Can't take you through the looking glass to a parallel world, but can lead you into my Garden of Versus," and he spelled versus, one letter at a time. "You see it's not Stevenson's Garden of Verses, and not a garden for growing Flower Children. It's a garden for growing ideas, one idea versus another, verse and adverse."

The young lions roared.

"My Garden of Versus has only one tree," the professor continued when the roar came to a purr, echoing round the marble rotunda. "It's the Philoso-tree."

Another roar! The professor waited for it to sputter down. "The Philoso-tree is rooted in three questions," he continued. "What is Reality? What is Good? How do we know?"

"The young lions went silent. The professor told them the three questions were carried up the trunk of the Philoso-tree, and branched out in opposite philosophies, Idealism and Materialism. Reality is idea, mental, spiritual, for the Idealist. Reality is matter for the Materialist. The Good is absolute for the Idealist, relative for the Materialist. The way of knowing is deductive and rational for the Idealist, inductive and scientific for the Materialist."

The young lions were silent.

"Double-talk," the hairy student leader snarled and waved the professor back to his seat. "He's full of Orwell's double-talk! Orwell taught us to beware of double-talk!"

"I think you fell into Orwell's memory hole," the professor countered. "Orwell wrote about doublethink, not doubletalk. Orwell's doublethink was no thinking at all. There was no difference between opposites. War is Peace!"

"See how the professor plays word games with us," the student leader roared out to his young lions.

The young lions didn't roar back.

"Games aren't good without opposite sides," the professor kept speaking out, still standing up. "Let's play my game of Dialectical Football, divide up into teams, pick out a topic, take one side or the other, get in huddles and prepare arguments for your side."

The student leader called for "time out!"

. . . .

Time was changing sides, from dark to light. Light was unraveling the campus from the folds of dark, polishing the copper dome of the Academic Building. The sun was beginning to gleam on the shields of police. A unit of the National Guard was backing them up, at parade rest.

A loudspeaker demanded students to come out, "peacefully!" Students hung out of windows, chanted "Hell no, we won't go!"

The police looked up. No figurehead appeared on the ledge around the dome. A whistle blew the ranks of blue on the move.

Far back, behind the police and national guardsmen, Alma Benedict was hovering under the bare branches of an elm tree. She feared for her Hart, thought he'd be hurt when the police broke in! She also feared for Professor Morrissee. The morning newspaper, folded under her arm, had reported the head of philosophy was a turncoat, stayed with the students when the other hostages were released.

Alma's copy of the Daily Times had a front page picture of students snarling and spitting at police. She couldn't believe there could be so much hate in such young people! Had the youths come from homes abandoned by fathers?

The sound of sirens began filling her ears, bursting them. Her eyes caught sight of police marching between the marble columns of the Academic Building, forcing open the bronze doors. Her eyes filled up with sights of bodies, kicking and screaming!

Night sticks seemed to be beating inside her head. She felt herself escaping into darkness.

....

Deep down in a well of blackness, Professor Morrissee felt himself getting drawn up to consciousness, aware of himself on a bench, pressed against a wall, buttressed on both sides by warm bodies. He didn't know where he was? His body remembered soreness. Night-sticks and handcuffs came to mind, and the "Black Hole" of the county jail. He felt like a bookmark, holding his place between arrested students. A book of Plato seemed to open up in mind. He imagined being chained-up in Plato's Cave, and he really saw shadows on the wall.

Plato's Cave was his favorite analogy for teaching students that material things are not always what they appear to be. Plato's cave was his analogy of the world where human beings were chained to their senses, unable to turn round to the real world outside the cave's opening. People only saw the reflected shadows of the real world on the back wall, thought the shadows were real.

In a moment of reflection, A.M. knew most of his students thought Plato's Cave was a fairytale, even if they believed in the invisible world of atoms. He wasn't selling Idealism, only offering it as an opposing philosophy. In another moment of reflection, he thought many of his students were living in a cave-world of drugs, thought it was the real world.

His reflections were blotted out by the sound of a familiar voice, a breath away. It was the whisper of Hart Benedict, asking, "you awake, Sir?"

"Awake, chained to Plato's shadowy prison of appearances."

"Always the teacher," Hart whispered back, "but we're chained in the Establishment's phony world. Can your Platonic Mind's Eye see a way out?"

"Reason tells me we'll be brought up for charges in the morning, and released on bond to the outside world."

"The outside world's a prison to us. Didn't you come over to our side?"

"Took your side to help you see both sides."

"You have to choose! Both opposite sides can't be true."

"I'm still in thought."

"Know I'm on the right side."

"Are you on the right side of morality when you're cavorting hand in hand with a woman not your wife?"

"I'm not on the Establishment's side of morality! Hope there's not a wall between us."

II

The Wall Between

The wall between students and faculty at Trinitarian University stood standing, even after the revolt was put down. Arrested protestors were let out of jail, classes resumed, but many students remained sullen, cut off.

The University president convened a special committee of Deans, Regents, and selected faculty members to help break down the wall. He asked the committee what caused the wall to rise between faculty and students, and answers ranged from anti-intellectualism to the war in Vietnam! He asked what could be done to pull down the wall?

"Start reforming the university!"

"Maybe society needs reforming?"

"The university is to serve society, not lead it!"

"We're in the business of the Mind, should mind our own business."

"Students are of a mind to run the university. Can the uneducated lead the educated?"

"We're divided ourselves," the Dean of Liberal Arts brought up. "There's a wall between the sciences and Liberal Arts. We need to bring the two cultures together."

"One wall at a time," the president put him down. "First of all, we must get together on what to do with the radical students! Do we make formal charges? What charges? Should we drop charges?"

"We can't tolerate the destruction of property!"

"How can we throw the book against so many students?"

"We throw the book at all of them in all our classes," someone jested.

"No time for frivolity," the president charged. "I agree we can't let destructive behavior pass, but we can't charge the whole student body."

"We can cancel scholarships for the leading participants, cancel draft deferments for protestng men. We can suspend some, expel others."

"Won't that keep up the walls?"

"Let's drop all formal charges."

"Let's charge the Snooks," the Dean of Liberal Arts suggested. "The boy's chairman of the Student Action Committee. The girl figured on the dome of the Academic Building."

"They come from a prominent family," President Godwin noted, looking down at his file. "The father was a chief executive in a Chicago meat packing company. Mother was a movie actress."

"Are you suggesting that the university might lose financial contributions if it disciplines these troublemakers?"

"I'm suggesting compassion. Records show the father died, and the mother's in the State Mental Hospital."

"They should be in the State Mental Hospital," the Dean of Liberal Arts raised his voice again.

"The radicals seem to be centered in your college," President Godwin talked back to the Dean of Liberal Arts. "Are you getting too liberal?"

"We have a radical head of philosophy," the Dean talked back. "He took the side of the revolutionaries, served a night in jail with them."

The president lifted both arms, told the Dean he was in charge of the College. He should do what he wanted.

....

"Back to the restored monarchy," Professor Morrissee said to his secretary when he showed up at his office.

"Good to have you out of exile," the Essential Bagley hailed him, getting up to fill his cup of coffee to the top. "Hated to think of you behind bars."

"Chained in the shadow world of Plato's Cave," he said with a forced smile at his lips. "Back in the real world."

"Are you sure this is the real world," his secretary smiled back.

"I'm sure you're a real good secretary," the professor told her, letting himself into the chair next to her desk. He intended to tell her about his change of status, but choked on a gulp of coffee, couldn't get the words out.

"I see you lost your glasses," Mrs. Bagley observed, "and found a black eye."

"Have been in the dark of Plato's cave, need to get fitted for Mind's Eye lenses."

"Hope you can see your way into department business," his secretary said, toying with the ballpoint pen dangling down front. "Your In-Basket's full, Out-Basket empty."

"I may be in the Out-Basket myself!" The professor swallowed his coffee and choked on his words.

"Do I need to break-in a new head?" The secretary tried to laugh.

"I'm breaking-in a new life," the professor let out, and he handed his card to the secretary, his new address scribbled on it.

"It was no secret," Mrs. Bagley confided. "Rufus King confided in us when you were indisposed! It came out in the Yell Leader. Some of the papers in your office got printed, some of your poems in the wastebasket."

"Published my verses of adversity!"

"Is love as mortal as the heart?"

"I should leave poetry to my assistant, Mr. Benedict."

"He still hasn't shown up!"

"Must be out of jail by now."

"And out of his marriage, too. Divorce must be worse than bereavement." She turned her face aside, showed the back of her head, and the gray bun. "Love lives after a loved-one's death, but surely dies after a divorce."

....

Divorce in mind, A.M. tried to put it out of mind in his private office, but couldn't get down to preparation for classes. He was relieved to be interrupted. Alma Benedict appeared at the door.

"Remember me, wife of your teaching assistant? Mrs. Bagley said I could see you."

"Of course," he said, seeing her as a picture of contrasts, white of dress, dark of hair, tears in eyes, smile on lips, and knowing his teaching assistant had made a break with her.

"I'm losing Hart!"

"He's the losing one."

"He's a different person!"

"We all change."

"You look different without glasses."

"You do see a changed man."

"When I tried to see you at home, your wife said you didn't live there anymore."

"I got suspended from home," he said, beginning to feel better about admitting it. "Seems we're both losers." He reached for his cigarettes, asked Alma if she'd object to a little smoke?

She nodded. "When a lovely flame dies, smoke gets in your eyes."

"That's the love ending song that brought me and my wife together," he said, lighting up, blowing smoke away from the young lady.

"Why does God let a lovely flame die?"

"Are you asking me to judge God?"

"Are you a God-fearing Christian?"

"Raised a Catholic," he said, sitting back, "religious still, but haven't kept up with the Church."

"My mother was Catholic," Alma brightened, glad to find something in common with the professor. "Mother gave me Hispanic hair and eyes, and her life. She died bringing me in the world." Alma dabbed her eyes again, said her mother didn't give her the Catholic religion.

Clearing her throat, she managed to tell him that her "Anglo" father remarried, gave her a Protestant mother, and a "fire and brimstone religion."

"That's good fire insurance against hell."

"My husband gave up his religious insurance. What makes a man put away his religion, and wife?"

"Things change, it seems."

"God only granted divorce for unfaithfulness!"

"Faithful to my wife," A.M. assured her.

"Faithful to my man and Church," seemed to echo out of Alma, and a word of reverence for the Church.

"Weren't your Protestant forefathers unfaithful to the Church? Didn't they get a divorce from the Church of Saint Peter?"

"The Church of Saint Peter went astray."

"Isn't that what every spouse says about the other, to justify divorce?"

....

Alma loved God more than me, Hart Benedict told himself as he lay in bed with the Maxy Snook, and Alma was beneath me, unable to get her mind up to mine! Unable to sleep, he tried to justify himself, began comparing his abandoned wife with the woman in bed with him. Maxy gave him her body, held back her mind and heart, told him she needed to live in her own "space." Alma gave him mind and heart, held back her body. She thought sex was only for making babies. In the dark of the bedroom, and his thoughts, he heard himself call out Alma's name.

"Don't want another woman in bed with me!" Maxy's voice vibrated next to him.. "You're the only woman I want in bed," he told her. "Want to marry you."

"Marriage is the Establishment way of enslaving women! Women are now liberated."

Hart felt the bed quiver. Maxy was sliding out of it, one part of her at a time, and he heard the weight of her body shake the opposite bed, the twin bed that held her brother. The bed across the way groaned as the brother made room. Hart felt the distance between her was greater than the distance between the beds. He'd been living with the Snooks since they bailed him out of jail, but he wasn't sure if he'd made it into her novel triangle of boyfriend and brother. He knew for sure that he didn't love the brother.

The sound of the phone shook him all the way awake. It rang once, twice, sounded off. After a moment the phone rang again. Two rings and a hangup. That was the signal! The former member of Maxy's love triangle was in town, registered at the College Inn as "Cliff Self." The signal was worked out in case the phone was bugged. The police were after Maxy's boyfriend for robbing a bank.

"Zany's in town," Maxy's cry burst out of the dark. The light snapped on and she appeared glowing white and shiny in Hart's eyes. She was feeling her way into dungarees. Her brother's hairy arms were pulling up pants, hitching them together.

Hart turned over in bed, buried his head full of jealousy in the pillow. Was Maxy still crazy about Zany? They broke up after high school when he took off to the University of Michigan to study physics. Maxy told him Zany blossomed into a "flower child," but grew wild, went from the Students for a Democratic Society to The Weathermen. He fell into the underground, helped rob a bank. Hart's thoughts were roughed out by the growl of Maxy's brother. Harry Snook was demanding that he get his "ass in gear.!"

"Worked butt off waiting tables. Need shut-eye."

"Council time! Need your savvy."

"Zany's gonna help us make bombs," Maxy said over her shoulder, zipping herself into a tight sweater.

....

Contained in her usual tailored tweeds and stiff collar, Mrs. Bagley looked up from her typewriter to see the professor burst out of his inner office.

"Another bombshell," A.M. gasped at her, waving an opened letter. "Campus Mail dropped a bomb!" His eyes were magnified in new glasses. "Another black eye," he was saying, handing the letter to his secretary. "Get a load of this!"

Mrs. Bagley put glasses to her eyes, read aloud. "I regret to inform you that you are removed immediately as head of the Department of Philosophy, and your tenure at this university has been revoked." She looked up in disbelief, went on reading. In accordance with Section 5-A of the Faculty Regulations, and with the recommendation of the Academic and Tenure Committee, your services will be terminated at the end of the semester. Should you wish to resign, I'll do everything in my power to recommend you and assist you in relocating. Should you want a hearing before a Committee of your peers, please meet in the Board Room on January 5, 1970. You may bring counsel. Please let me know your intentions in this matter within five days of receipt!

Mrs. Bagley handed back the letter, let her glasses slip off and dangle on the chain next to her ballpoint pen. "My eyes must be deceiving me," she said, looking away. "On what grounds can your tenure be taken away?"

"My police arrest is unprofessional."

"You got arrested in the line of duty, attending the needs of your students."

"Attending the needs of the wrong students, it appears, and our Dean mentioned my impending divorce as another mark of moral turpitude."

"Take a stand," Mrs. Bagley urged. "Isn't this a case of Academic Freedom?"

"A stand would hurt the university!" A.M. took off his new glasses and rubbed his eyes. "It would bring down the wrath of the AAUP, stir up publicity. My family problems would come out in the open, hurt the children."

"Our department will be hurt without you."

"With you around, the department will do well."

"What new head will I have to break in?"

"The Dean didn't ask for my recommendation, but I suspect it will be Rufus King, our new man. He won't be a threat to the Dean, not for awhile, and he's got a good head on his shoulders."

"Your wish is my command." Mrs. Bagley reached for the pen hanging next to her glasses.

The former head of department dictated a letter requesting a Hearing. Mrs. Bagley typed it up, handed it to him. Signing it, he told his secretary he'd been assigned an office down the hall, "that hole in the wall."

"Won't be room for all your books."

"Need to box them. Would you give me a hand?"

What to do with all your books?"

"I'll make a requisition order. How many boxes will we need?"

He led her into his inner office, waved a hand at the walls of bookcases, picked up a framed picture on his desk, turned it down. It was a family portrait. He was remembering when he was a part of the picture!

"A lot of book boxes," Mrs. Bagley said. "I'll put them on order."

....

Book in hand, Mrs. Bagley was assisting the professor pack them.

"What's Plato's Cave and Skinner's Box all about," she asked, dusting the book. "Don't remember typing it."

"You didn't," the professor set her mind at rest. "It was published before I came here."

"What's it all about?"

"I compared and contrasted Plato's Cave and Skinner's Box, and the opposing philosophies that went into them."

"I know about Plato's Cave, never got into Skinner's Box."

"Skinner's box is our material world, and we're stuck in it. We're not free. Our behavior's conditioned by the environment."

"Isn't our behavior conditioned in Plato's Cave?"

"We are free to use our reason to figure our way out."

"Sometimes my life seems to be trapped in a box."

"Maybe we all end up in a box," the professor sighed as he put away the book in hand.

"You're not in a box yet.

What are your plans?"

"I'll start looking for another position."

"Will you be looking for another wife?"

Her question took him by surprise. He hadn't thought of it, said "this old sailor's not looking for a second mate." He asked why she didn't remarry? She said she didn't want her son to have three fathers, two on earth. He thought well of it, feared his children would have three fathers. He asked how her son was doing?

"Has his own family," she said. We need to live our own lives. Children have their own lives, and go away."

....

"The last great war will be between the young and the old," Harry Snook predicted from the driver's seat, "not between the rich and the poor."

From the back seat, Hart Benedict contended that there would always be a younger generation! "War every generation?"

"Our generation will get it right," Maxy broke in, and her brother nodded as he wheeled the car into the motel parking lot. They checked in, got the room number of "Cliff Self."

When they knocked at his door, it opened to a beardless young man with open arms that sweptHarry and Maxy into the room.

Harry wanted to know what happened to Cliff's lion's mane. "Shaved off my lion identity, kept lion inside."

"You're still my old Zany," Maxy greeted him, slipping out of his grip, "but you know I got a new man," and she pointed to Hart, introduced him as "our grad student, Hart Benedict."

Zany tossed a look at the new man in Maxy's life, looked him up and down, looked away, told Maxy they were now a foursome.

Hart didn't like the thought of being in a love quadrangle, or being in the room with the Zany guy. He dropped down on the suitcase rack by the door. The former threesome sat together on the edge of the bed, the one they all loved, in the middle. Hart thought Harry was the one who loved himself the most.

"Everything's going our way," Zany announced, arms around the Snooks. "Just got back from the Mall in Washington. Hundred-fifty thousand people rallied round our Cause! Time to make our move here at Tnitarian!"

"Got our Counter-University up and going," Maxy bragged.

"Got courses going on hallucinogenic drugs, political action, gay and lesbian sexuality," Hart contributed, "and courses on Black and Gender Studies are on the drawing board."

"Can't wait on education," Zany put it all down.

Hart, stunned, asked how Zany could be against higher education?

Zany said it was too slow and relied too much on literacy.

"Are you against literacy?"

"Literacy's the weapon of the Establishment. People believe what they read, get led around by words. Printed words go a lot farther than the oral. Establishment's got the presses."

"We'll teach people to interpret words!"

"We'll control the meaning of words," Harry Snook joined in on Hart's side.

"We're past words. Time to use urban guerrillas, build a Liberation Army."

Benedict said they didn't have the manpower to take over the country, not yet.

Zany said the Weatherman underground had above-ground support, and after a pause, complained that he couldn't make another move without a drag. He reached into his pocket, pulled out a crumpled cigarette, lit up, said it was time to get tuned up together.

"One for four, four for one," Maxy puffed, "that's our Declaration of Interdependence."

"Trinitarian took away my deferment," Harry brought up with a blast of smoke in his turn.

"Draft Board gonna take away my independence," and he handed the cigarette to Hart.

"Lost wife and draft deferment, too," Hart complained, choking on a drag.

"Burn draft cards," Zany snorted. "Cut your hair, doff the leather jackets, come underground with me!"

"How we make a living underground?"

"We break new ground, break the banks, break the system with guns and bombs!"

"Can bombs build a better world?"

Zany shrugged, said the whole universe was created by a big bang, said it was the newest theory in Physics, with proof! "We burst out of a Primeval Atom, and a Big Bang."

"We all began with a seed and a big bang," Harry Snook quipped.

"I'm not into Physics, or biology," Hart talked back, "but what set off the Big Bang? Philosophy looks for a First Cause, or a prime mover."

"We don't need a father-God anymore," Zany sneered.

Maxy said she never had a father God figure. "My old man was always at the office."

"No father God in the sky for me," Hart agreed. "I've got the Atomic God, atoms in me!"

"What's the gospel according to St. Benedict?"

"We came from the atom, not Adam! We're in the image of our Creator, atoms."

"It's a big bang of a theory," Zany conceded.

"We're good and bad," Hart went on, "made of positive and negative charges."

"The atom's the creative force," Zany agreed, "and the destructive force."

"Got me a fear of the Atomic Bomb," Maxy said.

....
—

"Morality begins in fear, and ends in the will to do the right." Professor Morrissee was summing-up his lecture," but thought his words were left hanging in air. Seats of the lecture hall were mostly filled again, but the students seemed absent-minded. He knew their minds were focused on vacation. He heard the shuffling of feet and closing of books, and dismissed the class with wishes for happy holidays, and the promise of an overall review when they returned. As he watched the students rush out, he thought they were anxious to leave all his teaching behind.

Alone with himself, he gathered his thoughts and notes, headed for his cramped office. On the way he passed the Faculty Lounge, had been avoiding it since his fall from power, now wanted to pass a little time in its snug and tweedy atmosphere.

Opening the door, he looked at a transformed world. Trashed during the student uprising, the lounge was refurbished, except for the carpet that still bore some cigarette burns. Only a few members of the Liberal Arts were scattered here and there among the easy chairs. No close colleagues, and none gave him any notice. He felt like a ghost, invisible in his old haunts.

He passed a member of the Music Department, a cellist in the university symphony and string quartet. He didn't know her well but had made an effort to remembered her name, Clara Kreutzer, Clara for Robert Schumann's wife, and Kruetzer for one of Beethoven's sonatas for violin ad piano. He respected her as a longtime faculty member, and campus leader of the Women's Liberation Movement. She always dressed like a man, in a gray flannel pantsuit. A.M. waved at her as he passed, but she didn't look up from the folds of a newspaper. He seated himself in a nearby leather chair, put the musicologist out of mind and a cigarette to his lips, filled up with smoke, and thoughts of his children. They'd gone off for the holidays with grandparents in New York. He had nothing to look forward to, except the next cigarette.

In a filmy haze he looked up to see the musicologist overshadowing him. "Sorry to hear you're leaving us," she said through the smoke of his cigarette. "You'll be missed!" He stood up, waved at the adjacent chair, asked her to join him.

"No time," she said, "class coming up."

"You're a class lady!"

"A lady of classical music," she agreed, motioning for him to sit back down. "Hope you make it to our concert tonight, Beethoven's string quartet, the C-Sharp Minor."

"Beethoven's minor mood," he said, "fits my mood."

"Like Beethoven, you're always searching for the profound," she was saying as she walked off, waving a hand behind her back.

She left him thinking that music and morality were based on rules. Beethoven broke the musical rules of his time! Students were breaking moral rules, and rocking and rolling the old musical rules away.

"Care for a brew and a break from thought?"

A.M. was startled out of his thoughts, got a look at Rufus King, the new Head of Philosophy. A.M. nodded, saying, "coffee up to the top, black."

"Black like me," Rufus King grinned, heading for the coffee urn.

A.M. hadn't seen much of Rufus King, or anyone, since losing his chairmanship. He'd helped King get established as head of the department, but wanted to stay out of his way, out of everyone's way.

"Here's to you," Rufus King said, returning with a cup of coffee in each hand. "And here's to my new head," A.M. toasted as soon as he got cup in hand.

Rufus King thanked him, and asked what was in "my esteemed former head's head these days?"

"Furniture of the mind's getting rearranged."

"Any prospects?"

"Still looking."

"Your Hearings coming up. Hope you don't have to leave."

"Not much chance of beating the Dean. Tenure doesn't protect a professor who goes against the university."

"What made you take the side of the Hippie Flower Children and Yuppie sons of guns?"

"They were divorcing the university. I wanted to counsel them out of it."

"Your own divorce final?"

"Have to wait it out. House is up for sale, books and personal possessions in storage."

"Divorce must be hell!"

"It's an after death purgatory. Seems like I already died."

"Have you found out what threw your marriage off course?"

"Still lost at sea!"

"Heard about Cas Koczur's marriage going on the rocks?"

The cup rattled in A.M.'s saucer. He asked if the whole world was coming apart?

"Was it ever all together? Humans have always been in separate bodies, separate minds and separate perceptions."

"That's why we have different philosophies," A.M. agreed. "You're an Analyst, I'm the last of the Romantics, perhaps not romantic enough."

"Perhaps marriage, like philosophy, needs less romance," Rufus King said with a wink, "and more Analysis."

....

In analysis of his marriage failure, A.M. got back to his office, kept wondering if there was another man? He even wondered if there might be a woman! Had Lil changed sexual orientation? He put it out of mind at the sound of high heels, and the sight of Alma Benedict fluttering into a chair, brushing back a wing of dark hair. "My life's come to nothing!"

"What is nothing? Philosophers have been writing about nothing for years," he said in hopes of getting a smile from her.

Without a smile, Alma said Hart had left her for another woman, and there was nothing left of their marriage!

"Something can come out of nothing," the professor kept trying to settle her down, "if you believe a big bang brought the world out of nothing."

"The world came out of God's word!"

"I wish I had a word of hope for you, but haven't seen your Hart since we shared a cell in jail."

"Did you get a hopeful word from your wife?"

"No word. My date in court is still coming up!" He was thinking he'd be sentenced to solitary confinement for life.

"Courts make divorce easy nowadays," Alma sniffed through her handkerchief. "Church doesn't have a say, but my church got a Group Therapy session started for people going through the ordeal. I came here to invite you to join the group."

The shriek of a siren blew his thoughts away.

ATTENTION! PRESIDENT'S HOUSE BOMBED! CLASSES DISMISSED!

The professor heard Alma scream something about Hart being mad enough to throw a bomb. Leaping up, her chair unfolded under her and crashed to the floor. She took to the opened door and disappeared in the crowded hallway.

"Another chapter for my next book on student unrest," Cas Koczur gasped to A.M. when they collided in the hall.

On the run, A.M. asked his friend about the "unrest" in his marriage?

"Not for publication," Cas said, leaping ahead, jumping down the stairs, three steps at a time.

A.M. chased after him, and they both joined the procession of students and faculty going across campus, coming to a stop in front of the president's two story Colonial house, front door blown off, smoke pouring out. The grounds around the house were blanketed with students sitting, standing, or whooping it up.

"Natives are restless," Cas Koczur observed, his voice bellowing over the roar of the crowd.

"The big bad wolf is huffing and puffing," A.M. heard himself saying, "trying to blow the house down."

"Kids aren't playing Mother Goose anymore," Cas talked back," but sure are giving me goose bumps!" He called out to one of the passing students, asked who threw the bomb! The young man kept going, leaving behind muffled words.

A.M. called out the question to a co-ed flying by. She yelled back that his generation threw the "big one!"

"They blame us for the Doomsday Machine," Cas said of the atomic bomb. "They're the children of the bomb, first generation of the Atomic Age."

"Our fathers," A.M mentioned, "thought they were the Lost Generation."

"Our students think they'll be the Last Generation," Cas said, "and they will be if there's a big bang atomic war."

"And they'll be the Last Generation of Civilization if they abandon their studies!"

"This generation learned its lessons well," the sociologist kept the train of thought on track, "went to school with nuclear bomb drills, crouched under school desks, huddled in windowless hallways. They didn't know if there would bebe a tomorrow, made them think they had to live for the day, made them the Now Generation."

"No use studying for the future, if there won't be a future," A.M. said.

"Education is future oriented," Cas continued. "That's why underclass kids don't always do well in school, don't think they have much of a future. Hamburger in hand's worth more than three ways to spell the word two."

"Thought you came up from the lower class. You had to give up the pleasure of the moment to study for the future!"

"School was always easy for me. Figured I had a future when coming out of the war in one piece."

"Seems like you and Teresa are giving up on your future together!"

"Time to noodle it out, Man! She's a used-to-be!"

"You seem to be digging the hipster slang, but might be digging your professional grave. Tenure can be taken away for moral turpitude."

"Morals are changing, as you moralists should know. The pleasure principle's now in. Is pleasure immoral?"

"Is it good to get pleasure out of bombing somebody's house?"

"Somebody thought it was good."

"Fire's out, good or bad for some people," A.M. said, pointing to the president's house. Firemen were rolling-up hoses, calling for people to stand back, "go home!"

"Where's your home these days?" A.M. asked his colleague as they headed back to their offices.

"Got jungled-up with one of my graduate students. She's got a good pad, wants to make good grades under me."

"Aren't you too old for the Now Generation?"

"I'm not too old for the Sexual Revolution! The pill now makes sex free for every generation."

"Death of marriage might be the pill's side effect?"

"I've got a home to go to. How about you?"

....

Feeling homeless, A.M. made his way back to the College Inn, stopped off at its Coffee Counter for a drink and a snack. There were vacant booths but he took a stool at the lunch counter where students of the Counter- Culture held sway.

"Don't let me freak you out," A.M. said as soon as he sat down and the buzz at the counter fizzled out. He knew students accepted him for taking their side in the showdown with the police, but they were always suspicious of anyone over thirty. "I'm on your side of the counter," he called out. "Anybody know who threw the bomb?"

One of the young men said, "bombing's not our kind of hip-a politics. We make love, not war!"

"Man, it got to be somebody's power trip!"

"Could be the Weathermen from off campus."

"Weather, or not," one student punned, "the climate's changed round here."

"Let's blow!"

Students began spinning off the round stools. The professor was left at the counter, alone, got up and found the comfort of an empty booth, and the enjoyment of a newspaper left on the table.

An early edition, it carried no news of the bombing. A.M. paged through news of battles and body- counts in Vietnam.

The waitress took his order as he was reading about the court-martial of a murderous platoon leader in Vietnam, and the prospect of the "helter-skelter killers' trial." His day in divorce court was coming up and he thought the whole world was on trial, just as his order was put before him. As he sipped coffee he began thinking he had no future, no need to prepare for the future, like the underclass Cas Koczur was talking about. He turned the page, caught sight of the chamber music concert advertisement. He knew it would be cancelled. Clara Kreutzer came to mind and he carried thoughts of her to his room, and bed, pictured her with a cello between the legs, and wondered if the best things in life were between the legs, or between the ears?

....

As A.M. lay between the sheets, between sleep and wakefulness, he began wondering what life would have been like without Lil. He pictured the time he lay eyes on her. She was ahead of him in the buffet line at the wedding reception of his Brooklyn College colleague, Paul Vandermeer. She turned to him, wineglass in one hand, plate of chips and dips in the other, introduced herself as "Lilith." He introduced himself as "A.M.," and she asked if that meant he was a morning person.

He returned her a smile, told her his name was "Ayers Morrissee, too much of a mouthful." She asked him to call her, "Lil."

They took their drinks and dips to an empty corner by the window, shared the view of Central Park and the skyline of skyscrapers on the far side. The young woman told him she was a friend of the bride, "Starla," hardly knew the groom. She wondered who was holding the reception, thought they really lived the "high life," hoped the newlyweds would always live the high life.

A.M. said he knew the groom, a good man, about to make tenure at Brooklyn College.

He lay in thought of Paul for a moment. He hadn't kept in touch, but learned he'd lost his wife. Could Lil be seeing him on her frequent trips back to Brooklyn?

His memory returned him to Lil at the reception, and their talk as they parted the smoke between them, and learned about each other. The skyline view was dimming, turning into an outline on the horizon. Their talk turned into a game of guessing the occupations of the many strangers standing around in groups. Lil guessed one of the women was a "circus bareback rider." A.M. guessed one of the men was a spy for the Russians. They got around to guessing their own occupations. She guessed he was a professor. He said, "only a lecturer." He guessed she was a teacher or nurse. No. She was a "buyer" for a dress shop on the North Side. As they exchanged words, and smoke, a phonograph began playing Smoke Gets In Your Eyes.

"May Starla and Paul never get smoke in their eyes," Lil said, toasting the newlyweds with a glass in one hand, crushing out her cigarette with the other.

The reception was breaking up. Lil suggested exchanging phone numbers, and "crossing wires sometime." Phone calls were still wired in his memory, and the dinners and Broadway shows. They ordered the same dinners, liked the same shows, but not the same books or operas. She liked Science Fiction, he liked science and philosophy. A Met performance of Tristan und Isolde was too long for her, not long enough for him. When he asked her to marry him, she couldn't give him an answer, not right away, said she'd have to think about it! She took her time, and when she phoned to say "yes," he'd almost forgotten what she was agreeing to. When their bodies came together in marriage, he thought he'd finally become a whole person. Now he was half a person again, and without a home!

....

"I'm home," Hart Benedict called to Maxy when he opened the door, late at night, after waiting tables at the College Inn. He found Maxy out of mind and body, strung-up in the lotus position.

"It's Horizontal time," he said, trying to get her out of a meditation trance and into bed. "I'm in the Triangular," she mumbled, still sitting on crossed legs. At the sound of the doorbell she unfolded herself in a hurry. "Too late for visitors!"

They both knew no Council Meeting had been scheduled. A warrant was out for Harry to testify in a police inquiry about the bombing. The police might be on the other side of the door!

"I'll put them off," Maxy promised as she draped herself in a robe, got to the door, opened it a crack, stood back on bare heels. The shrouded figure huddled in the dark of the hall was her mother!

"It's the old hag, got herself outa bag!"

The woman was hunched-up in a mangy Persian Lamb coat, her face half-veiled in a scarf. "Bugged outa Bug House," she said with a laugh.

Maxy pulled her mother inside, closed out the dark. "Cops after you?"

"Gave pigs the slip."

"This is the first place pigs gonna sniff round for you."

"Harry gonna protect me!"

"Harry's hiding out in Canada!"

"Take me to Harry!"

"Sneak you up to him, but gotta hide you out for now."

"Gonna be hard to hide a star."

"I'll get you in a motel, registered under your old stage name, Kat LaKatz."

"Kat LaKatz is my name," the mother snorted as she shook off her scarf, arranged her blond- tinted hair that lay stringy around the furry coat collar.

"You were a star before I saw light of day, but you were Catherine Katz off stage, Catherine Snook when you married Daddy. Cops don't know your film name."

"Scenes with your daddy ended up on the cutting room floor."

Maxy knew her mother no longer could tell the difference between real life and movie reel life. "Think I found a new role for you," Maxy made up,"Trinitarian University is staging a play about Anne Frank, the girl who hid out from the Nazis. You can play the mother."

"Don't like hiding roles. Played one in old Germany." She lifted her chin for a pose.

"Not yet time for closeups," Maxy told her mother while helping her out of the wooly fur coat. "Fur's for animals," she said. "Isn't this the Persian Lamb Daddy gave you?"

"Bought it for me, so I'd give him Harry. He got you for nothing."

"Hope I'm worth more than nothing."

"Worth a lot to me," Hart interrupted, breaking into the scene with bow tie hanging loose at the collar of his waiter's shirt.

"This swishy character's my associate at the Free University," Maxy explained to her mother, and introduced him.

Hart bowed to the mother, told her he knew she was a movie star. He also knew she'd been confined in the state hospital and thought she was a political prisoner.

"She just got away from the Thought Police," Maxy told Hart, with a wink. "You know she was hidden in a hospital because courts couldn't jail her. Gotta find her a hiding place at the College Inn."

"Gonna hide myself in a stage character," the mother told Hart, "could use a leading man like you."

"We'll sign him up," Maxy said, "but need to get you backstage before Thought Police show up!" She waved off to get dressed and find "costumes" for her mother.

She and Hart soon got back to wind the mother up in her Persian Lamb coat, get her to the motel and registered under her stage name, "Kat LaKatz." The name raised the eyebrow of the desk clerk.

"I couldn't send her back to the Loony Bin," Maxy told Hart when they left the mother and got back to their apartment.

"Maybe we're all political prisoners in the loony-Bin world," Hart said, stripping off his tie and shirt.

"Mama's on and off the wall."

"A shadow in Plato's cave," the philosophy student cracked with a smile.

"I'm not into Plato, and his cave," Maxy talked back, pulling off her sweater. "I'm into Shakespear, and his stage."

"As you like it," Hart said as he slipped naked between sheets. "What's the story for getting your mother up to Canada?"

"Same way Harry and Zany got over. Get to border, sneak through the woods. Have to make Mama think she's playing a role. She really did sneak out of Nazi Germany. I'm half Jewish, you know."

"Half divine!"

Maxy asked which half, "top or bottom?"

She let both halves of herself get under the covers before Hart could make his choice, let herself get wrapped in Hart's arms and legs, but her mind wasn't thinking of him. It was full of her mother, scenes of her mother flipping through movie magazines, flipping out of mind, forgetting her roles as wife and mother. There were memories of her making radical speeches in Jackson Park, and running naked protests on the Gold Coast. In one scene of memory, cops brought her home. She'd been found wrapped under newspapers in the railroad station. She'd hocked the family silver to buy a ticket, and a life, in Hollywood. Memory blurred at thought of her mother's attempted suicide. It got her put down in the state hospital.

"You need to put the old woman out of mind," Hart said, trying to get in better touch with Maxy's thoughts, and body.

Maxy said she couldn't get the mother out of mind, "the mother who's out of mind."

....

Almost out of mind with worry, A.M. gave up grading papers in his motel room, and took himself to the Coffee Counter. He found relief in coffee and ham sandwich, but no relief in the pages of his newspaper full of war and hate.

A shrilling voice, aimed his way, shook him out of the war in Vietnam. He looked over the headlines to see an angry woman in a wooly fur coat. She was screaming at him, getting a rise out of customers at the fountain counter.

He thought he heard her accusing him of spying.

"Only reading my paper," A.M. protested, embarrassed by the grins of students at the counter.

"You're a policeman in disguise."

"I'm no policeman," he insisted, but remembered his students of the counter-culture charged him with policing their thought, using morality as an invisible policeman!

"You been sneaking looks round your paper, spying on me," the woman kept bombarding his ears. "Can't get me. I be in free country."

Her screaming voice carried a German accent, took the professor back to his prewar year of study in Berlin, reminded him of the hysterical screams at Nazis rallies. He tried to calm her, said she was worth looking at.

"I sure am worth looking at," she said in a lowered voice. "I was a rising cinema star in Germany before the war."

"I was a graduate student in Germany, before the war!"

The woman in the fuzzy fur coat put on a smile. He saw a look of refinement behind the mask of makeup, didn't think she wasn't the kind of woman who rented rooms in the motel by the hour.

"Take another look," she said, "see if you might remember me on screen." She posed, showing her profile. "See me in German pictures?"

"Movie houses were school houses for learning conversational German," he said, "but don't think I could recognize you, after all these years."

"Remember Kitty Kat LaKatz on screen credits?"

The professor shook his head at the sound of the name, crazy as the woman who sounded it out. He tried to think of a way to get himself out of the picture.

"Let me help you remember me," the woman said, saluting him with a cup of coffee in hand. She ducked into his booth, balancing herself and coffee cup, maneuvering into position across the table from him.

Not wanting to make a scene, A.M. introduced himself as a professor at the university, former student of philosophy at the University of Berlin, "back in the last year of peace."

She said it was no year of peace for her, told him it was the time Hitler took her out of pictures, and she had to take herself out of the country.

The professor told her he had a hard time getting out of Germany, and his thoughts stretched back to the time the American Embassy warned to get out of Germany. He had a hard time getting a train, finally got standing room in a railroad car stocked with young men called-up for military service. He had to change trains at the border of Holland, lost a suitcase in the transfer, had to rot in Rotterdam for weeks before he could book passage on a neutral ship.

The woman across from him broke into his reveries, told him she had a really hard time getting out of Germany, and the Nazis were st ill after her, just threw a bomb!

He knew the woman in the gray wooly fur coat was fuzzy in the mind, and kept wondering how he could get away without making a scene. When she fitted a cigarette to her lips, he flicked his lighter her way, said American students were only making a scene, like the Hitler Youth, but weren't burning books, only shutting them.

She told him she could put him on the stage. He said he was under contract to another woman, and got away. He was telling the truth, scheduled to take Mrs. Bagley out to dinner.

....

"I believe I'm on the agenda for dinner," Mrs. Bagley said to A.M. when he appeared at her door. She saw him in a black topcoat, hat in hand, red hair parted in the middle with that streak of gray.

"You're the whole agenda," he said, seeing his secretary looking so different. No tight suit with a ballpoint pen hanging down. She was shaped in a loose gown with a string of pearls hanging down. Even her gray hair was unbound from its usual bun.

"Is this the real Mrs. Bagley?"

"I thought philosophers knew what is really real?" They both forced laughs. They both were uneasy.

"This is not a real date," the professor pointed out. He didn't know how to play the dating game, had forgotten the rules, and suspected there were no rules anymore. "Dates are for kids," he said.

"I don't care a fig about a date," Mrs. Bagley said with her usual smile. "This old lady's happy to go out for a change." She handed him her wrap, let him fold her into it. He was already thinking about bringing her home. Would she expect a kiss? Was he supposed to jump into bed with her? He wasn't ready for getting involved.

"You look like a different person," he said, opening the door and following her out. "I'm one person at work, another person at home, two people in two worlds."

"Two in one," A.M. said. They both laughed as they walked to his car in the driveway.

"A '69 Ford," Mrs. Bagley observed as the professor helped her in. "You're really up to date."

"It's rented," he said, "can take us in style to the College Inn for dinner."

"It's the best place in town for dining, very expensive," she said, reminding him that she signed all the vouchers when he entertained professorial prospects there.

"Did you think I'd treat you to a box dinner for boxing my books?"

She offered no response, pulled the coat collar up. He kept his eyes on the road, hoped she'd think he was repaying her, not dating her. Snowflakes were dancing in and out of the headlights, reminding him of the times Lil wanted to go dancing, and he said it was too snowy to go out.

Mrs. Bagley took his arm as they stepped out of the car, let go when they were greeted by a uniformed doorman. They checked their coats and walked down the hall to the dinning room. The headwaiter escorted them through a maze of tables to the far side, next to the fireplace. As he helped his secretary into a chair, he hoped he wasn't seen by anyone who knew him.

As they sat down and unfolded napkins, A.M. looked up to recognize the waiter as his teaching assistant, Hart Benedict! The young man had shaved off the beard, cut back the long flaxen hair, and was standing stately in dark suit and bow tie. He looked like a member of the Establishment!

"I'm your server," he said stiffly, "now serving stomachs instead of minds."

"You always served well," A.M. said, standing back up to shake his hand. "You know our secretary, Mrs. Bagley, who also serves well."

"Good to see you, Mr. Benedict," the secretary spoke up.

The waiter nodded, turned to the professor, said he hadn't seen him since they were chained- up in "Plato's Cave."

"It's good to be back in the real world," his professor smiled back, sitting down again. "I expect you've been busy freeing minds in your Free University."

"Free University is underway, set up in a storefront for now."

"The first universities were in makeshift settings, free to move around," the professor said, as if in lecture.

"Student Guilds, back then, hired the professors to teach them what they wanted," the philosophy student lectured in return.

"What do students want to learn these days?"

"Courses that expand consciousness!"

"Thought protestors used drugs to expand consciousness?"

"Let me take your orders, expand your stomachs!"

"I'd like to get you back to the main course," the professor kept talking, "The Existential Contributions to Progressive Education."

"It's not on the menu. Can I interest you in drinks?"

"I'll have a white wine, any kind you recommend," Mrs. Bagley spoke right up. The professor said he'd take a martini, "gin with olive."

"A white wine, any kind, for the lady," the waiter noted, "and a gin martini with an olive for the gentleman. Your waiter used to serve up history to high school students. You might like to know the grape and the olive symbolized body and mind in Classical Greece. The grape stood for Dionysus, god of revelry, and the olive represented Apollo, god of wisdom."

"Descartes separated the grapes from the olives," A.M. added.

Mrs. Bagley said, in the curve of a smile, "I thought Apollo was the space project that just landed men on the moon?"

"The Apollo olive in a dry martini will fly the professor to the moon," the waiter said with a smile of his own. "I'll be back with the gods of grape and olive."

"Your teaching assistant made a good lecture out of the aperitif," Mrs. Bagley said when Hart Benedict was gone. "I wonder what he'll make out of the main course?"

"He's made a mess out of his life, turned from Apollo to Dionysus!"

"How's your mess?"

Before the professor could gather his thoughts, the waiter returned with the drinks, asked if they were ready to order?

"What do you recommend?"

"The Leg of Lamb is choice meat."

"It's my choice," the professor said, raising a martini glass to the waiter. "And mine," Mrs. Bagley said with a toast of her own.

The waiter turned on heel, left an empty space, and an embarrassing silence between the professor and his secretary. They sat at opposite sides of the table, in separate thoughts, unable to get a conversation going. The clatter and chatter of dishes and diners filled the space between them, until a piano struck a chord that hit the professor with a familiar melody.

"Smoke Gets In Your Eyes," the professor said, identifying the melody that was drifting through the air. "It was our song, Lilith and mine." He lit his cigarette, let memory circle round his head with the smoke, and the swing of music. The melody carried him back to the wedding reception where he met Lil. Memory showed him in their two-room Flatbush apartment. He was beginning to get published and she was getting pregnant. He remembered holding his first born, and second born, holding the meaning of life in his arms. Smoke kept getting in his eyes, with thoughts of his children.

"How are the children?" Grace Bagley asked.

"I don't get to see them very much," A.M. managed to say, taking the cigarette out of mouth to make room for words. "They have their own, separate lives." He took a sip of his drink and blamed his watery eyes on the gin.

"What do you do with your life?"

"No research. Try to keep up with my teaching, stay in my room at night, and all day on weekends, hoping to get a call from the children. I phone from time to time, but Lil puts me on hold. Most of the time the children aren't there."

"Visit them?"

"Help with their homework, but visits are uncomfortable with Lil avoiding me. I can't get the children to talk much. They only want my help to find answers to their school assignments."

"Do they visit you?"

"Not much for them to do at a motel. They'd love to come to the swimming pool, next summer. In the meantime I get to take them to the Student Center for video games, and ping-pong. Not many movies appropriate for children! I take them to Sunday School. Their mother doesn't go to church anymore."

"How's she doing?"

"Children are instructed not to tell me anything."

"You live in separate worlds!"

"My mind's still in both worlds."

....

"We live between two worlds," Maxy said as she looked up to Hart from Matthew Arnold's Collected Works, "One dead and the other powerless to be born. What's he's getting at?"

Hart put down the book he was reading, said the Father of Modern Philosophy thought we lived in two worlds, one Transcendent.

"Come back down to earth!"

"I don't know what Matthew Arnold meant. When I wrote poetry I didn't always know what I meant."

"I think," Maxy speculated, "Matthew Arnold, way back in the beginning of the Industrial Revolution, was bemoaning loss of Medieval community, and unity of faith! The world was no longer a village, and industrialization would never let it become one again. I think our Communes will bring back the world of community!"

Hart put lay aside his book, said he was living between two marriages, one dead and the other powerless to be born.

"You know marriage's not for me!"

"Isn't marriage like some kind of Commune?"

....

Communing with Alma Benedict in group therapy began to seem like a good idea as A.M. felt more and more alone, more and more isolated. His children had been taken away to share Christmas with grandparents in Brooklyn, might never return. Students were leaving for the holidays in homes all over the country, but would return for finals, and his final days at the university.

At loose ends, he joined the therapy group which met at the Wesley Foundation within walking distance of the College Inn. He was surprised to see Cas Koczur's wife, Teresa, and Clara White Kreutzer, the cellist, in session with Alma, all sitting in armchairs around the leader, Dr. Adams. He was wearing a suit, no tie, collar opened to a few strands of chest hair. He had a thick neck and an enormous Adams Apple. It was going up and down as he welcomed A.M. to the group. "I understand you need no introduction," he said. "The other members call you A.M.! May I?"

"I AM what I AM."

"I am what I am, too, glad to be at your service."

"Now that there are four of us," the musicologist brought up, "we're a Quartet." A.M. noticed her legs. She was wearing a dress instead of the usual pants.

"A Quintet," the leader corrected the musicologist. "I'm one of you."

"Quartet, Quintet, there's only dissonance in divorce," Clara Kreutzer brought up. "We all sing the blues."

Dr. Adams said he hoped to bring happy music back to them all, asked "A.M." to "strike the first note, get the session off with something of himself."

A.M. said divorce is shameful and embarrassing, and he only wished to erase himself, like a blackboard.

"You should erase you sense of guilt. Chalk up divorce as a learning experience."

"Divorce is a good experience," Clara Kreutzer brought up. "Happy marriages don't end in divorce."

"Marriage was happy for me," A.M. let his private lifeout, "until the wife started turning me away."

"Divorce is sin," Alma Benedict said. "Marriage is sacred!"

"Reminds me of a dream I had last night," A.M. felt free to reveal. "Dreamed I was at the wedding of God and Mother Nature!"

"What do you make of them apples?"

"What apples?"

"Just one of my expressions," Dr. Adams explained, with his Adams Apple going up and down at every word. "Apples came off the tree of knowledge, and we're trying to get at knowledge."

A.M. shook his head, said he wouldn't find knowledge in dreams!

"There may be more in dreams than are dreamed of in your philosophy! How did you picture God in your dream?"

"As a childhood picture in a book."

"As a child, did you think God was married?"

"No. There was only one God."

"God isn't married," Alma Benedict intervened.

Clara Kreutzer challenged her, said God had a son, should have married the mother, made Christianity legitimate!"

After getting looks of surprise and scorn, she said she was joking.

Dr. Adams said Freud thought humor was a way of releasing forbidden impulses.

"Plato thought humor was a form of mockery," the philosopher contributed, "the way for an inferior to put down a superior."

"That's why we should never make jokes about God," Alma Benedict said.

"God made a lot of jokes on us," Clara Kreutzer challenged again, "if marriages are made in heaven."

The leader asked the musicologist if she believed in God.

"Not sure God believes in me," the musicologist sighed, crossing her legs with a swish of nylon. "How could She keep track of me and everyone else?"

A.M. thought Clara had shapely legs, thought God was neither male or female. Dr. Adams asked the group to get back to interpreting the professor's dream.

"Mother Nature's a joke," Clara Kreutzer started it off. "Can't imagine a woman giving birth to a planet!"

"Nobody believes in Mother Nature," Alma Benedict rushed to inform, "and nobody believes God is married."

Dr. Adams asked her if it wasn't written that God married Israel? "And Israel was unfaithful," Clara Kreutzer spoke up, "like my ex."

"Want to tell us about your ex?" Dr. Adams asked, "get him off your chest?"

"Already got him off my chest. Let's get back to A.M.'s dream. I'd like to know who was the minister?"

"Good question. Who could minister to God?"

A.M. agreed that God was above all, but after collecting his thoughts, said he couldn't remember the minister in his dream."

"Look within," Dr. Adams requested. "That's what your Socrates and my Freud asked us to do."

"My Socrates thought the soul was eternal, knew everything, but forgot at birth. Education was remembering, a look within."

"My Freud thought everything came from outside, and the subconscious was hiding troubling things, needed to be probed."

"Isn't the subconscious beyond consciousness, by definition?"

"Methinks ye thinks too much. We don't live by thought alone."

"Thinking's my job. I think, therefore I A.M."

"I think, therefore, I am sure you're a Cartesian, and Descartes separated mind and body. Perhaps God was Mind in your dream, and Mother Nature was body! Are you thinking Mind and Body should not be separated?"

A.M. nodded, said he was getting to be against all kinds of separation.

Dr. Adams suggested that he was the Mind in his marriage and his wife was the Body, and A.M. looked within and nodded. The leader suggested they move on from the dream of God's marriage to the nature of marriage itself.

"Marriage is holy," Alma Benedict spoke right up.

"It's the civilized way for having children," Teresa Koczur made her point.

"It's a game, like Chess," Clara Kreutzer affirmed, crossing and uncrossing both legs. "Men make the moves. It's always checkmate for women."

"Marriage should be more like the game of bridge," Dr. Adams suggested, "and we need to learn the rules for being a good partner."

"Marriage isn't a partnership," Alma Benedict interrupted. "Marriage makes a man and woman one body, but man is the head."

Clara Kreutzer scoffed, held that men and women should be equal, at least get equal pay for equal work.

Dr. Adams agreed with the musicologist, but asked the group if the equality of the sexes was a problem for the stability of marriage?

"Equality makes marriage more harmonious," the musicologist proposed.

"Marriage seems to be out of tune today," the leader offered. "Roles are changing and men and women don't know what to expect of each other."

"In the old days," Teresa opened up, "everyone knew the wife was to stay home and care for house and kids, but I had to keep my job, put my husband through college. Now he says I'm not educated, says I bore him. Hell, I bore him two sons!"

"Men only think of themselves," the musicologist muttered.

"I always put my wife's interests before my own," A.M. countered. "I wonder if Lil wanted the traditional Lord and Master for a husband?" He turned to his former neighbor, asked Teresa if Lil ever complained to her about him?

"Lilith only told me you weren't a handyman, like men were supposed to be, said you didn't know which way to turn a screwdriver, but never said you didn't turn her on!"

"Rather have a drippy faucet than a drippy husband," Clara Kreutzer piped up.

"If your marriages can't be repaired," the leader asked the group, "would any of you like to be re-paired, married again?"

"It's the solo life for me," the musicologist shot back, crossing her legs with a swish. "Won't get strung-up with another man. Men and women should be separate as strings on a cello, but still make music together."

Teresa Koczur said she was too old to get a man.

Alma Benedict said she didn't believe in remarriage, and God didn't either.

While the women were talking, A.M was looking within, imagining what life would be like with another wife. Alma Benedict was desirable, but too young. The Essential Bagley was of the right age but less desirable. He would always think of Teresa as another man's wife. The musicologist's legs, crossing and uncrossing, made music for him, but she was married to her career. He didn't think he could ever remarry. All at once, he realized he wasn't listening, everyone looking at him as if waiting for a response. He remembered Lil accusing him of not always paying attention to her, complaining that he was always thinking of something.

Dr. Adams repeated his question, asked the professor what philosophers had to say about marriage. A.M. said Socrates didn't like it, got out of the house to get away from his wife. "Not many philosophers had wives, or opinions on marriage," he concluded, "but the philosophy of love, that's a different matter."

"Whatever love is," the leader summed-up, "you all seem to be out of it, and we're out of time. Next session we'll consider the love life, and the disconnected life."

....

Cut off from their world, Harry Snook and Zany Self were hiding out in a Montreal apartment. They'd sneaked across the Canadian border. American draft-dodgers were accepted in Canada, but not those with warrants for arrest.

"Underground's got us buried alive," Harry Snook complained as he paced from wall to wall in their square little living room.

"Soon be getting back to life with new identities," Zany promised from the sofa where he was stretched-out in briefs and undershirt. "Weathermen be getting us forged papers."

"Can't shave off our old selves," Harry complained as he stopped pacing to look out the bay window. The street below carried invisible lives in moving cars. The apartment windows on the other side of the street were curtained. Apartments on both sides of the street, he'd learned, had been converted out of warehouses. He thought they were still warehouses, storing humans! He started pacing again, thinking about changing who he was.

"Do yourself a favor," Zany called up to him, "drop a little acid, take a trip."

"Sick of trips, going nowhere!" As he walked, Harry traveled back in memory. His mother was always changing identities in movie roles, and in real life, finally didn't know who she was. "I want to be myself," he told Zany on his next trip around the room. "Her doctor said changing identities gave Mama something called anomie, a French word for no name! She lost all identity, couldn't cope, had to be put away."

"Pig Establishment wanted her out of the way, wants outsiders out of the way."

"Getting tired of being an outsider," Harry complained as he paced. "Mama was an outsider, a Jewish outsider in Nazis Germany, a German outsider in America. Married to a Christian

243

she was an outsider to Christians, and Jews. Divorced, she was an outsider in a world of couples!"

"Yap, yap, yap," Zany yawned, sitting up, scratching armpits, "rap, rap, rap. You're running off at the mouth."

Harry turned on heel and paced off, carrying thought about his mother. He'd learned from his sister that their mother escaped from the hospital, had been recaptured. He recalled the times he'd visited her hospital ward, pictured her amid sterile linens and sterile faces, had thought it must be hell to be half-sane in an insane world! He turned back to his friend, asked how they ever escaped from the Establishment. "My old man was Mister Establishment," he said, "a big cheese in the meat industry."

"You and me and Maxy came out of the Establishment," Zany agreed, rolling off the sofa, standing up on bare feet, wiggling toes, "got born at the top, had to get to the bottom to see the light."

"We're at the bottom, all right," Harry groaned, dropping into the cushioned space Zany had vacated, sinking into the warmth he'd left behind.

"We'll be on top, one day," Zany predicted as he took up the pace. "You getting cold feet, figure on skipping out of the Movement?"

"Been considering a Commune."

"Get planted with all the flower children?"

"Get down to earth, get connected."

"We'll make the whole country a commune." Zany predicted. "Our time will come."

"Time for mail," Harry noted, checking his watch. "Time for the good word and good greenbacks from Maxy."

Zany stopped pacing, wrapped himself in a robe, let himself out. When he reappeared, waving an opened letter in one hand and cash in the other, he said the Free University was "falling by degrees, college degrees." He read from Maxy's letter. "Students have a fix on the opiate of college degrees, aren't going for the anti-university." Zany handed the letter to Harry with word "Maxy's having second thoughts about her new man."

"If he's a fallen man we'll be a threesome again."

....

"Heard you're a fallen man," A.M. said as he opened the hospital door to see Cas Koczur at rest in a bed cranked-up to the sitting position. Bandages were wrapped round the top of his head like a turban, his face masked with a stubble of red and gray whiskers. Red pencil in hand, Cas sat slumped over a pile of papers in lap, but a smile deepening the cracks in both cheeks at sight of his colleague.

"The forbidden fruit caused me to have a great fall," he said. "Thought I could fly."

"You joined the drug culture?"

"Researching the drug culture. Drugs are the cake of custom for the hippies."

"I see your cover's the bandage head."

"Undercover sociologist, I'm studying the hospital class system."

"I assume you found doctors a class above nurses, and nurses above patients?"

"Only working on the culture of patients."

"Aren't you isolated from other patients? You don't even have a roommate."

"Some of us ambulatory patients get together for a meal or two, down the hall, in the Serving Room." Cas put the red pencil behind his ear, set the papers aside, put himself in the lecture mode.

"Some of us are higher than others on the mortality list. Pajama and robe patients stand above the crutch and wheelchair patients, way above the bed patients. Patients also classify themselves by the food they eat, solid diets rank higher than liquid. Some of us are gruel people, some salad people. Meat and potato people, upper class."

"I suppose patients don't get equal treatment!"

"That's for sure."

"While you've been here in research," A.M. said, sitting down next to the patient's bed, "I've been in therapy with your wife, and other damsels in distress. Teresa's broken up about your breakup."

"Broken-up as much as me?"

"She's a wreck, but not in bandages!"

"How's your wreck of a marriage?"

"My bandages don't show either."

"You need a nurse or woman to bed you down."

"Are you still bedded down with a Now Generation girl?"

"Now and then," Cas admitted. "Hot and cold! Teresa tells me you're now interested in a younger woman."

"So, you've been talking to Teresa."

"She brought me those flowers, told me about you and told me off!"

"Maybe your marriage is off and on again?"

"Maybe. What about your marriage?"

"It's almost off the charts, but I do have a younger woman in my sights."

"See her in bed?"

....

A.M. was in bed with Alma!

One leg struck sparks against her leg, shocked him into full wakefulness. Coming out of a dream, he realized his own legs were touching. He was under the covers, alone, between dreams and remembrances of the night before. He'd taken Alma home after a therapy session, remembered an awkward moment when she was searching her purse for the house key. He wondered if she'd let him in, wondered what she was thinking? What did a woman of the younger generation expect of a man on the first date? Would she expect a kiss? Would his kiss miss? It finally came to him that he left her at the door.

....

Leaning against her front door, Alma Benedict was so tired from a day of substitute teaching first graders that she could hardly fit the key in the keyhole. She managed to get the door opened, just as her neighbor's door flew open and Cheryl came out to prepare Alma of a surprise! The surprise was her Hart. Hat in hand, he came out of Cheryl's apartment without the look of his previous self. Beard and long hair were gone.

"Let you two have a go at each other," Cheryl said, and closed herself out of the scene. A breeze was blowing Alma cold.

Hart greeted her with a smile, asked if "the man of all time" could have a little time with her?

"It's about time! You look naked without your beard!"

"Feel naked, like a sinful Adam," he said."

"Have you found your Existential Self?"

"Found it can't be found, not until it's complete, all lived out."

"You left me and Little Hart incomplete."

"How's our baby son?"

"Gone with Mom and Dad. He doesn't think his Daddy loves him anymore."

"He thinks as a child. Can I come in, speak to you as a man?"

Alma leaned against the open door, let him pass by, closed out the cold. She collapsed on the couch, waved Hart into the chair across from her, kicked off shoes, rubbed feet, asked how a father could take off from his own child?

"Fathers have to grow up, too."

"Apart from wife and child?"

"We lived like robots, programed by the Establishment."

"We were programmed to the Good Lord.."

"I thought God abandoned the world, disappeared in that mushroom atomic cloud!"

"You abandoned God, and love!"

"Socrates believed love could only exist between equals, and men and women aren't equal, not yet."

"If love is only between equals, how could there be love between us and God?"

"Didn't God come down to our level, on earth?"

....

Feeling let down, A.M. struggled to keep up with his remaining work at the university. Group therapy helped him find peace in himself. Writing letters of inquiry to universities advertising openings in philosophy helped him find hope for the future. Phone calls to the children kept him wired-up to them. Phone calls to old friends at Brooklyn College got him word that his former colleague was dating again, but no former colleague let him know who. It would be ironic, he thought, if the man whose marriage brought him and Lil together ended up with her. He still wondered why Lil put him down.

The only lift he got in the lowlife was a new position. A letter from Texas A&M informed that the all-male college of agriculture and mechanics was seeking university status, becoming co- ed, developing a College of Liberal Arts, needed a man of his reputation to lead the way. Chairmanship of the new philosophy department was offered to him! Without hesitation, he took himself to the departmental office, asked Mrs. Bagley for "a type-up job," his letter of acceptance. Right away, she rolled a sheet of letterhead stationery in her electric typewriter, lined it up, asked what the A and M of Texas A&M stood for?

"Agriculture and Mechanics," A.M. informed her, "a Land Grant college very strong in the productive arts, building-up the liberal arts."

"I think A.M. and Texas A and M should make a good fit."

"Need to fit somewhere," A.M. said with a smile, wishing he could take the Essential Bagley with him, wondering if he could make arrangements for her at Texas A&M, and wondering if she'd accept. He didn't dare think of her as the Essential Morrissee.

"It's a long way from the children," he said when the letter of acceptance was finished. "Not so far in flying time,'" Mrs. Bagley reported. "My son and grandchildren live in Oklahoma, next to Texas, only three and a half hours away."

....

Hours later, A.M. was at work in his hole-in-the-wall office when a pain hammered him in the back. The pain turned into waves of highs and lows. He clinched his fists each time the pain reached a high, let go when the pain settled down. It was like riding out a storm in the rise and fall of a ship at sea! After a time of hanging on to himself, he managed to stagger down the hall get to the Essential Bagley!

"Feel like I've been torpedoed," he gasped, unable to straighten up. Mrs. Bagley called Rufus King out of the inner office. They both walked A.M. to the elevator and down to the parking lot, drove him off to the hospital emergency ward. Rufus King had to get back to the office, assigned Mrs. Bagley to take over, said he send a car for her.

She helped her professor check in, talked with a doctor, waited until the professor was put out of pain with a shot of morphine, wheel-chaired away.

"Doctors think you have a kidney stone," Mrs. Bagley told him when she was allowed to visit him in his room. "Maybe it's only the pit of a Martni olive?"

"Feel like I'm floating in air, rising up to Kant's transcendental world."

"It's the morphine," Mrs. Bagley tried to make him smile. "You're in the arms of Morpheus, god of sleep."

When A.M. looked up again, Mrs. Bagley was gone. A nurse was in her place, told him he'd passed a kidney stone, rattled his bedpan to prove it. He was so relieved of pain he joked about passing all his students!

Waiting for discharge, he got a visit from Cas Koczur. On crutches, Cas pointed one at him, sang out "my data done told me, when I was in research, you'll be out of my data base pretty soon.'"

They laughed and talked together. Another time, A.M. got the visit of an angel. Her wings were folded tightly in the golden knit of a sweater, and a golden halo seemed to be shining over the black shine of hair. The angel came into focus as Alma Benedict. She was hovering at his bedside, asking if he were out of pain. He said he was just out of it, asked if she thought pain was God's punishment for sin? She said sin caused pain, and pain told a body to stop doing what it was doing. She mentioned to him he was talking to God all the time she was waiting for him to wake up.

"What was I talking about?"

"Asking God to take care of your children."

"Always on my mind."

"We miss your mind in therapy."

"Our group helped me get through the ABC's of divorce, but not the XwhyZ's."

"Why worry about why?"

"Philosophers and scientists always ask why! It's their job."

"If you knew why Lilith left you, would it bring her back?"

"It might help me become a better person!"

"You are a good person. I'll let you go back to sleep."

....

"Had another dream," A.M. brought up at his therapy group as soon as he got back. "Dreamed I was in the Navy again, at my battle station. My ship took a hit! When the smoke cleared, my body had been blown away. Only the head of me was left. A disembodied head, I could think, couldn't get around."

"What do you make of them apples?"

Alma Benedict answered for A.M., said his wife was the body he lost. Teresa Koczur thought A.M. only lived in the head.

Dr. Adams suggested that they look at the ship in the professor's dream. "It wasn't A.M.'s fault the ship got blown out of the water. The dream might be telling him the divorce was not his fault! Another man torpedoed his marriage!"

"Another man was always in my mind," A.M. was quick to respond, "but he hasn't shown up." Paul Vandermeer came up, and out of mind.

"A wife doesn't abandon ship," Dr. Adams kept up, "unless she's got another ship on the horizon."

"Not easy for a woman on her own," Alma Benedict agreed. "We live in a world made for doubles."

"A divorced woman is like an odd sock in a world of matched pairs," Teresa Koczur contributed.

"It's still a man's world," Clara Kreutzer complained.

"Half a man's world," A.M. protested. "Half of all I own goes to the wife, and all my treasure, the children!"

III

The Gate Between

A.M. refused to believe the gate between himself and family was closed forever. Gates close, and open. He had visitation rights to his children. The gate was ajar. Protesting students were back in class, might open up their minds again.

One night, he asked the women in his therapy group about the possibility of opening the gates to their marriages. Alma Benedict said it takes two to open the gate, and Teresa Koczur added that opening the gate wouldn't make things the same. The musicologist said the gate to her marriage was closed and locked for good.

"Didn't the man grow on you, after years of marriage?"

"Only lived off me," the musicologist snapped back. "Blamed business failures on the trauma of the Korean Conflict, made himself a prisoner of that war all these years!"

"There are hidden casualties of war that never get cured."

"He wounded me! Would you believe he had a wife and kid, and no divorce when he married me?"

Her words, charged with feeling, struck shock in all members of the group. Handkerchiefs went out to her, but she pushed them away, said she needed to let a good cry come out!

"How in hell did you find out he was a bigamist?"

"His kid showed up, a grown man, said he was looking for his Dad, had been told his father was killed in Korea, got told differently when his mother was on her deathbed!"

"What was the dad's story?"

"Claimed his wife disappeared with the kid, left him with a note, told him not to look for her. She was going into hiding, starting a new life, couldn't live with him or with the shame of divorce."

"A man can't get a divorce if he doesn't have a wife to sign papers," Dr. Adams tried to speak up for the husband.

"If the wife's dying," Alma Beneict broke in, "your husband won't be a bigamist anymore. You could open the gate to him."

"There's no music in him, no music in our marriage. He has a son now. That should do him."

"A marriage shouldn't go up in smoke," Alma Benedict cried out, thinking of the song that brought the professor and wife together. "Smoke gets in your eyes," A.M. said.

....

A.M. smoked away the holiday season. The campus was blanketed with snow, asleep. Group therapy helped hold him together during the "Holiday Break." The campus awoke with the New Year, and the dawn of the Nineteen-Seventies. Faculty, staff, and students returned for the end of the Fall Semester, the beginning of a new decade.

A.M. got word that Texas A&M would hire his secretary, and Mrs. Bagley accepted the chance to be closer to her only son. He felt good about the future while going through finals and getting grades in. He didn't feel so good about his anonymous student evaluations. He was considered a friend of the "student movement," and one of the "good ones," but of the dominant generation. One student thought he was a good teacher, but why didn't they give him something good to teach. Many objected to the study of "dead white men!" Some objected to his method of teaching. He made them think, didn't give them answers, made it hard to prepare for tests and make good grades.

He thought they were more interested in grades than knowledge, but felt like a failure, unable to make students love learning, unable to make his wife love him. It was time to move on.

....

Life is a procession, A.M. thought, marching in his last Commencement at the university.

Life is a continual march, he kept thinking, step after step, from the time we take our first step to the time we fall out of step. Life is one commencement after another, he kept thinking and marching, one life change after another, step by step.

Following the Mace Bearer, keeping in step with other faculty members, his thoughts turned to the graduates marching behind. They would be leading the procession in the recessional, and leading the nation in the fullness of time. Would they follow the lead of their professors, or take a different turn? While his feet kept in step with the beat of the ceremonial march, his mind was out of step. Something must be wrong with him. Should he get a divorce from himself?

His feet kept carrying him forward, but his mind kept carrying him back. Had he lived too much in books? Paging back through his past, he couldn't find the answer. He stopped marching, got seated in the front of the auditorium. He looked out at a black mass of caps and gowns and hanging hoods. All bodies were draped in the fashion of the Middle Ages! He'd often wondered why academic regalia didn't keep up with academic knowledge, and his mind began marching again, going back. Teaching methods went back to the Middle Ages, too. Professors professed, as priests sermonized. His eyes came to focus on the college president at the podium. He was standing like a Medieval monk at a pulpit. He was sermonizing, lecturing the graduates to keep books open, after graduation. The Latin word for lecture was reading, and Medieval professors read from their rare book, students made their own copy. Now, books were plentiful, but it was expected that professors tell students what was in them.

Thoughts kept marching through his head. Why had academic gowns and academic teaching methods been carried on? The Cultural Lag stepped into mind, but he didn't know why a changing culture dragged useless relics of the past with it? It came to mind, all at once, that his own life was changing, like a culture. He couldn't go on without carrying some of the past with him. He carried baggage, like his tattered old slippers.

His thoughts were wiped out up by the shuffle of feet, graduates rising from seats, lining up for diplomas. His thinking began marching again. Diplomas were rolled-up scrolls, much older than Medieval books. The text, he thought, was related to textiles, stories woven together. It came to him he really did think too much, just as Dr. Adams put it to him. He let himself pass time by counting each graduate passing by, calculating how many passed in a minute. As minutes passed, he noticed some of the passing graduates wore black armbands, almost invisible on their black velvet sleeves. He knew they were demonstrating grief for the death of their Movement.

His memory marched him back to his year of study at the University of Berlin. The German students he knew didn't protest the rule of Hitler. Unlike the students he knew today, his fellow students in Berlin were uninterested in politics. Student organizations in Germany actually supported the rise of Hitler. They didn't know what Hitler would do to them. Now, students didn't know what a really repressive society could do to them! He thought of the crazy woman in the fur coat and the fury Hitler put her in, and the world!

Time passed and students passed, until the Commencement ended with the Benediction. It brought A.M. to thought of Hart Benedict and his blessed wife. Their reconciliation let him know gates could be closed and opened again.

The recessional music brought him to his feet, brought up thought of what lay ahead at Texas A&M. Marching out, behind the graduates, A.M thought one gate was closing, another gate opening.

AFTERWORD

"I had a dream last night," A.M. brought up at his final session of group therapy. "God and Mother Nature divorced! Mother Nature got the earth and custody of the children. God got visitation rights."

"What do you make of them apples?"

Edwards Brothers Inc.
Ann Arbor MI. USA
March 15, 2018